DISCARD

A Million Times Goodnight

A Million Times Goodnight

Kristina McBride

Sky Pony Press
New York

First Edition

Sky Pony Press books may be purchased in bulk at special discounts for sales promotion, corporate gifts, fund-raising, or educational purposes. Special editions can also be created to specifications. For details, contact the Special Sales Department, Sky Pony Press, 307 West 36th Street, 11th Floor, New York, NY 10018 or info@skyhorsepublishing.com.

Visit our website at skyponypress.com.
www.kristinamcbride.com

10 9 8 7 6 5 4 3 2 1

LIBRARY OF CONGRESS CATALOGING-IN-PUBLICATION DATA
Names: McBride, Kristina, author.
Title: A million times goodnight / Kristina McBride.
Description: New York : Sky Pony Press, [2016] | Summary: Told in alternating storylines, a teen must decide whether to confront her boyfriend or go on a cross-country road trip after he posts a compromising picture of her online.
Identifiers: LCCN 2015025639| ISBN 9781510704015 (hardback) |
ISBN 9781510704039 (ebook)
Subjects: | CYAC: Dating (social customs)—Fiction. | Online identities—Fiction. |
BISAC: JUVENILE FICTION / Social Issues / Dating & Sex. |
JUVENILE FICTION / Love & Romance. | JUVENILE FICTION / Social Issues / Friendship.
Classification: LCC PZ7.M1223 Mi 2016 | DDC [Fic]—dc23
LC record available at http://lccn.loc.gov/2015025639

Printed in the United States of America

To all my sister friends,
A million times *I love you*.

A Million Times Goodnight

1

Oak Grove, Ohio – 9:07 PM

"Are you sure we should be doing this?" Mia asked from the backseat as I eased my boyfriend's BMW off Main Street and up a steep hill on Old Henderson Road. A dense canopy of trees closed in above us. I could hear them overhead, the branches swaying, the waxy spring leaves hushing and shushing.

"This *is* kinda creepy, Hadley." Brooklyn stared at me from the passenger seat. "I mean, we've all been back to visit where she died, but to drive up here at night?"

"Don't focus on that," I said. "Tonight's about honoring her memory. Her death is all anyone seems to remember anymore. She was so much more than that."

"If we're not supposed to be thinking about how she died, why are we going back to the place where we lost her?" Brooklyn asked.

"It's the anniversary." My hands gripped the wheel tightly. "Isn't that what you do?"

"It's also the first Saturday of spring break," Mia said. "The party's just getting started. If you ask me, the best way to honor Penny is to head back and have a drink or two, dance like no one's watching, and kiss a few random guys just for fun."

I started to wonder if I had it wrong. If maybe I was the

one who'd forgotten how to remember Penny Rawlins: the girl who'd stand in the middle of a mass of writhing people, face tipped to a star-filled sky, twirling to the beat of a crazy-fast song. The girl with a triumphant smile spreading across her freckled cheeks as someone called out her name, announcing her reigning champion over the senior football players in a beer pong tournament; the girl who could just as easily lose herself in a moment of quiet, pouring her soul onto the pages of the sketch pad she carried with her everywhere.

But those thoughts didn't stop me—didn't turn me around. Instead, they kept me rolling up the wooded back road that twisted itself away from everything until it reached the Witches' Tower, a structure that looked like an old lighthouse missing its glass-topped chamber. It was the scene of the worst accident in Oak Grove's history—the accident that took our Penny from us.

"The party can wait," I said. "I want to drive through the trees, top down, music blaring, my two best friends along for the ride. We agreed we would do this. Together."

"That was back when it was just an idea." Brooklyn's words surfed the air streaming through the open convertible top. "You know, a throw-it-out-there-and-see-if-it-sticks kind of thing."

"Well, I threw it out there. It stuck. That's why we left to go to Circle K. It's why I grabbed the—"

"Yeah, I know," Brooklyn interrupted. "I'm just not sure anymore. This feels wrong."

"It's not wrong." I followed a curve in the road, wondering what it would feel like to drive off the pavement and crash into the thick band of swaying trees beyond. "It's the only right thing. Trust me."

"Fine," Mia said, a shiver tightening the word. "We'll do

this. For her. Even if it is creepy."

"It's only as creepy as you make it." I looked in the rearview mirror, catching Mia's eye, trying to forget about the curve in the road where Penny took her last breath.

Brooklyn laughed then, tipping her head back against her seat. "You sound like her, you know."

"That's exactly why we're out here." Strands of hair whipped my face. "To remember her as she was."

"Loud. Wild. And totally free." Brooklyn stretched her legs across the passenger floorboard, her loosely curled hair turning from a silvery glow to dark shadow and back again as we drove in and out of the moonbeams streaming through the trees.

I pressed my foot on the gas, suddenly needing to go faster. To get to the tower. To be in the last place Penny had been. "We're all in? For Penny?"

"For Penny!" they both shouted, just as the trees thinned and the starry sky seemed to break open above us.

I reached for the volume on the stereo, cranking it up before either Brooklyn or Mia could say another word. A remix of some pop song burst into the night, rolling down the steep ravine that dropped off to the left, bringing a blast of life to everything that had been shadowed since Penny's death.

I felt good—so incredibly good—to be alive, to be driving that car with my best friends by my side. With the music and fresh air and moonlight washing over us. It was one of those forever moments that I knew I'd never forget.

I pictured Penny along for the ride, the wind tossing her caramel-colored hair, eyes closed, with her arms raised through the open convertible top, hands pumping in time with the beat of the bass. I felt her with us, her lightness and wonder, the way she'd be laughing at Mia for freaking out, at Brooklyn for feeling the same way and trying to hide it, all the while cheering me on for leaving the party in the first place.

After we'd rounded a few more bends, we reached the six-story building, and I eased the car onto the shoulder. My eyes tripped across the grass that stretched from the road to the base of the building. The tower stopped me—held me in place—the stone glinting in the headlights as my eyes followed the walls from the door, which had been stuck three-quarters open for as long as I could remember, all the way up to the parapets that gave its top a crowned look. I breathed a sigh of relief. What we were doing felt right. More than right. It felt necessary.

"Ready?" I asked as I turned the radio down.

"I don't know," Brooklyn said with a grimace. "I hate to say it, but this place radiates bad mojo, Hadley."

"That's just because you have a negative emotional attachment to it." I tried to shrug off the bad memories, but it wasn't so easy.

"A 'negative emotional attachment'? You think?" Mia asked.

"We're here for a reason." I put the car in park and turned to Mia. Her face was so drained of color, she had a slight glow-in-the-dark vibe going. "We weren't here for her a year ago. Shouldn't we be here now?"

Mia sighed. "I kind of hate you for being right about this."

Brooklyn opened the passenger door, slipped out, and tugged her seat forward so Mia could climb through.

My phone vibrated in my pocket for the fifth or sixth time since I'd turned onto Old Henderson Road. My nerves vibrated right along with it. But it wasn't time to deal with anything beyond the scope of Penny. I opened the driver's-side door and walked to the front of the car where Brooklyn and Mia stood waiting, all of us caught in the glare of the headlights. I'd left them on. The last thing we needed was to face this place and all of its history in total darkness.

"I still can't believe she came up here that night." Mia stared at the shadow that pooled behind the tower and disappeared into the line of trees just beyond. It was impossibly dark in there, a black-hole gloom, swallowing all traces of light and seeping into the labyrinth of trails that extended, fracturelike, from this point.

"I know," Brooklyn said. "I hate thinking of her walking those trails by herself. Thinking that she was up here all alone when—"

"She wasn't afraid," I said. Penny wasn't afraid of anything. "She loved the woods at night."

"Yeah," Mia said, "but—"

"But nothing." I tipped my head toward the boulderlike monument that had been installed between the tower and the road. It was rough-hewn, chiseled around the edges, giving it an ornamental flare that Penny's artistic eye would have appreciated. "We're here for her."

We walked together, the plastic bag from the convenience store swinging from Mia's arm and hitting my thigh with each step.

"I still can't believe it," Brooklyn said when we stopped, all of us linking arms as our eyes locked on the name etched in the center of the stone—PENELOPE RAWLINS—and the starburst pattern beneath. It was the same design Penny had painted on her headboard when we were in ninth grade, the one she said represented a dream taking shape. "I can't believe she's gone."

"I know." I swayed, dizzy with the thought that we would never see her again. "I'm not sure it'll ever feel real."

I grabbed the bag from Mia's arm and pulled out the item that had inspired our trip to the tower—a pint of gin. I'd found it back at the party, deep in the bar, stashed behind the stack of red plastic Solo cups I'd been sent to search for. The bottle reminded me of Penny. Her drink of choice had always been gin and tonic. When I saw it, I knew we had to drive out here. That it was some kind of sign.

"Remember how much everyone loved her?" Brooklyn took the bottle from my hand and cracked open the seal. "God, I used to hate her for that. Made me so jealous."

"Yeah," Mia agreed. And then she laughed. "Everyone did love her. All the time. Which was kind of amazing because she could be *such a bitch* when she felt like it."

We all laughed, because it was so true. A pissed-off Penny was never good. She'd get eerily quiet and brood until it was time for her to lash out. Brooklyn took a long swig from the bottle and passed it to Mia.

"I miss her so much it hurts." Mia tipped the bottle to her mouth and cringed, squeezing her eyes shut as she swallowed and passed the bottle to me. "Oh my God, how did she stand this stuff?"

"I have no idea." I held the bottle in the air in a salutatory toast before taking my own drink. "Remember her laugh? That snorty hiccup thing she did when she really got going? I can still hear it. If I try really hard."

"I remember everything." Mia took the bottle from my

hand, pouring a looping stream of gin across the grass at our feet. "The way she hopped up and down a little when she gave hugs. Her warp-speed texting. And the insanely fierce loyalty she showed all of her friends."

"Especially us," Brooklyn added. "She was *especially* loyal to us."

"Do you think she'd be alive if we'd stopped her from leaving the party that night?" I asked. And then I wished I hadn't. The obvious answer was yes.

"We didn't know," Brooklyn said, her voice cracking. "There was no way to know what was about to happen."

"One of us should have gone with her." My eyes pricked with tears.

"Stop," Mia said. "Just stop. We agreed—after the funeral—we swore we wouldn't do this again."

"But it's so hard." My voice caught in my throat. "When I think back to that night. God, guys, we seriously let her down. She would have done anything for us—"

"She would have." Brooklyn swiped at her eyes. "And because of that, we need to do the most important thing for her. We need to *live*."

"You're right." I reached into the plastic bag and pulled out the other item we'd brought to honor Penny's memory: an oversize package of Skittles that had been hanging on a peg back at Circle K. "We need to live for Penny."

The bag crinkled in my hands as I tore a corner open, a tangy sugar-laced scent invading my senses as I spilled a handful of candy into my open palm. I held them out, an offering Brooklyn and Mia both accepted.

"I'm addicted to these things," Mia said, choosing red and

dropping it into her mouth. "It's totally her fault."

"Ditto," Brooklyn said, taking a yellow. "Skittles are delish."

I chose a purple and popped it into my mouth, my eyes watering with the flavor and an overload of emotion, and then tossed the remaining candies out into the night. Penny wasn't there—her body was buried at the cemetery on the outskirts of town—but I felt closer to her here. Maybe because here, she had been alive.

"Look!" Mia said, bending down and plucking something from the grass near one of the green Skittles, holding it in the air between us. It was a small, wooden bobblehead turtle with a yellow shell and an orange flower painted on its back.

"You think it's one of hers?" Brooklyn asked.

"Probably." I thought of Penny's turtle collection. She had at least thirty more displayed on a shelf in her bedroom, each intricately decorated. "Maybe her parents stopped by earlier? Or Tyler? It doesn't look like it's been out here very long—the paint is perfect."

"She would love that this little guy is here," Mia said, placing the turtle on the top edge of the memorial stone, its tiny head bobbing. "So, this is it?"

"The point is that we're thinking about her, right?" Brooklyn asked. "What we just did, it would make her smile. And then she'd give us shit for missing the party."

"Okay, then, not to be insensitive, but can we go?" One glance at Mia's heart-shaped face—her pinched eyes and scrunched nose—and it couldn't have been more obvious. Mia had to pee. Mia Hughes *always* had to pee.

"If you have to go that bad, why don't you just—"

"Don't even say it, Hadley." Mia scowled. "You *cannot*

expect me to go here."

"It's not like I'm suggesting you pee on the memorial."

"If Penny were here," Brooklyn said, "she'd dare you to go in the woods."

My phone vibrated again. I took a deep breath, knowing I was out of time.

"I don't even think I *can* go here." Mia looked at the tower and beyond, to the woods stretching into total darkness. "Too freaking creepy."

"You"—I tipped my head, trying not to laugh—"can pee anywhere."

"She's got a point," Brooklyn said, pulling out her phone and using it as a flashlight. "Come on. I'll go with you."

As they walked away, I tucked the bag of Skittles into my fleece jacket and slipped my phone from my pocket, heading back to the car. I slid into the driver's seat and took a deep breath. By now, Ben had to have realized his precious car was missing. He'd be pissed, but he'd finally stop ignoring me and listen to what I had to say.

Staring at the screen, my eyes squinting as they adjusted to its light, I realized that my phone hadn't been vibrating to alert me to calls. I had twelve new notifications on Facebook. I didn't care much about party updates—who was wearing what, who was making out with whom—but since I was waiting alone in the car, I pressed my finger to the app.

After a few seconds, a picture popped up on the screen. A picture of a very naked teenaged girl. A picture that looked oddly familiar, but I wasn't sure why. Then I saw my name and a sense of dread settled in my chest, spreading out in waves that echoed the frantic beating of my heart.

2

The Witches' Tower – 9:24 PM

My hands shook as I stared at the little screen. I squeezed my eyes shut to block out the string of comments posted by my classmates.

It wasn't me, no way it was me, it couldn't be me.

First of all, I was not a fan of the cheerleaders at Oak Grove High—only one of the reasons I would never, ever strip naked in front of a camera and pose like a varsity squader mid-cheer with one leg kicked high in the air, spirit hands the only covering for a pair of very natural pom-poms. Whoever the mystery girl was had to feel lucky that she'd angled her body so that nothing major was visible.

And then something caught my eye. The girl in the picture wasn't *completely* naked. She was wearing a ring. When I zoomed in, my heart almost stopped. She was wearing *my* ring. My favorite silver and turquoise ring. The one I never took off my right hand.

I thought of someone from the admissions board at Ohio State seeing this post, and my stomach twisted. I wondered if they could revoke my acceptance—my scholarship—because of one stupid picture. And then I thought of my parents, how OSU probably didn't matter anymore because, if they saw this, they would never let me out of their sight again.

But somehow, none of that seemed to matter as much as everyone else who would see this. Everyone else mattered *right now*. Everyone else was five minutes away, back at the party, and there was no way to avoid facing them. I wondered how many news feeds currently featured that picture, how many of my classmates had seen me totally exposed.

And then my mind did a trippy kaleidoscope twist, taking that single image and turning it live, kicking loose a few of the lost memories I'd been trying to find since a few weeks ago, the night Ben and I had spent alone, celebrating his eighteenth birthday. A celebration that was scattered in bits and pieces through my mind.

I heard the echo of my voice shouting out, "Go! Fight! Win!" Felt my hair rise off my bare shoulders as I spun around an already spinning room, spirit hands thrust high in the air as I went from performing his birthday present (a private dance that I thought was totally brilliant) to a naked cheer (making fun of Sydney Hall and her minions, of course).

I wanted to scream. Or melt into the leather seat of Ben's car. Instead, I opened my eyes, threw the door open, and puked all over the ground.

Looking at the screen again, I saw that the picture was still there. And it was still me. The worst part, though, was when I realized who had posted the oh-so-private and embarrassing image—the *only* person who could have a picture of me naked from that night. My boyfriend. Ben Baden.

Running my finger along the screen of my phone, I scrolled to Ben's contact information and stabbed his smiling face with my finger, brought the phone to my ear, and listened as the line attempted to connect. One ring. Two. Thr—

"Where's my car, Hadley?"

"How can you even think about your stupid car after posting that picture?"

"You saw the picture?" His voice was smooth, like warm honey. "Don't be pissed, Hadley; it's not a big deal."

"Not a big deal?" I asked, my voice shaky, shame smoldering deep inside my chest. "Exactly how is a naked picture of me, posted on Facebook by my boyfriend, not a big deal?"

"You look hot in that picture. Besides, it's not like anything's showing."

"Seriously? Ben, you have got to be crazy if you think—"

"Hey, all I did was post it. I had no idea someone would start tagging all the people in our class."

My heart stuttered—threatened to explode—and the shame I'd been trying to hold at bay caught fire, blazing white-hot, searing me from the inside out. "What are you talking about? That's like three hundred and some people, Ben. A picture of me *naked* is currently posted on the news feed of every single person in our senior—"

"Well, not *every* single person. Definitely not the losers like Jo—"

"I cannot believe this is happening."

"You *stole my car*, Hadley. You didn't think I'd do anything to retaliate?"

"I *borrowed* your car. To make a point. There's no way—"

"What a coincidence. I uploaded that picture *to make a point*. Did it work?"

"You can't even begin to compare the two, Ben. Take the picture down. Now."

"I can take the picture down. But I'll need my car back first."

"You think this is some kind of game?"

"Not really. It's simple. You have something I need."

"What's that supposed to mean? Just take the damn picture down and—"

"Get your ass back here." His voice turned hard. Cold. "Then I'll take it down."

He said something else, but static sliced the words in half. To avoid losing the connection, I walked to the front of the car, crossing the beam of the headlights and leaning back on the hood, one foot tucked behind me so that the bottom of my shoe ground into the hood ornament and the shiny black paint. It would have driven Ben crazy if he'd been there to see me.

That's when I noticed Brooklyn and Mia stumbling back from the shadows, both of them holding phones that illuminated their faces, which were pinched with anger. I knew that they knew, and seeing them, feeling their rage, gave me a burst of strength.

I didn't want to go back to that party to face Ben, knowing what he had done. To face everyone else, knowing what they had seen. "You're really going to play this game, Ben? Because I swear to God, I'll win." I wasn't sure where that last part had come from—maybe a little spark of my inner Penny—but it sounded good. I just wished I believed it was true.

"You can't beat me, Hadley. Don't even try." He sounded so calm. I was starting to *feel* a little crazy. Daring, too.

"Wanna bet?"

"Hadley. I'm serious."

"I am, too. Take the picture down."

"Listen, you don't understand what's going on here." I noticed a change in Ben's voice, a hint of weariness settling in. "You need to get your ass back to this party in the next five minutes or else—"

"Or else what? You'll post a naked picture of me on Facebook?" I laughed, slicing my finger across the screen, ending the call.

"What's going on?" Brooklyn asked, turning her phone toward me until I was facing that naked and way too happy version of myself again.

I squeezed my eyes shut, ducking my head. "I kind of gave Ben a private dance for his birthday a few weeks ago."

"And you let him *document* it?" Mia asked.

"I didn't *let* him," I said, my eyes snapping open. "Look, to be honest, I hardly remember anything from that night, okay? But Ben says he's not taking the picture down until I bring his car back."

"I'm sorry, what?" Brooklyn asked. "The car he *loaned you*? I know you didn't tell him about our little tribute to Penny, but he knew we were going to Circle K. Didn't he ask you to get him a pack of cigarettes?"

"That's not *exactly* how it happened. . . . I kind of snagged the keys from the pocket of his jacket and left. After he told me not to."

Mia bit her lip. "You didn't."

"It was stupid, I know. But he's been distracted lately. I wanted to see how long it would take him to notice I'd disappeared. The cigarettes were supposed to be a peace offering."

"So, that's the reason for the picture?" Brooklyn asked. "Payback?"

"I thought this thing with Ben was going to be different for you." Mia sighed. "Let's get out of here." She waved a hand in the air and started for the passenger-side door. "We'll go back to the party and *make* him take that picture down."

"Not so fast," I said. "I need to think."

"What's there to think about?" Brooklyn leaned against the car's hood. "We take the car back, and he'll pull the picture off Facebook, spewing apologies until you forgive him. Or break up with him. No pressure, but after this, I totally vote for option two."

I shook my head. "Everyone's already seen the picture. I have to do something. Something to take him down."

"Ben Baden?" Brooklyn and Mia asked simultaneously, staring at me as if I'd lost touch with reality.

I nodded, feeling a shift deep inside me. It was as though the Ben I thought I knew had never really existed.

"What are you gonna do?" Mia asked. "Ben's, like, untouchable."

I rolled my eyes. "No one is untouchable. And you're forgetting that I have something he wants." I pushed off the car, reached my hand in the pocket of my fleece jacket and felt the bag of Skittles, then started walking toward the tower's door, which was centered in the bluish beam of the headlights. "I need a few minutes, okay?"

"Hadley, where are you going?" Brooklyn called after me.

"You can't go in there!" Mia shouted, her voice echoing through the trees.

I made my way through the opening, my eyes locking on an abandoned umbrella, popped open and leaning against the brick. It glowed in the headlights—a tiny, fallen star against the shadowy tower wall.

"Don't you dare make us come after you!"

Swallowed by shadows so thick I felt blind, I walked up the spiral staircase, my footsteps echoing throughout the round chamber. It was steel—such old, cold steel. It creaked and it shuddered, but it held. It had always held me.

My hand slid along the railing.

My feet glided with no effort, even in the darkness.

And then I was at the top.

Walking across the open, flat roof of the tower.

Watching the trees toss themselves in a wild show.

Seeing the stars winking and blinking.

Feeling the air wash me clean.

Gripping the stone wall and peering over the edge, I didn't know if I felt like laughing or crying. The only thing I knew for sure was that I had to act. Fast.

My eyes locked on the memorial. I thought of Penny and wondered what she would do. She was as fearless as she was loyal. Nothing ever held her back. I wanted that kind of freedom. I would have done anything to claim it for a single night.

And then I heard him.

I'm not sure if it was the scuffle of his shoe against the stone floor. Or maybe the zipper of his jacket grazing the wall. It could have been his hand, rustling something as it dipped into the open pocket of his backpack.

Suddenly, he was there. Sitting beside me, hiding in the shadows as if he'd been waiting for me all night. Staring up with his eyes wide open, reflecting the moonlight and the starlight and maybe even a little of my fear.

He was the last person I'd ever expect to find at the top of the tower, and in one instant, as I stood there looking down at him, I remembered everything. Everything I'd spent nearly a year trying to forget.

"Josh," I said, my voice shaking, trembling. "Josh Lane."

. . . .

3

The Witches' Tower – 9:33 PM

I STARED at him, taking in all the details: how after that first moment of recognition, his eyes wouldn't meet mine; the way his hand seemed to be hiding in the depths of the backpack propped against his side; how his legs stretched out in front of him, looking as strong as they'd ever been, even though I knew they weren't.

He pulled his hand free, lightning fast, and zipped the main pocket of his backpack closed, tossing it over his shoulder as he stood. And then we were face-to-face.

"Last person you'd ever expect to find up here?" he asked.

I flinched. I couldn't help it. "You could say that."

He smiled. For a moment, he looked like his old self. The one I remembered from cross-country meets before he was forced to quit running. The smile he wore when he led me through the woods during practice, taunting me with his favorite line: *catch me if you can*. But his smile was sad and was gone as quickly as it had appeared, a too-familiar emptiness washing away any trace of the guy I had once known. Josh hung his head, his sandy-colored hair falling to cover his eyes, as if he'd just remembered that the thing we had between us was as dead as Penny Rawlins.

"Sorry to intrude." I wasn't sure what else to say. "I walked up here and . . . I didn't see you."

He grunted. "Most people try not to these days."

An awkward silence fell over us, stretching out like a string of the taffy I'd passed on the shelves back at Circle K.

I wanted to get away from him—no one talked to Josh Lane, not anymore, and with all of our history, the emotions swirling through me were actually making me dizzy—but if I turned at that moment, it would have been obvious I was running. And I hated thinking I'd become that kind of person.

So I reached into my pocket and yanked out the bag of Skittles just to have something else to focus on.

He looked over the side of the tower. "You with them?"

I followed his gaze to find Brooklyn and Mia standing in front of Ben's car, backlit by the bright headlights, staring up at us with craned necks. "Yeah."

"Is someone up there with you?" Mia shouted, her voice echoing.

"Get your ass down here, Hadley!" Brooklyn punctuated her demand by stomping her sandaled foot, the sound crack-crack-cracking the night in two.

Josh took a step toward me and looked down at my friends. "It looks like they're about to explode into a mushroom cloud of glitter and silly string."

"They've always been afraid of the tower." I let out a short laugh. "I'm pretty sure they think it's cursed. They're freaked that I'd even consider walking up here by myself."

"Oh, yeah?" Josh turned back to face me. "They must not know you very well."

I thought about that, how my history with this tower went

further back than the night we lost Penny. The irony was that this guy, whom I really didn't know at all anymore, knew something about me that neither of my best friends ever had. As I stood there, the stars spinning above us, my eyes met his, and another memory fought its way to the surface: my back pressed against the rough, gray stones of the tower's chamber, the heat of his hands on my skin, the silk of his lips against mine, the rise and fall of his chest—

"No way!" Josh said, one finger pointing toward the purple-tinted sky, breaking my memories into a million pieces and flinging them back to the past.

I looked just in time to see a star racing through the night sky, its tail a fiery, sparkling white.

"Make a wish?" Josh asked.

I did. A silent wish that I'd be given everything I needed to make Ben regret what he'd done.

Shaking my head, I focused my attention on finding the tear in the bag of candy. It crinkled, my fingers slipping across the plastic, but I couldn't get it open. I wasn't sure if it was just nerves from being alone with Josh or if it was my anger at Ben over that stupid picture.

Josh grabbed the bag from me and, in one swift movement, unwrapped the corner I'd folded over to keep the candies from spilling out.

"Can I have some?" he asked.

I nodded, feeling a strange sense of déjà vu. For a moment, it was comforting and familiar, and it almost wiped everything away—my history with Josh, Ben and his threats, Penny's death. . . . But the moment passed, and I pulled myself back to the reality that nothing about Josh would ever be comforting again.

He turned the bag sideways, pouring a few Skittles onto the palm of his hand, popping one into his mouth. "Grape," he said. "My favorite."

My gaze darted to the ground, to Josh's dark-green Converse shoes, and traveled up his legs, pausing on his scarred knees, before moving up his cargo shorts, over his wrinkled Heineken T-shirt, across the straps of the black backpack he always wore, and stopped on his face. Standing there, staring at him, I realized I *had* been granted my wish. My way to switch things up. To do something drastic. I wanted to get it right. To get my revenge against Ben so that I'd have no regrets. Now I knew exactly how to begin.

"Hey, Josh. You need a ride?"

His eyes crinkled with confusion, as if he hadn't heard correctly. I was supposed to hate him, just like everyone else. I had more reason to. But I couldn't.

I knew my idea was crazy. Dangerous. Like purposely triggering a trip wire just to see how big the explosion would be. But I couldn't help myself. I didn't want to.

"There's this party." My eyes never left his. "Or I could take you wherever you're going. Whatever. I just thought you might need a ride since—"

Everyone knew Josh's car had been totaled last year, and now he walked or rode his bike everywhere. I blew out a deep breath, wishing I'd just kept my mouth shut. Using Josh Lane to get back at Ben was a bad idea. Besides, it wasn't as though he'd ever take me up on my offer.

But then Josh met my eyes. Parted his lips. And spoke grape-scented words: "Are you referring to *the* party? Up in

Spring Heights?"

All of a sudden, he was this normal version of himself—the Josh he would have been if everything that happened last year hadn't—as if heading to the closest kegger was standard operating procedure.

"You know about it?"

"Who doesn't?"

It was like time stopped. Spring Heights said it all—top of the line as far as popularity at Oak Grove High. Money and shiny new cars. Alcohol. Drugs. And people who hated Josh Lane.

He pressed his lips together for a few seconds then swiped his hair out of his eyes, straightening up and pulling his shoulders back.

"Yeah," he said. "I could do a party. Why not?"

4

THE WITCHES' TOWER – 9:43 PM

"JESUS, HADLEY, I thought you were never going to come down." Brooklyn stood in the beam of the headlights, breaking the glare, so Josh and I remained in shadow as we exited the tower door and started toward the car.

Mia swayed in and out of the light. "Wait, who's with you?"

"Josh." My voice was solid and sure. "Josh Lane."

"As if," Brooklyn said.

"Isn't it, like, sacrilege to say his name around here? Especially tonight?" Mia huffed. "Besides, that freak would never in a million years come back to this tower."

Brooklyn swatted at Mia's arm and said something I couldn't hear, obviously recognizing the figure looming behind me.

"Holy shit. It really is him." Mia's voice tensed with anger.

I looked at Josh, who was staring at those dark-green Converse shoes.

"He's coming back to the party with us," I said, stopping in front of my friends.

"What?" Brooklyn crossed her arms over her chest and tipped her head to the side. Prime bitch stance.

"Is that really a good idea?" Mia asked. "There's the

obvious reason, obviously. But considering everything that happened between you two . . ."

"It'll piss Ben off, won't it?"

"Wait a minute," Josh said, taking a step back. "You only invited me to piss off your boyfriend?"

I looked Josh right in the eyes, thinking how much more there was to it than that. "If I remember correctly, you always thought Ben Baden was a self-centered prick."

"Well, yeah, but—"

"So you're in by default, right?"

"Depends," Josh said. "What'd he do to piss you off so badly that you want to drag me to a party?"

"Nothing."

Josh shook his head. "No way I believe that."

"Fine." I shrugged. "He did something. And you don't need to know what."

Josh looked at me—hard—and I half-regretted asking him to join us. But he was the answer, the best possible ammunition I could use against Ben. I knew it was selfish, but Josh had to get in that car. For a minute, as we all stood there, I thought I'd lost my chance. I imagined myself walking into the party alone, the joke of the century as a zillion pictures of a naked me floated around the house and spun to the farthest reaches of the Internet.

"I know you're pissed," Brooklyn said, "but this, Hadley, is not the answer."

"I'm pretty sure there aren't any answers at this point. But one thing I'm sure of—Josh has to come with us."

He cleared his throat. "I don't *have* to do anything."

"I need you." My voice sounded strong. "And you owe me."

"Hadley," Brooklyn said, "think about it for one second and you'll see. This—it's crazy."

I shrugged. "Maybe. But it's the perfect kind of crazy." I looked Josh in the eyes. "You in?"

I almost expected him to turn and walk away. Part of me wanted him to. Things would be easier that way. But tonight wasn't about easy.

"Shotgun," Josh said, brushing past me, swirling the cool night air. So close that I breathed in his scent—boy mixed with trees and earth and night.

Relief washed over me. I wasn't sure exactly how I would use him, but knowing I could made all the difference.

"You can't call shotgun," Brooklyn complained as she traipsed after Josh.

I stared at the reflection of the stars sparkling on Ben's windshield. My mind hit fast-forward, scrolling through all the different options I had, all the different outcomes I could possibly face.

"You don't have any rank." Mia propped a hand on her hip. "To call shotgun, you have to have rank."

Josh stopped short of the passenger-side door, pointing my bag of Skittles at Brooklyn and Mia. "Which one of you wants to sit in back with me?" he asked, then poured some of the colorful candies into his mouth.

Brooklyn and Mia locked eyes.

"Right," Mia said. "You can have shotgun."

With the engine still purring, I slipped into the driver's seat, sliding my hands along the steering wheel as the others hopped in through the passenger side. My eyes were drawn to the winking flash of silver wrapped around the middle finger of my right hand, its three turquoise stones glowing in the light of the moon. I remembered the day I'd bought it, heat rising off the pavement as I'd walked through the annual street fair with Penny and Brooklyn and Mia. It had been the Fourth of July between sixth and seventh grade. I'd plucked the ring from a table display, sliding it on my finger as a woman counted my cash, and had never taken it off.

But seeing the ring now turned my stomach. It would always remind me of the moment when I realized the naked girl in the picture on Facebook was me.

I tugged the ring free, slipping it straight off my finger, and almost tossed it out of the window, down into the ravine. But I couldn't. I might have hated that ring, but a part of me loved it, too. I tucked the little silver circle into the front pocket of my jeans, burying my shame right along with it.

"We going?" Josh asked.

"Yeah," I said, putting the car in drive and steering Ben's BMW back toward the road.

I saw the headlights racing straight toward us. Knew that we'd all seen them because a collective gasp whirled through the car.

Mia let out a high-pitched scream.

Brooklyn shouted something about sweet baby Jesus.

Josh grabbed my arm, his fingers squeezing tight.

Everything flipped into slow motion, giving the scene a dreamy feel of detachment. I sat there, trapped, with no place to go, hearing the echo of a scream as I stared into the blue-tinted light from the oncoming car, seeing wisps of long hair streaming through an open convertible top, watching the mirrored image of the BMW's hood ornament gliding toward us.

Josh lost his grip on the bag of Skittles, and an explosion of color flew through the car.

Then came a sweeping gust of air, the feeling of floating through space.

The world around me fractured into a million tiny pieces.

And I turned right and left in the space of one single breath.

5

THE ENTRANCE TO SPRING HEIGHTS ESTATES – 9:51 PM

UP THE hill we climbed, the deep, thumping bass urging us forward, swells of wind pulling us on and on and on, and the moon hanging in the sky, its glow a silver pathway stretching before us.

"I can't believe that car almost hit us," Brooklyn said, her eyes meeting mine in the rearview mirror. "I warned you, Hadley. That tower? Bad. Mojo."

I glanced at Josh. My heart was still racing, but he, more than any of us, had a right to be totally freaked. His expression gave away nothing, but his cheeks had drained of all color, his skin practically glowing in the moon's light.

Rounding the last curve, the headlights arced, sweeping across the large stone wall marking the entrance to Spring Heights Estates.

The music faded, crackled, and a cloud crossed in front of the moon, blanketing us in deep shadow.

I stopped at the corner, the car idling beneath me, wondering what I would do when I walked into the party and faced Ben. Wanting, needing, seeking something I could use to make him feel regret.

Josh looked at me. Blinked. And took a deep breath. "I'm sorry," he said.

"For what?" I hoped he'd say he was sorry for everything that had happened since last year's spring break. Maybe if he did, I could, too.

He held the nearly empty bag of Skittles in the air. "I spilled."

"Oh," I said. "No big deal."

Josh tilted his head to the side. And then he leaned down to the floorboard and started picking up the shattered rainbow of colors, plopping the round candies back into the bag with a succession of little *click click click*s.

I took a deep breath and offered them all one last chance to escape. "Things are going to get ugly."

Brooklyn placed a hand on my shoulder. "We know."

"We're here for you, *chica*." Mia's voice was solid. Sure.

Josh looked at me, his bottom lip caught between his teeth, and nodded in silent agreement.

I felt better then. Stronger with the girls by my side. Strangely comforted that Josh was there to back us up.

I pressed the button for the convertible top. Listened to the sound of it rising, stretching, falling. Imagined Penny—always fearless, forever daring—cheering us on.

And then I turned right into Spring Heights Estates and steered us toward the party, the lights, and my now ex-boyfriend, Ben Baden.

6

The Entrance to I-75 South – 9:51 PM

Down the hill we spiraled, the rich tones of acoustic guitar urging us back, swells of wind pressing us on and on and on, and the moon hanging in the sky, its glow a silver pathway stretching behind us.

"I can't believe that car almost hit us," Brooklyn said, her eyes meeting mine in the rearview mirror. "I warned you, Hadley. That tower? Bad. Mojo."

I glanced at Josh. My heart was still racing, but he, more than any of us, had a right to be totally freaked. His expression gave away nothing, but his cheeks had drained of all color, his skin practically glowing in the moon's light.

Turning on the main road, the headlights flashed, sweeping across a small blue sign marking the entrance to I-75 south.

The music faded, crackled, and a cloud crossed in front of the moon, blanketing us in deep shadow.

I stopped at the traffic light, watching cars zoom toward us and then away. The highway overpass vibrated beneath us, filling me with a sense of urgency. In the red glow of the light, my body tingled with the thrill of possibilities: revenge, adventure, transformation.

Josh looked at me. Blinked. And took a deep breath. "I'm

sorry," he said.

"For what?" I hoped he'd say he was sorry for everything that had happened since last year's spring break. Maybe if he did, I could, too.

He held the nearly empty bag of Skittles in the air. "I spilled."

"Oh," I said. "No big deal."

Josh tilted his head to the side. And then he leaned down to the floorboard and started picking up the shattered rainbow of colors, plopping the round candies back into the bag with a succession of little *click click click*s.

I took a deep breath and offered them all one last chance to escape. "Things are going to get ugly."

Brooklyn placed a hand on my shoulder. "We're not heading back to the party?"

I shook my head. "I'm thinking *no*."

"Where, then?" Mia asked, the glow of the red light a veil frosting her skin.

"If it's away from this town"—Josh turned to face me—"I'm in."

Brooklyn snorted.

"We're with you, Hadley," Mia said. "No matter what."

I felt better then. Stronger with the girls by my side. Strangely comforted that Josh was there to back us up.

I reached forward and pressed a button on the dash, resetting the trip odometer to zero. Imagined Penny—always fearless, forever daring—cheering us on.

And then I turned left, onto I-75 south, and steered us away from the party, our little town, and my now ex-boyfriend, Ben Baden.

7

Spring Heights Estates – 10:05 PM

"Holy shit! The entire senior class must be here." Brooklyn climbed out of Ben's backseat, smoothing the front of her tank top as she looked up and down the tree-lined street, where parked cars wrapped around the corner and slipped into the shadowy darkness.

"Cops are gonna bust this up," Josh said.

"Well, if they do, they'll only send their standard two officers to scare everyone away without actually doing any work." Mia grabbed Brooklyn's hand and started walking toward Ryan Peterson's front yard, where several people were standing in a cluster at the open front door.

"Just make sure you get out the back," I said. "Run the course and you're free."

"Seriously?" Josh asked, his eyes darting to mine. "The golf course is still the escape route up here?"

Brooklyn stopped and turned back to us. "What'd you expect? A hovercraft?"

"I don't know," Josh said. "But it's senior year. I figured things would have evolved a little."

As we stood under the branches of a half-grown maple tree, it hit me that while Josh had pretty much ceased to exist for most of us, he'd gone on living his life.

"We'll see you in there, Hadley," Mia said. "We've got your back with Ben and all, but there's no way we're walking in with *him*."

Josh looked toward the party as if he hadn't heard, but there was no way he'd missed the comment.

"Right," I said. "No problem." I took a deep breath, wondering if I'd made a mistake inviting him, but shoved the thought away. Josh was the best tool I had to work with. If he could handle the pressure.

"You're sure you want to do this?" I asked, bending into the open driver's-side door and grabbing my purse, my phone, and Ben's keys. I stayed like that, half in and half out of the car, fumbling around while I waited for Josh's answer. He surprised me when he ducked into the passenger side, crouching down in the dim light.

"I'm sure."

"Why? There are people in there who wouldn't hesitate to—"

"Like you said, I owe you."

I felt a sense of victory hearing those words. But then I remembered the red paint–splattered accusations dashed across his garage door, the rumors that people had thrown threatening notes rubberbanded around rocks through his windows, the way he always walked with his head down, his body stiff and alert. My victory suddenly didn't feel all that sweet.

Josh leaned down to the floorboard, reaching under his seat.

"I thought you got all the Skittles."

"Just want to double-check now that I have more room to maneuver." He stretched his arm farther into the dark space. "You ready for this? Facing whatever's going on?"

"I have no idea." I closed my eyes. Shook my head. Tried to ignore the hurt and shame that were smoldering beneath my anger. I wondered if I'd made the right decision, driving Ben's car back to the party instead of taking off to some mysterious location. "But at this point, I have no other choice."

"Sorry," Josh said. "I didn't mean to—"

"Don't be." I opened my eyes, watching as Josh closed the zipper on his backpack and yanked it from the floor. "It's a good question."

Josh's eyes were the same deep green I remembered. For a moment, it felt like before. Like we were living another life. The life before we lost Penny.

"Things with Ben were good," I said, feeling the need to defend my choice even though I knew it didn't matter anymore. "But after tonight, I'm seeing him a little differently."

"Finally seeing him for the asshole he is?"

I opened my mouth, my instinct to defend Ben, to say that he could be a pain but that deep down he was a good guy. And then I remembered the picture.

Josh tipped his head toward Ryan's house. "Now or never?"

"Definitely now." I stood tall, pulling my shoulders back, then pressed the lock on the door handle until it beeped twice. My heart raced a little as I thought of what I was about to do. Flinging my purse over my shoulder, my eyes trained on the pack of cigarettes I'd shoved into a slot under the stereo, I took a deep breath as I tossed Ben's key ring into the dark space of the center console. And then time seemed to speed up, rushing me toward that first moment with Ben—the first moment I'd spend with this new version of him, that I felt like I'd only just met.

Slamming the car door, I turned, hearing Josh's door bang closed behind me. The echo of music rippling from Ryan's house hit me in the chest just before Ben's voice.

"You decided to make the smart decision, I see?" He was standing in front of me with his chocolate-brown hair flipping up and away from his chocolate-brown eyes. The light from the house outlined his body in an eerie way.

"Your phone," I said. "Take it out and delete that picture. Now."

Ben smiled, but it was forced. "You're the one who stole my car. And now you're giving *me* attitude?"

"Don't be so dramatic."

"I told you not to take it. I made myself very clear."

"Believe me, Ben, if I stole the car, you'd know it."

"Whatever. Just give me the keys."

"Delete the picture first."

Ben sighed, rolled his eyes, and reached into the back pocket of his jeans. "Touchy, touchy." I watched his fingers dance across the screen, opening Facebook and pulling up the shot. "I didn't want to do this, Hadley, really. But you didn't leave me any choice."

"I'm not even going to ask you to explain that. Whatever game you're playing, it's over."

He raised his eyebrows, giving me a curious look. "Trust me, this is no game."

With his phone between us, Ben hit the DELETE button. I watched the picture disappear, wishing my shame could vanish along with it. Wishing that his action had wiped the picture from existence. But I knew the image was saved to his phone. Asking him to get rid of it was pointless. I'd have to find a way to tackle that later. For now, at least, the picture was off Facebook, which meant it—and all the comments below it—had disappeared for everyone but Ben and me.

"Now let's go have some fun, shall we?" A smile stretched across Ben's face. A genuine smile that was soft and sweet and, for a split-second, reminded me of why I'd chosen him in the first place.

I looked at him and couldn't say anything. Did he seriously think I was about to go into that party with him?

"Keys?" he asked, holding his free hand between us. "I gotta grab something really quick, and then we can head back inside."

He was acting as if what he'd done to me was nothing. As if I was just going to slip back into my role as his girlfriend, no questions asked.

I started with my pockets, natural, like the keys should be right there. As I fake-searched, I looked down at the ground. Ben was wearing his favorite Columbia sandals—the pair he bought online one night while we were eating cold pizza, half-naked in his bed. Only a month had passed, but God, it felt like a lifetime ago.

"Come on, Hadley. I don't have all night."

"Gimme a sec," I said, shoving my hands in my purse and fishing around. "I can't see a thing."

Ben reached into his pocket and pulled his hand out, lightning quick, flicking a lighter in my face. "This help?"

I searched for another moment, faking relief when I heard

the muffled jingle from the bag.

"Here," I said, tossing the keys in the air. The flame from the lighter died as Ben's hands fumbled for the key ring, which fell to the ground with a thunk.

As Ben leaned down, Josh rounded a nearby tree. He was standing in the shadows, both hands in the air, asking me what I wanted him to do. I jutted my chin toward the party, hoping he would go on without me. It wasn't time for Ben to see him. Not yet. Ben stood as Josh stepped out of the shadow and turned toward the roiling sounds of music and laughter, his feet stepping from the grass onto the pavement.

"What the hell, Hadley?" Ben's voice was quiet but hard, as if he was trying to remain calm. "These are not my keys."

"What?" I crinkled my eyes with confusion.

He jiggled the key ring between us, the silver charm my mom had given me for my sixteenth birthday swinging in the air. "Not. My. Keys."

"Oh, shit, Ben," I said, turning toward the car. "I think I fucked up. I'm sorry, but—"

"Hadley—"

"What did you expect after posting that picture? I freaked, wanting to get back to you as fast as I could." I flashed him a nervous smile. "I think I locked the keys in the car. But I bought you a pack of smokes, because I noticed you were almost out and—"

"You what?" Ben asked, his voice tinged with something that sounded like panic as he shoved me out of his way and raced toward the car. He yanked on the locked door handle before pressing his nose to the driver's-side window. "Jesus Christ, Hadley. How could you be so—"

"I said I was sorry." I gave him a little shrug.

Ben leaned against the car, his elbows propped on the roof, hands covering his face. He looked defeated, and I almost felt sorry for him. But then his phone rang, and he snapped upright, spinning around, his face twisted with emotions I couldn't read, a silent word escaping his lips.

He yanked his phone from the pocket of his jeans. "'Sup?"

I heard the muffled sound of a guy's voice coming from the other end of the line.

"Yeah. She's back."

More jumbled talking.

"Look, there's a little issue with—"

A few quick words.

"Right. No worries, bro, I swear."

And then it was over. Ben slid the phone back into his pocket. He stood there, eyes focused on the ground, lips pressed together. Then he turned and slammed a fist into the windshield so hard I expected it to splinter.

"Shit, Hadley, I did *not* need this tonight!" His voice echoed, anger and frustration echoing along with it, and I began to wonder what was really going on.

"Calm down, will you?" I was still pissed, but starting to feel worried, too. "I can go find someone to drive me to your house to get your spare key, okay? It'll only take a half hour."

"Hadley. I don't have that much time." Ben took a deep breath, then blew it out. "Just leave me alone, okay?"

"Are you sure?" I asked, taking a step back. "Do you want me to find someone to give you a—"

"Hadley, go. Now."

I turned, biting my lip so the bubble of nervous laughter

that was threatening to escape wouldn't have the chance. Then I rushed across Ryan Peterson's lawn, my purse swinging back and forth as I made my way through the front door.

And that's when I saw him, Josh Lane, surrounded by six of the biggest football players on Oak Grove High's team. That part was bad.

Worse? Standing directly in front of him was Tyler Rawlins—Penny's twin brother.

8

CINCINNATI, OHIO – 10:44 PM
TRIP ODOMETER – 42 MILES

"HADLEY, CAN you *please* hurry?" Mia's face popped up between the front seats for the zillionth time since we'd veered off the exit ramp, her eyes and cheeks scrunched.

"Mia, I swear if you don't stop whining, I'll—"

"You'll what?" Brooklyn asked with a laugh. "It's not like you have much of a choice. Take the next right."

"I seriously have to pee," Mia squealed. "Like, right now."

"You always have to pee," I said, rolling my eyes. I turned onto Pavilion Street, searching for a parking spot, slowing the car as a group of college students dressed in skinny jeans and tank tops took their time crossing in front of us. "I don't know what I was thinking, taking you on a road trip."

"Road trip's over," Brooklyn announced as she looked from the bright lights of one bar front to another. "We have officially arrived!"

"Yeah," Mia said. "We're as far from Oak Grove as we can get, about to take over the coolest bar district in Cincinnati."

"We're hardly as far from Oak Grove as we can get," I said, wishing we were still cruising south on the highway.

"Yeah. And *take over*?" Josh swiveled to look at Mia.

"Hell, yes, we're gonna take over!" Brooklyn shouted, her words streaming out the open windows.

"This is Mount Adams. You really think you'll get into one of these bars?"

"You, Josh Lane, must not remember my brother," Brooklyn said with a tilt of her head. "Eddie is a miracle worker."

Josh leaned back in his seat. "A miracle's exactly what you'll need."

"There!" Mia practically shot over the seats, her arm extended, finger pointing to the right side of the street. "Parking space. Right! There!"

"Okay! I'm not blind. Or deaf, for that matter." I eased the car into the space, listening to Mia tap her fingers impatiently on the seat back the entire time. Finally, I put the gear in park and let out a big sigh of disappointment. Cincinnati was not the destination I'd had in mind when I veered Ben's car onto I-75. But it would have to do.

"Holy crap, that took long enough." Mia pushed Josh's seat forward and practically crawled over him.

"Do *not* pee on me," Josh said, jumping out of the car and away from her.

"Where are you even going?" I shouted through the open door.

Mia stumbled onto the sidewalk, nearly toppling right onto her ass. A guy walking by grabbed her shoulders and righted her before moving on. She gave him a flirty wink-nod and said, "Hey, baby," which made me feel like I might throw up all over Ben's dash.

Then, as if nothing had happened, she looked at me again. "There are a bunch of narrow alleyways down here. I got lost in them with Penny when we all came down to visit Eddie for Little Sibs weekend." She started hopping from one foot to the other. "I'll be back in a few." Mia hobbled past a couple of bar fronts, then turned between two buildings and disappeared.

"Can't she be arrested for public indecency?" Josh asked.

"Says the guy who narrowly escaped life in prison." Brooklyn muttered the words under her breath, but she might as well have shouted them. She pulled a tube of gloss from her purse and started swiping it across her lips.

Josh crouched down, placing his hands on the leather seat to face her. "Is that the best you've got? Because, trust me, I've heard worse."

Brooklyn shrugged and smacked her lips, shoving the gloss back into the front pocket of her purse. She looked down at her phone as if Josh was a total bore. "My brother just texted me. They're at Monk's Cove. And they have one-dollar Jell-O shots!"

"Unbelievable." Josh grabbed the bag of Skittles from the console, stood, and walked toward a trash can. Part of me wanted to protest—those had been for Penny—but after seeing the candies on the floor, I knew he was right. I watched him toss the bag as groups of wobbling twenty-somethings pranced by in dangerously high heels.

A phone chimed from somewhere outside the car, and I was glad that it wasn't mine for once—that it had nothing to do with Ben or Facebook or that naked picture of me. Thinking of the image made me cringe, and I wondered if I'd made the right decision, driving Ben's car to Cincinnati instead of taking it back to the party. But I reminded myself that no matter what I did, Ben was going to do whatever he wanted with that picture. At least this way I had some leverage.

I just had to figure out what to do with Josh, who was leaning against the side of the car.

"What's your problem, Hadley?" Brooklyn asked, her words clipped. "I said *one-dollar Jell-O shots*. And since you need a clue, think about this: hanging out with my brother is the perfect way to stick it to Ben. Eddie has a bunch of hot fraternity brothers, and I say that dancing in the middle of a bar—hell, *on top of a bar*—all pressed up against some hunk of actual college man is exactly what you need."

From outside the car, Josh said something that sounded a lot like *No fucking way*, but I couldn't be sure with all the laughter and shouting from people on the street mixing with the music pulsing from the bars. Then he pushed off the side of the car, leaned down, and looked right at me.

"What?"

Josh shook his head.

"No, don't do that," I said. "What?"

"I just . . . Getting back at Ben this way? I thought you were a little more creative. Especially considering . . ."

"Considering what?"

Josh's eyes flashed, the lights from the bar fronts turning them electric. Then he dropped his forearm flat on the seat between us and opened his fingers.

And there I was. Resting in the palm of his hand. Totally and completely, utterly, and shamelessly naked.

"How did you get that?" I asked.

Josh shrugged. "Is that really what you're worried about right now?"

"*You* are on Facebook?" Brooklyn asked.

"Impressive deduction." Josh flashed her a smile. "I used to have a life, you know."

"Not anymore, loser." Brooklyn batted her lashes. "Delete that picture or you'll regret it."

"Like it'll make any difference? From what I can see, it's already gone viral."

I grabbed the door handle and shoved my way out. Brooklyn stumbled out right behind me, and suddenly we were standing in the middle of Pavilion Street, on top of a hill overlooking the bright lights that blanketed Cincinnati, right next to my ex-boyfriend's stolen car. I pressed the button to lock the doors and shoved the keys in the pocket of my fleece, looking directly across the black convertible top and into Josh's eyes.

"Have you forgotten that we're an hour from home? That I drove you here? Because if you don't listen to her, I swear to God I'll leave your ass right where it is, and I won't look back."

Brooklyn wrapped an arm around my shoulders and pulled me tight. "Who's gonna drive all this way to rescue you, Josh Man? No one, that's who. Because everyone back in Oak Grove hates you. Just like I hate you. And Mia hates you. And Hadley hates you, too."

"Brooklyn," I said. But my voice was weak, and her anger swept the word away as if it had never existed.

"I only let Hadley bring you along because I thought it might chap Ben's ass, since he hates you just as much as we do. You did kill his best friend's twin sister and all. But this plan of Hadley's is obviously a bust. So, we're done with you." Brooklyn shrugged. "Bottom line: you want a ride back to town when we're through here, you delete that picture. Now."

Josh stood there, frozen.

Brooklyn tightened her grip around my shoulders. *"Delete. It."*

Josh closed his eyes. Pressed his lips together.

Watching his chest rise and fall with a deep breath, the memories came at me in flashes: Josh and me in the woods, our hands clasped tight, faces tipped together, lips melting with the heat of a million perfect kisses.

"That's enough, B," I said, my voice cracking. "Just forget it."

Josh's eyes snapped open.

Brooklyn's arm dropped from my shoulders, and she took a few steps away. "Forget it? Hadley, that freak should not have a picture of you—"

I shrugged. "What's it matter? Everyone else does. Can we please just stop talking about it? The whole thing makes me feel sick."

I looked down at my hands, watching his shadow as Josh stepped away from the car.

Mia skipped up a minute later. "Tonight is going to be epic!" she shouted, practically knocking us down. "Penny would be so proud you decided to screw Ben over. It's gonna be a blast making him pay."

A car honked, and we all rushed to the sidewalk where Josh was standing, leaning against a red-brick wall, watching us. Off to his side, the doorway of Monk's Cove cleared as a group entered, and Eddie Simpson surfaced from the mix.

He glided down the steps in his übercool way, crossing the distance in a few short strides. He was wearing pastel patchwork shorts and a white polo shirt, which made him look like he belonged on some ritzy golf course, not in the middle of a college-bar district.

"Brooklyn, baby, so good to see you," Eddie said, moving to flick her on the forehead.

She ducked, barely escaping her brother's attack, just as Mia hopped forward, twirling a brown curl around one finger and looking up at Eddie with mischievous eyes. He was three years older than us, a junior in college and way out of Mia's league, but she'd been trying to get her hands on him since about sixth grade.

"Hey, Eddie," she said, her words soft and slow. "Thanks for bailing us out."

He held his hands up in the air. "No details, please. I don't want to be named an accessory to any of your devious, girly missions."

Mia giggled and kept twirling that strand of hair.

"You guys are lucky I have friends who look like you." He pulled three IDs from his pocket and handed one to Brooklyn, one to Mia, and one to me. "You're Suzette, Candy, and Sarah for the evening. Perfectly illegal in all ways. And don't let me catch you doing anything too crazy or I swear to God I'll tell Mom." He narrowed his eyes at Brooklyn as he said the last part, ever the big brother, then turned and started up the steps. Mia followed with one of her little skip-hops.

And that's when I looked back at him—Josh Lane—still leaning against the brick wall, his hands in his pockets, one foot propped behind him. He was staring at me, his eyes a window to the past, pulling long-lost memories up from a place I thought had ceased to exist. Memories like the way he used to look at me, a lazy smile on his face, unaware that we could ever run out of time; how when he was driving, he'd leave one hand on the wheel, the other always resting on my knee; the way he'd scoop me up and twirl me around when we hit the halfway mark of our favorite run, through the trails and right up to the top of that tower. My heart had closed him out nearly a year ago. But I'd dragged him all the way to Cincinnati—he'd *let me* drag him all the way to Cincinnati—and that meant he was my responsibility.

"Wait," I said. "Do you have one for Josh?"

Eddie turned, his entire face screwed up in confusion, and walked back down the steps, whispering so the bouncer couldn't hear him. "Brooklyn said you needed three IDs. *Female* IDs. Who the hell is Josh?"

Josh stepped forward and waved a hand in the air. "Hey, man." The hope in his voice gave away exactly how lonely he'd been.

Eddie sucked in a breath, his chest puffing up with air.

"I guess I forgot to mention that part," Brooklyn said, looking at the ground.

"I remember your face from the news." Eddie was no longer whispering. "Josh Lane, right?"

Josh's face fell. He gave a single nod, and I watched him shrink into himself.

"With my sister?" Eddie gave Brooklyn a look that was a mixture of confusion, anger, and grief. "You brought Josh-fucking-Lane to Cincinnati to hang out for the evening, Brooklyn? I don't understand."

"It's a long story." She tucked her hair behind her ears.

"Yeah," Mia agreed. "A very long story."

"Well, you can keep your story to yourself," Eddie snarled, taking a step toward Josh. "And you, if you know what's good for you, will get out of here before I decide to leave this bar. Penny was like a little sister to me, man, and if I see your face again tonight, I'm going to smash it in so far—"

"Eddie," Mia said, grabbing on to the arm he'd raised, wrapping her fingers around his fist, which was inching closer to Josh's face. "Let's just forget about him. Go inside. Maybe choose a song from the jukebox. They do have a jukebox, right? Because I'm seriously ready for some tunes."

Eddie relaxed a little under Mia's touch, and I half wondered if she might have a shot with him after all. But I forgot that thought when Josh leaned down and plucked his backpack from the sidewalk, flinging it over one shoulder.

That's when things got confusing—I heard a guy talking about the kick-ass convertible BMW parked on the street, and then someone stumbled into me from behind. More like plowed into me, because I found myself in Josh's arms. We were too close, and I smelled musky boy scent. It reminded me of the tower, the trees, and the cool night air back on Old Henderson Road.

"Caught you," he said in a slow whisper. And I heard it again, his voice from life before Penny died, calling out to me as he jumped from behind the sister trees, wrapping his arms around me and pulling me tight: *You can't catch me, Hadley. But I will* always *catch you.*

Except he had been the one who pushed me away. I'd spent too much time making a new life for myself, and I wasn't about to lose that over Josh. So, this time I shoved him, swiping my hands up and down my arms as if to wipe off his touch. He turned and started down the street. I had a little pang of regret, but the feeling was washed away by an image I would never be able to erase from my memory: Penny Rawlins, lying still in an open casket, eyes closed, and the crowd of mourners spilling from the chapel on the day of her funeral.

As Josh walked away, a voice inside of me screamed to just let him go. So when Brooklyn and Mia hopped up the steps, chattering about a sorority they'd barely heard of, as they handed their borrowed IDs to the doorman, as Eddie pressed a hand to my back and twisted me around, pushing me up the steps, I went.

I turned back only once as the doorman placed Suzette Collins's ID in the palm of my hand, just in time to see Josh's green T-shirt and sandy-blond hair swallowed by a crowd of people who would all want to kill him if they had any idea what he'd done to the wild and free Penny Rawlins.

Problem was, if they knew my secret, they would want to kill me, too.

9

Spring Heights Estates – 10:13 PM

"I asked you a question, punk." Mike Yates, the senior captain of the football team, jabbed his hand into Josh's shoulder.

The circle of players tightened around Josh, but he didn't seem to notice. His eyes were locked on Tyler's, as if he was seeing Penny's last moments all over again through the window of her brother's face. Like he was frozen in a slice of time, one year ago.

I'd pushed my way past two rocking chairs on the front patio, the music and heat from all the bodies inside like a thick wall as I stopped dead in the doorway. My hand gripped the cool handle, and my eyes darted around the oversize entry, recognizing every one of my classmates crowded around Josh, or lining the staircase, staring at the scene below. He hadn't even made it ten steps into the house.

"Answer the question," someone said. The voice was deep. Angry.

Josh didn't move. His lips were pressed together, his hands clenched, his eyes locked on Tyler's.

Someone turned off the music, and a heavy silence invaded the air, pressing against all of us.

"I'll give you one more chance," Mike said. "What the *fuck* are *you* doing *here*?"

I stepped forward, taking a deep breath as someone coughed the word *killer* into the charged space. I had to do something. Say something. But I couldn't find the words.

"I'm here to talk to Tyler," Josh replied, his voice quiet, but steady.

A few of the football players stumbled back as though they'd just been pummeled by the largest offensive lineman in the state. Others, including Mike, puffed out their chests, pulled their shoulders back, and stepped forward, closing Josh in even more. But Tyler did nothing. He just stood there.

"No way in hell you're talking to Tyler," Mike said.

Josh ignored him and kept staring at Tyler, who showed no sign of the emotions that I was sure were sweeping through his body as he stood face-to-face with the person who had killed his sister.

"I can't do this anymore, Tyler." Josh shook his head. His hands slid up the shoulder straps of his backpack, his fingers gripping them tightly at the top. "This just . . . my life, Tyler, it's not—"

"*Your* life," Mike said, gripping the top of Josh's backpack and pulling him back a few steps, "is *nothing*. Do you hear me?"

He twisted Josh around, but Josh's eyes remained focused on Penny's brother's. "I can't keep doing this. You have to forgive me."

Mike's hand was on Josh's face in an instant, his fat fingers gripping Josh's cheeks like a vise. "Forgive you?" Mike shouted, his words bouncing off the champagne-colored walls, pinging around the people crowding the open staircase, which wrapped around the right side of the entry. "No one in this town will ever forgive you, Josh Lane. You killed her. What else do you expect?"

Josh closed his eyes and tried to shake his head.

"You got balls coming here, man," Mike said. "Who the hell brought you anyway? No way you rode your bike."

Josh remained still, seeming to know that trying to escape would only give Mike and his friends a reason to tear him apart. At least, that's what I thought at first. But when I saw Josh's blank stare, I wondered if he just didn't care anymore. About anything.

His silence saved me. I'd used Josh to get to Ben. Because of my selfishness, Josh was in danger.

"Let him go." Each word was so soft, I wasn't sure if I'd imagined them. Until I noticed the glares, swiveling from Mike and Josh to me.

"Hadley?" Mike asked, confused.

There were whispers then. A giggle from the landing.

I cleared my throat and looked at Josh. "I told you to let him go."

"We're gonna take care of this kid once and for all." Mike widened his eyes as if I should have seen this from the start.

I shook my head. "He came to the party with me, Mike."

"Why the hell would you—"

The front door hit the wall with a thunk. I didn't know what was behind me, but it had taken everyone's attention off me. And I was grateful.

Until I heard his voice.

"He *what*?" Ben's words pelted my back.

I took a deep breath and turned to face him.

Ben ran a hand through his hair and tilted his head to the

side. He would have looked beautiful if his face wasn't so distorted with anger.

"You gave this piece of shit a ride? In *my* car?"

"Ben, enough! I know I screwed up, taking your car, locking the keys—"

"Screwed up? You let a murderer get into my car, Hadley."

"Don't call him that. The cops and the courts—everyone ruled it an accident." I looked around the entryway, taking in faces twisted with shock and horror. They all thought I was on Josh's side.

Ben's eyes flashed in the light from the chandelier, the energy in the room surging. He'd been pissed before, but seeing Josh, knowing I'd brought him with me, had pushed him further than I'd imagined I could. It was more than a little thrilling.

"Penny is dead because he hit her with his car. He might have been in juvie when he pulled his little disappearing act right before winter break. But juvie's too easy after what he did. It's time we make him pay."

Behind me I heard grunts, shouts, feet pounding the slick wooden floor. I turned just in time to see Josh break free from Mike's grip, tear through the bodies around him, and shove his way past Tyler Rawlins. The last thing I caught was a flash of Josh's green T-shirt and sandy-blond hair as he raced through the hall leading to the family room and kitchen and was swallowed by a crowd of people who all wanted to kill him for what he'd done to the wild and free Penny Rawlins.

"Nice, you two," Mike said. "Really nice. We had the son of a bitch, and your little drama ruined it."

"He hasn't gotten far," Ben said, waving a hand in the air.

"I need to deal with something here. You guys go after the piece of shit. Text me when you find him."

Mike looked at Ben, then me, and back again. "Yeah, dude. We'll let you know where to meet us. It won't be long."

"Don't worry, Ty," Ben said, thrusting his chin at his best friend. "We'll get him. Tonight."

Tyler didn't say anything, but his flat-line expression gave me chills.

That's when everyone started moving again. The football players broke apart, some heading out the front door, others following Josh out the back. Traffic on the staircase began its normal flow.

As the party came back to life, I started to decode some of the whispers ricocheting off the walls.

"I can't believe he actually thought Tyler would speak to him."

"I hope they kick his ass. For Penny's sake."

I felt bad for Josh. Protective, almost. It was something about that look in his eyes and the way he'd sounded when he asked for Tyler's forgiveness. There were feelings, too, swirling around inside of me, brought on just from being at this party exactly one year after my last night with Penny. And, of course, the memory of that year-old lie tripping off my tongue.

"Girls' night," I'd said to Josh, my cell pressed against my cheek, watching Brooklyn twirl her car keys around her finger as she, Mia, and Penny waited to head to Ben's for what was supposed to be the most epic party of the year. The party Josh was boycotting because he thought Ben was a self-centered prick. It felt like I was betraying Josh. I'd sucked in a deep breath, convincing myself that it was easier—more respectful—to lie.

"Sorry to bail out, but I'll make it up to you. I swear. Tonight's movies and pizza at Brooklyn's. No boys allowed."

But then I heard something that made all of that disappear. Suddenly, the whispers weren't about Josh Lane or Penny Rawlins. They were about me.

"Can you believe she's here?"

A wave of giggles, and then, "After *that* picture, no way in hell I'd be caught in public!"

"Well, the secret's out. Hadley Miller *obviously* wears a push-up bra."

"And she likes to slut it up."

"On camera, no less."

More giggles, then full-on laughter that swelled and spiraled around me.

I swiveled toward the voices—so close I could still feel the sting of the words—and found myself face-to-face with Ava Riggens. Varsity cheerleader. Barbie look-alike. Besties with Sydney Hall, who was, hands down, the most desired girl at Oak Grove High. And Ben's ex-girlfriend. It was obvious from the way she stared when she thought no one was watching that she'd never gotten over him.

Sydney was standing next to Ava, wearing a white mini tank dress that highlighted her sickeningly perfect combination of long legs, windswept hair, and tanned glow. Their eyes were trained on me, and it took everything I had to keep my head up under the weight of their stares. I didn't move. I wasn't about to give them the satisfaction.

But Sydney, the world's most accomplished snark, simply stared back at me. I dared a glance at her face, catching a flash of her satiny smooth skin, überlong eyelashes, and upturned lips. After flicking her gaze to Ben for a moment, she shook her head and turned away, leaving behind nothing but the faint scent of tropical fruit. I realized then that none of the voices mocking me had been Sydney's. Ava stood there for a second longer, her mouth parted in surprise, and then turned to follow her friend. Their gaggle of minions trailed after them, and they were lost in the crowd before I could register what had happened. Even before I could be grateful that Ben's ex-girlfriend hadn't taken the perfect opportunity to exact revenge.

"A word, Hadley?" Ben's hand gripped my elbow.

"Not in the mood," I said, trying to yank free.

Ben tucked his face close to my shoulder, his breath hot against my neck. "You screwed me, Hadley. Stole my car. Locked my keys inside. And now I find out you gave that freak a ride? The least you can do is follow me, nice and quiet, to the master suite so we can have a little chat."

"Whatever." I jerked my elbow from his grip and swiveled to face him, ready to end this thing once and for all. "But it's gonna be quick."

With his hand pressed against my back, I shimmied between the people pouring down the staircase and the faux-finish wall, inching my way up each step, dreading the scene that would play out when I reached the top landing. As someone hit the volume and music blared through the entire house, I took a deep breath and reminded myself that I was in charge—and that tonight was the night I was going to take Ben Baden down.

10

Cincinnati, Ohio – 11:02 PM
Trip Odometer – 42 Miles

"I HAVE an idea," Mia shouted—the way you have to when you're in a crowded bar, and the jukebox is cranked high. The way we'd have been shouting if we'd stayed in Oak Grove and headed back to the party.

She reached across the table and, with a flirtatious smile, grabbed her phone from one of Eddie's friends, who was looking at a picture he'd just taken of us posing with our Jell-O shots.

"We've got an entire night ahead of us," I said as Mia's fingers worked the screen. "I'm open to ideas."

"Lemme guess," Brooklyn shouted. "Your idea involves a bathroom."

Mia picked up an empty plastic shot cup and launched it at Brooklyn's head.

"What was that for?" Brooklyn tossed the plastic cup back at Mia. It arced over her shoulder, missing.

"My idea has nothing to do with peeing." Mia giggled. "Unless pissing someone off counts."

"Impressive wordplay," Brooklyn said.

"You wanna talk impressive? Let's discuss what our friend

here did tonight."

"I'm intrigued," Eddie said, leaning on the table. "What'd she do?"

"She got us here, for one thing," Mia replied. "Hadley's the reason we're sitting in the middle of the UC college district in the coolest bar ever."

"Not to mention the fact that she stole her boyfriend's car." Brooklyn's words hung in the middle of the dark little bar, music vibrating each syllable, giving them life.

"*Ex*-boyfriend," I said with a shrug.

Eddie raised his eyebrows. "Remind me to never cross you."

Mia giggled again. Her breath was strawberry-and-tequila-scented, heavy on the tequila. Mine was the same, I assumed. We'd just finished our third Jell-O shot, and I was feeling warm and happy, like I could do anything I wanted before the sun came up. Have anything I wanted. In any place I wanted. The deep bass thrummed in my chest, filling me with the feeling of freedom, of being in charge of my fate.

"So, my idea," Mia said. "We need to hit Ben where it'll hurt."

"I thought we already did that."

"That was phase one. This bar offers the perfect opportunity for phase two."

"Phase two?" I asked.

"What would be worse than Ben losing his car?"

Brooklyn's eyes popped wide. "Losing his car *and* his girlfriend? All in one crazy-ass night."

Mia smiled.

"He's already lost me."

"But he doesn't know that. We're talking about Ben Baden here. The kid who has everything he wants before he even knows he wants it. He takes the words 'spoiled rich kid' to a whole new level. Trust me, even if he's as through with you as you are with him, he wants to be the one making that call."

"So? What's the plan?"

A huge smile spread across Mia's face. "We play his game."

"And how, exactly, do we do that?"

"We show him that you've moved on and left him behind." Mia held her phone in the air. "We give him a visual of you with another guy."

I rolled my eyes. "News flash: I'm not actually the slut that Ben's picture makes me out to be. I'm not thrusting myself on some random—"

Mia's eyes scrunched together. "I did not say anything about *thrusting*. I'm talking about an illusion. See Eddie's friend down there at the end of the table?"

I didn't need to look. I knew exactly who she was talking about. The guy was the epitome of gorgeous. He'd probably been featured in some national Calvin Klein campaign.

"All we need is a picture," Mia said with a shrug. "Just one little picture, Hadley."

"Admit it. The plan is brilliant." Brooklyn hopped off her seat. "Seeing you with another guy—especially Jerry—would kill Ben. You have to do it."

Brooklyn was around the other side of the table in a flash, whispering in Jerry's ear. He smiled and looked up, finding my eyes in an instant. I couldn't look away. He was the perfect guy to help with phase two.

He winked and waved me over.

With precision timing, my phone vibrated in my pocket.

Ben, no doubt. Again.

I didn't know if he was calling or texting, and I didn't care. I walked over and stood behind Jerry, draping my arms around his shoulders and pressing my body against his, losing myself in the beat of the music. It was loud. So loud, I could hardly hear Mia count down. Jerry tipped his head back just before the camera flashed, pressing his lips to my ear, his warm breath lighting my skin on fire.

I was blushing when I pulled away, thanking him with a string of fumbling words, but I didn't care. All I could think about was how totally, incredibly awesome I felt standing there in the middle of that bar. And how totally, incredibly pissed Ben would be if he could see me in this moment. *When* he saw me in this moment. Just as soon as I approved the picture.

And then I saw Brooklyn and Mia, heads bowed, four hands on the phone, devious smiles lighting their faces.

"Wait, guys. What are you doing?"

"Texting Ben," Brooklyn said without looking up.

"Duh." Mia rolled her eyes and shook her head.

"Before I see?" I looked at Eddie, hoping for backup, but all he did was shrug.

"It's not the first one they've sent." He gave me a look that said he thought it was petty and immature but kind of funny at the same time.

"Please tell me you're lying."

"He isn't." A look of pride washed over Mia's face.

"First there was the shot Mia took from the backseat. You and a mysterious guy sitting in the front of Ben's precious car. From behind, Josh Lane looks kinda like Jerry over there.

Same color hair, right?" Brooklyn grabbed another Jell-O shot and started working her tongue along the edges.

"That's exactly what I was thinking." Mia held a hand up in the air. Brooklyn threw her a high five.

"What the hell, you two? Ben's going to freak if he thinks I've been driving around in his car with some other guy."

"Hadley," Brooklyn said, leaning so far forward I was worried she might topple off her bar stool, "Ben freaking out . . . I thought that was the point."

"The point," I said slowly, "was to make him jealous. Not homicidal."

"Three pictures," Mia said, holding the phone up for me to see. "That's all. They tell the perfect story of Hadley Miller moving on."

The image on the screen was the one of Jerry and me. It was dark, and the whole scene was kind of hot in a mysterious way. It would make Ben seethe. Which meant the girls had been right after all.

I breathed a sigh of relief. Until I scrolled back. If Ben had seen this picture, there was a problem. A big problem. And I had to deal with it fast.

"You sent three? The one of Josh and me from the car. There was no way to identify Josh, right?"

"Give us some credit," Mia scoffed.

"Then the one of Jerry and me?"

They nodded.

I turned the phone around so they could see the image of all three of us, wide-eyed and carefree, holding bright red Jell-O shots in the air. "And this one? Did you send it?"

"Of course!" Brooklyn clapped her hands. "Girl power

beats everything."

"We contacted Facebook, too," Mia said, "reporting Ben for harassment and lewd content. Hopefully, the Facebook team will delete the picture of you since Ben sure as hell won't after the little incident with his car."

"Thanks, guys." I stared at the picture on Mia's phone. "I appreciate you trying to take care of me. But you know as well as I do that the Facebook team can't delete the picture from his phone."

"We'll deal with that later," Brooklyn said. "Until then, focus on the three of us together. Penny would love it, the picture and the whole idea of this night. It's perfection, showing the world that you can't be broken, that you will prevail, and that Ben can—"

"Guys, I have to tell you something."

Mia raised her eyebrows and cocked her head to one side, causing her to sway a little in her seat.

"That you *luuuv* us?" Brooklyn held her hand in the air, and Mia gave her another high five.

"Um. No." My mind was swirling from the alcohol and the music. Only one thing was clear. I had to get out of that bar. Fast. "I'm leaving."

"What?!" Brooklyn and Mia cried at exactly the same time. "You can't. We just set up the most—"

"Insanely wrong situation possible!" I shouted, shoving the phone closer. "See the right side of the shot, the person sitting next to Mia? That's Eddie, leaning his elbows on the table, looking right at the camera. Sure he's a little cut off, but it's obviously him. An excellent clue for Ben, right? If I'm with Eddie, that means I'm somewhere near UC. Even better, though, is that huge Monk's Cove sign hanging in the background, just behind our heads. If Ben's looking for me—and I'd bet my life on that, since I stole his car, and you guys texted him two pictures of me with another guy—he'll now know exactly where to find me."

Brooklyn snatched the phone from my hand and squinted at the picture. "Shit."

"Hadley," Mia said, "it doesn't mean he's going to notice the sign. And even if he does, that doesn't mean he'll—"

"I'm not taking chances. I can't deal with Ben tonight. I'm not just leaving this bar. I'm getting out of Cincinnati. Are you coming with me or not?"

I turned toward the crowded entrance of the bar, ready to make my escape. It would take Ben about an hour to schmooze someone for a ride and then get to Cincinnati, assuming he'd seen the picture and taken action the minute he received it. That gave me roughly an hour to get as far away as I could.

I looked back at my friends, who had both slid into their seats. Neither would look at me.

"You got me into this mess. You're not going to help get me out of it?"

"We could stay a little longer. . . ." Mia's eyes slid toward Eddie.

"No. No way. No chance. Just . . . *no*."

"Agreed," Brooklyn said. "You need to leave. But what if we can help you more from right here?"

I sighed. "How exactly would you do that?"

"We could throw Ben off track," Brooklyn said. "Tell him to go to some frat party to look for you, or something random. Like a scavenger hunt with no prize at the end, because you'll be long gone."

I bit my lower lip, thinking. It could work. It might even be the best option. Ben would never in a million years believe that I'd go off on my own, leaving Brooklyn and Mia behind.

"Eddie?" I asked, swiveling to face him. "You'll help? Plan out the craziest places to send Ben?"

"Someone messes with you, he messes with me." Eddie gave me a little wink, his eyes glittering with the promise of a wild mission to lead Ben off course. "Throwing his night into a tailspin will be my pleasure."

"It does sound like the best option."

"I hate thinking of you leaving on your own," Brooklyn said.

"I'll be fine. Just don't let me down." I shoved a hand in my pocket and yanked out Suzette's ID, tossing it on the table in front of Eddie. "Thanks for getting me in here."

"Wait," Mia said, grabbing my hand. "Where are you gonna go?"

"I have no idea." But that wasn't entirely true. The highway was calling me. Problem was, after three Jell-O shots, I couldn't exactly get behind the wheel.

"You'll text us?" Brooklyn asked. "When you figure it out?"

"Just come up with some good places to send Ben. I want him to spend the entire night searching Cincinnati for his stupid car."

"We're all over it," Brooklyn said.

Mia giggled. "He picked the wrong girls to screw with tonight."

I blew each of my best friends a kiss, then turned, trusting Eddie to guide their moves for the rest of the evening.

As soon as my feet hit the sidewalk, I breathed in the crisp spring air, trying to ignore how light-headed I was from the shots, trying to shove away the fear that swept over me when I thought of heading out on my own. I could handle this, I told myself. Nothing to it.

I pulled my phone from my pocket. Ben had texted me twenty-seven times and left seven voice mails in the last hour.

"Sorry," I said, shoving the phone back in place without reading or listening to a single message. "I'm currently unavailable."

Standing in front of the bar, my gaze fell on the red-brick wall where Josh had been leaning, his backpack propped between his feet, before we'd gone inside. I felt a moment of relief, my first glimmer of hope that I could pull off a real escape.

Until I remembered him walking away.

And the truth of that bare, dirty, red-brick wall sank in.

Josh had been close. But he wasn't anymore.

"Shit." Josh Lane would have been the perfect person to save me from the disaster that was about to rock the Mount Adams bar district. The perfect person to save me from Ben.

I turned in a slow circle, looking at all the people moving up and down the street, hoping I'd see his sandy hair, his green eyes, the curve of his cheek.

But Josh was gone.

I stopped turning, sucking in a deep breath, when I realized that Josh Lane wasn't the only thing missing.

Ben's car was no longer in the spot where I'd parked it. In its place sat an extremely old, extremely rusty Volkswagen Bug.

"Double shit." I closed my eyes, wishing I could blink

myself back to the tower, back to the minute I'd been stupid enough to think I could take Ben Baden down. If I could do it all over again, I'd take it back in a heartbeat. I'd head back to that party and end things before they even began.

11

Spring Heights Estates – 10:19 PM

"Get your hands off me," I said as Ben led me through the door to the master suite. It was dark inside, and the air smelled faintly of men's cologne. I watched the shadow of Ben's body waver along the wall until he snapped the light on.

"Jesus, Hadley, my hands have been on every square inch of your body. It's not like I—"

"Dragged me up here?" I asked sarcastically. "Right. You'd never do that."

"What the hell is going on with you?" Ben kicked the door closed behind him, muffling the sounds of the party.

"Funny you should ask," I said, crossing my arms over my chest. "I've been wondering the exact same thing."

"I don't want to do this with you." Ben's voice was surprisingly soft. Almost sweet. "This is *not* how tonight was supposed to go."

Ben stepped forward. I stepped back, moving away from the bed, toward the master bathroom, my purse sliding down my arm and falling to the floor. I kept moving, making no attempt to grab it, not even looking at the brown leather bag. When he realized I wasn't about to let him get any closer to me, he stopped.

"We can forget about all of this, Hadley—believe me, I want to—after you tell me where my shit is."

"Your keys? They're in the car. Right where we—"

"I'm not talking about the keys!" He was angry, I knew that, but there was something underneath the anger. Frustration. Maybe even fear.

"I don't have any idea what you're—"

"*Don't* lie to me." Ben closed his eyes for a moment. Took a deep, calming breath. "Do *not* lie to me."

"I'm not lying. I swear."

"It was in the car. With you. I know it was there before you left because I checked right when we got to the party. And now it's gone." Fear. His words were definitely streaked with fear.

"*What* was there?" I shouted, totally confused. "*What's* gone?"

Ben looked right at me, his eyes pleading. "Hadley, you have to tell me."

Something about those words caught my attention, and even though I was still pissed, I was suddenly afraid for him, too.

"Let's go downstairs. I'll get a ride to your house and grab the spare keys, and then we can search your car and find whatever it is that you're missing. Okay?"

"You don't get it." He shook his head, then laughed, but there was nothing happy in the sound. "It's *gone*, Hadley."

"I didn't take anything."

"I'm not stupid. You found it, and you didn't like what you saw, so you decided to lock the keys in my car to buy yourself some extra time while you got rid of it." He ran a hand through his hair. "You have no idea what you've done. No idea."

Ben's eyes were frantic, almost desperate. I could hardly believe this was the same guy who had held my hand to keep me from falling as we slipped across the icy parking lot at the movie theater just a few months ago, the same guy who, three weeks back, had kissed the tip of my nose while we danced to the sound of the creek trickling through his backyard.

"Did you hide it?" he asked. "Or was it Brooklyn and Mia?"

"Wait. Why are you bringing them into—"

"We need to find them, Hadley. They were in the car and if they have any idea—" Ben closed his eyes and brought his hands to his face. "Holy shit!"

"What? What are you—"

"Josh Lane. Where was Josh sitting?"

"Why does that matter?"

"Hadley," Ben said, his hands balling into tight fists. "Please."

"In the passenger seat. Josh was in the passenger seat, but I don't see why—"

"Jesus, Hadley, you really don't have a clue, do you?" Ben laughed, the sound tearing through the room.

I shook my head. Swallowed. "I already told you that."

Ben nodded. Sighed. And then he stepped forward. "I'm sorry. I didn't mean to scare you. It's just . . . something went missing. Something important. And it looks like your little tag-along Josh Lane is the culprit."

"Ben, I—"

Ben put a finger to my lips. "I have to go and find him. And I want to be able to find you when I'm finished because we have some things to work through."

"Work through? You think we're just going to *work through* you posting that picture of me?"

"Jesus, forget about the picture. Just forget about everything until I get back." Ben wrapped his hands around my biceps, gentle at first, but then tighter, rougher as I tried to pull away.

"Get your hands off me." I jerked sideways but couldn't free myself.

"I know you're pissed, but you have to trust me." He practically picked me up off the floor as he backed me toward the dark opening that led to the master bath. "This won't be for too long."

"What won't be for too long?" I asked, hearing the shaky panic in my voice and hating it. I had to get a grip. I had stay in control. "And did you actually just tell me to trust you?"

He stopped talking then. So did I. The only sound was our feet scrabbling on the floor and my hands tearing at his shirt, his jacket, his face—anything they could grasp. I flailed, kicking and shouting, hoping someone would hear me because there was no way Ben was going to change his mind. I could see the determination in his eyes. But no one was going to hear a thing. Not with the music blaring, and people laughing, and the heated game of beer pong going on in the kitchen below us.

When he got me to the bathroom, he flipped the light on and wrapped his arms around me, squeezing tight. Pressed his cheek into my hair. I felt his hand slip into the back pocket of my jeans and realized he was taking my phone. I knew I wasn't going anywhere. I let myself go limp, my body pressing against Ben's, using him as my support so he'd think I was too weak to fight back. I was glad guys like Ben Baden don't know how many ways there are to attack an enemy.

"Please," I whispered. "Don't leave me."

"I'll be back for you," he said. "We'll work this out."

My arms slid up the sides of his body, fingers searching, pressing, pulling, rough and insistent. "You can't leave me here. What if—"

"Nothing's gonna happen, Hadley." Ben's voice was soft. Reassuring. He swept my hair off my face and tucked it behind my ears, pulling back, but not far. Just enough to look in my eyes. I could see our reflection in the large mirror hanging on the wall and wanted to shove this new version of him backward into the glass so that it splintered and rained down on him. But I stood there, tolerating his embrace—it was my only way out.

"You're coming back?" I asked, my eyes meeting his. I needed him to think I was counting on him. For him to feel he'd won.

"Of course. After I deal with Josh. I promise."

"What are you going to do to him?" I asked. As crazy as it seemed, I felt as if Josh and I were on the same side again.

Ben shrugged. "Let me worry about that."

"Just don't—"

"Don't what?"

I cleared my throat and found the right words. "Don't do anything to get yourself into trouble."

Ben chuckled, closing his eyes for a beat, and then kissed my forehead. I wanted to scrape the feeling off my skin.

"I'll be back before you know it." He pulled away and smiled. The bastard actually smiled. As if everything had flipped to normal, just like that.

I didn't rush after him, throw myself at the door, or try to keep him from shutting me in. I just stood there in the middle of the polished travertine floor, my arms at my sides, hands tucked behind my back, listening as Ben slid a chair beneath the door handle and pressed it tightly against the wooden frame.

"I swear I'll make it up to you, Hadley. And you might not believe it right now, but I'm doing this for you."

I heard footsteps padding away from the door, the bathroom, and me. A quick blast of music trickled through the crack along the floor. Then there was silence.

I faced myself in the mirror, flashing a wide smile, not even caring that I was trapped. Directly behind me, a second floor-to-ceiling mirror cast multiple reflections in the mirror over the granite countertop, as if I was standing on the cusp of a million different lives, all occurring in the same moment, seeing a million different versions of myself.

More importantly, the mirror confirmed again and again and again what I already knew to be true.

My fingers tightened their grip on Ben's cell phone. The one I'd pulled from the inside pocket of his jacket when I'd surrendered, leaning into him as though I was so afraid of him leaving me that I might collapse.

"Gotcha," I said, breaking into a little dance, shaking my butt and waving my hands in the air as I spun around, my hair swooshing wildly around my shoulders.

I gave myself a little wink, and all of the other Hadleys winked right back. Then I eased myself against the wall, sliding down the robin's-egg-blue surface, and got to work. I had to delete every last picture of myself from that phone. And then I had to find a way to escape the echoing prison of the master bathroom before Ben made his way back to me.

12

Cincinnati, Ohio – 11:26 PM
Trip Odometer – 42 Miles

"I'm dead." I was standing on the sidewalk in front of the entrance to Monk's Cove. The sky above me was stretched wide, but still, I felt trapped. Losing the car I'd stolen from my boyfriend was not an option. But looking at the VW Bug that had replaced Ben's BMW, it was clear that was exactly what had happened. "Ben's going to kill me."

And then I laughed. Ben Baden was getting exactly what he deserved.

Josh Lane, on the other hand, was not. I knew he was behind the missing car. I couldn't figure out how, but I would. And then I'd make him regret his little stunt.

I yanked my phone out of my pocket and found Josh in my contacts. I'd almost deleted his number a million times. But he was still right there where he had always been.

I started a new text and typed, one very angry finger stabbing at the screen.

Me: Where are you?

I hit SEND and then leaned up against that dirty brick wall and waited, debating whether to walk north or south on

Pavilion Street to try tracking him down. It wasn't like he could be in any of the bars. Maybe I'd even find Ben's car parked along the street.

I wasn't sure what I expected to happen. Josh ignoring me completely, I guess, as he had since last fall when he got out of the hospital. But before I could decide which way to walk, my phone chimed. And, for once, it had nothing to do with that naked picture or the person who had posted it.

Josh: Wouldn't you like to know?

I could practically hear him laughing.

Me: Don't play games with me.
Josh: But games are so much fun.

I almost screamed.

Me: Fine. I don't care where you are.
Where's the missing item?
Josh: Someplace safe.

Leaning my head back against the wall, I took a deep breath. I could do this. I'd stolen a car and driven it all the way to Cincinnati with Josh Lane sitting in the passenger seat. I could do anything.

Me: Enough, Josh. Just tell me.

I waited for his reply. Nothing. He was probably getting some kind of sick pleasure out of torturing me. He might even be watching. I turned in a circle, feeling he was close—that he had to be close—because if he'd just driven off and left me, I was totally screwed.

My phone chimed and I looked at the screen. He'd sent me a picture of a sign—oval shaped, blue—MOUNT ADAMS PAVILION in yellow block letters. Below the sign, he'd typed the words: *Clue #1*.

Me: Clue #1? No time for games.
Just tell me where to find you.
Josh: You want the car, you'll play.
Text me when you get there.

Josh Lane was the most infuriating person I had ever met, but I knew the only way to end his little scavenger hunt and get out of the city was to follow his clues.

I looked around, searched all the signs in front of the bars lining the streets, and found MOUNT ADAMS PAVILION. I started walking, looking across the street in case he was somewhere in the crowd, checking over my shoulder to see if he was following me. When I made it to the bar, I turned in a circle, but all I saw were throngs of drunk college partiers.

Me: I'm here. Send me the next clue.

A new picture came through. Another sign, neon this time and flashing, I saw, when I found it a block up the street. I ran to the bar and before I could even ask for another clue, he'd texted a third picture: a wooden bench, a tan napkin, and a bowl of purple ice cream—my favorite—black raspberry chip from Graeter's. Josh had remembered my favorite flavor.

But he was still the asshole who'd broken my heart, stolen my car (okay, Ben's car), and was turning the whole thing into a game. A game he would not win.

Josh was biting into the side of a waffle cone when I reached him. I knew without asking that he'd chosen chocolate chip cookie dough. I wanted to hit him, but in the same moment, I wanted to hug him. Now, we could actually get out of here.

"Have a seat," he said with the hint of a smile, tipping his head toward the open space where my bowl of ice cream was waiting.

The glint in his green eyes was so familiar. It was as if we were at the start of a practice run, his standard dare wavering in the air between us: *catch me if you can.* I had always wanted to. I had always tried. And, up until the end, he had always let me. We would press our hands together, fingers intertwined, and whisper the things we'd stored up over the day, our secrets and feelings spilling out in the darkness of the tower's chamber.

"No sitting." I shook my head, shaking all of that history free. "Only leaving."

"Why the rush?" He raised his eyebrows as if he didn't have a clue. He should have been more afraid than I was.

"Really? Can we not do this?"

Josh shrugged and licked a smudge of ice cream off his lips. "You expect me to just hand over the keys? After the way you guys treated me back there?"

"What do you want? An apology?"

"It's a little late for that, isn't it?" Josh swallowed another bite of chocolate chip cookie dough. "Besides, I get it. I know exactly why everyone hates me."

My mind flitted to Old Henderson Road, imagining for the millionth time the dark winding curves, the trees blocking out the moonlight, the sounds of twisting metal and exploding glass splintering the silence into a million pieces. Tires squealing as Josh's car veered off the road. Trees snapping as he slipped into the ravine. And, somewhere in that crumpled mess, Penny's broken, lifeless body.

I shifted my weight from one foot to the other, wanting to grab the bowl of deep-purple ice cream and run away from him . . . from all of it.

But I needed Josh. I needed his help.

"The way people feel about you, how Eddie treated you—"

"I know I can't hold it against anyone." Josh's voice cracked. Only slightly, but it was enough. "The whole thing was my fault."

That wasn't true. The problem was, I hadn't told Josh. I couldn't. Not then.

I wondered what he'd think if I came clean now.

"Look," I said, stepping forward until my knees were touching his, wondering if this was it—the moment I should spill everything. I wanted to pull back as soon as the heat from his skin seeped through my jeans, but I forced myself to lean in instead. *It would be so simple. . . .*

But then my jacket swept forward, my empty pocket grazing my hand, stopping me short. "Wait a minute. Back there, in front of the bar, you pretended to help me when that guy almost knocked me down—"

"I didn't pretend anything. You would have been flat on your ass if I hadn't caught—"

"You stole the keys from my pocket? That's how you moved the car?"

Josh took another bite of his ice cream.

"And to think I was starting to feel sorry for you," I said, smacking his arm. "Cute little prank. Now it's time to get out of here."

"What, like you and me? Together?"

I nodded. As much as it scared me to admit, I didn't have anyone else I could count on.

"Where are the glitter twins? You're just leaving them behind?"

"They're staying. We're going. That's all you need to know."

"What if I don't want to leave?"

I put my hands on my hips and leaned in even closer. Josh smirked, but I ignored it. Nothing was going to get in the way of my escaping my boyfriend—ex-boyfriend—and his rage. "If you don't want to leave, that's your call. But just so you know, Ben's probably already on his way here. He has everything he needs to pinpoint our exact location. I need to get out of here. Fast."

Josh ate the last bite of his cone and crumpled his napkin into a tight ball. "*You* need to get out of here. Me? Not so much."

"Have you forgotten how much Ben hates you? Penny was his best friend's sister. If Ben thinks you're part of this, he'll slaughter you."

Josh tossed the napkin in the air and caught it with one hand. "You make a strong point."

"So you'll show me where you hid the car?"

"I don't know. That sounds like something only a friend would do. And let's face facts. If you'd had the keys and found that car sitting right outside the bar, you'd be gone, and I'd be stranded here. Which would *not* have been friendly at all."

I remembered Josh in a hospital bed, his words echoing off

the sterile walls of the room as he told me to leave him alone. "Us not being *friends* anymore? That was your decision, not mine."

"True." Josh narrowed his eyes. "And then you ran straight from me to Ben Baden."

"You're really going there?"

Josh shrugged. "I'm just stating the obvious. The whole thing makes us a little more like enemies than former friends, don't you think?"

"Great. That should cut out any awkward moments."

Josh raised his eyebrows. "We'll be having moments?"

I sucked in a deep breath. "I kind of need you to drive. We can go back to not speaking as soon as we get through tonight."

"Right, and then you can go back to your dickhead boyfriend."

I smiled. It actually sounded like Josh cared.

He yanked Ben's keys from the front pocket of his shorts, then grabbed his backpack, swinging it over one shoulder. Without even looking at me, he turned and started walking away.

I grabbed the cup of black raspberry chip ice cream and started to follow him. But then I had a better idea. I turned toward the bulletin board beside Graeter's, my gaze running over the flyers for bands and art shows and wine tastings, and set my ice cream back on the bench. Then I snatched my favorite purple pen from my purse, smoothed a napkin out on my knee, and wrote a note for Ben:

Catch me if you can.
XOXO-Hadley.

13

Spring Heights Estates – 10:31 PM

I FOUND the pictures in no time, my fingers tripping across the screen of Ben's phone. They were saved in a folder labeled with my name. I wanted to fly through them without looking, hitting DELETE over and over until they'd all disappeared. But something caught my attention, distracting me.

There was more than one folder.

More than one name.

At the top of the list I saw *Sydney*.

And then *Jules*.

Becky.

And *Treen*.

But those names weren't what stopped me. They weren't the reason my blood turned cold.

There was another name. A sweet and simple name that everyone in town had repeated over the last year through whispers and falling tears. A name that had been tattooed on the surface of my heart.

Penny.

My stomach dropped as I pressed my finger to her name, as the folder opened and the first image popped up on the screen.

She was laughing, head tipped back, her caramel-blonde hair falling across one shoulder. One very *bare* shoulder. Her body was scrunched tight, as though she was trying to hide herself. But it was obvious. Penny Rawlins was not wearing a shirt.

Swiping to the next image confirmed that she was one small step away from naked. Her fingers were laced in the sides of the black-and-pink polka-dot panties. I remembered her picking them out during a trip to the mall the winter before she died. The photo highlighted her pouty lips, rounded in a wide O, and the way her wide eyes gleamed with surprise.

There were a few more like that—playful, silly—as if she had been enjoying herself. But the next shot told a different story. Penny was bending forward, one arm shielding her chest, her hand holding a bundle of clothes. Her forehead was creased, her mouth wide open. It was obvious she was protesting, maybe even trying to get away. She had been finished. But Ben hadn't been.

I needed to stop.

I couldn't.

I had to know how bad it had been. How bad *he* had been. I owed it to Penny to figure out what he'd done to her. She hadn't lived long enough to defend herself. I flipped through the next few pictures quickly, a sick feeling spreading from my stomach through my entire body. I saw Penny on a bed, blankets spilling around her, arms stretched above her head, her eyes hazy and unfocused. Penny curled up on the floor of a shower, her hair dripping and dark, pink lips shining in the light of the camera's bright flash.

My mind was reeling as I reached that last shot, my teeth

clenching as I took in the details. Because the image of her lying limp, barely conscious on that blue tile floor told me more than I'd ever wanted to know.

But the pictures of Penny gave me something, too: a way to take Ben down. Not a superficial act, like using Josh Lane to piss Ben off, but a real plan. Pictures like these could ruin a person's life. They'd destroy his dream of going to Ohio State in the fall. Penny had been a minor—these pictures might even land him in jail.

The thought of Ben paying for what he'd done burned brightly for a moment, then quickly dimmed as my shame kicked in. When I imagined showing these to anyone, especially the police, I was tempted to delete every image. Of myself. Of Penny. Of all the other girls. Penny would agree, I thought. She would understand how I felt. My finger hovered over the last shot. I selected it and watched as the option to delete appeared.

Then I heard a noise. A blast of music bursting through the crack under the door. I scrabbled to my feet, pushing off the wall, accidentally yanking a plush white towel off the rack above me, knocking my head as I put Ben's phone to sleep and shoved it into the pocket of my jacket. But if it was him, he'd search me. I knew he wouldn't stop until he found it.

I leaned down to the cabinets under the sink and yanked the door open. I was just about to pull the phone from my pocket and toss it into the darkness when I heard a knock on the door.

Looking in the mirror, my face was wild with the fear of discovery, the million versions of me reflecting from one mirrored surface to the other and back again, hunching down, preparing to hide a dark secret for myself and for Penny and for all those other girls.

"Ben wouldn't knock," I whispered to myself. "It can't be Ben because he wouldn't—"

"Hello? Is anybody in there?"

I laughed, loud and strong, releasing all of my nervous energy, then stood and walked to the door, zipping the pocket on my jacket to offer Ben's phone as much protection as I could.

"Mia Pia?"

"Hadley?!" Something scraped the door, and then the handle began to twist. As the door swung open, Mia shouted, "We had no idea where you were!"

"I was with Ben. Until he trapped me in here and took off."

"Are you okay? What's going on?"

I placed my hands on her cheeks, planting a kiss on her forehead. "What's going on is that you're saving me."

Mia laughed. "The bathroom downstairs has a line a mile long. No way I could wait. It's just lucky—"

"Look, Mia, I love you, right? But I gotta go." I started through the door, but she grabbed my hand and yanked me back.

"What are you going to do? Ben's on the warpath looking for Josh."

"The first thing I'm going to do is get as far away from this party as I can."

"Wait for me, then." Mia sat, her pinched expression softening with the release. "I'll get Brooklyn and we'll go with you."

I shook my head. "No way. You guys can't come."

Mia tipped her head to the side. "As if we're going to just let you face Ben on your own? The asshole *locked you in a bathroom*, Hadley."

"You'll do me more good here. You can keep me posted on what's going on and . . . Shit. Scratch that. Ben has my phone." I couldn't tell her I had Ben's. Not until I decided exactly what to do with those pictures of Penny. Of me.

"I have a phone." Mia stood, buttoning her jeans, and walking to the sink to wash her hands. "You can use it all you want."

"Thanks, Mia. You're a lifesaver." From behind, I grabbed her shoulders and squeezed tight, then held out my hand, waiting for her to make good on her offer.

"Not so fast." She grabbed a towel and dried her hands before turning to face me. "Only way I'm letting you use it is if you take me with you. Brooklyn, too."

"Mia, I—"

"No argument, Hadley. You wouldn't let me deal with this—whatever it is—on my own, would you?"

I shook my head, knowing she was right.

"We're stronger together."

"That's true, but—"

"No *buts*. Remember how we let Penny go?" Mia's voice dropped to a shaky whisper. "We knew something was wrong, and we let her leave that party anyway. Alone. No way you're doing the same thing."

"I don't like this."

"But you know I'm right. Right?"

I sighed. "Yes, okay? You're right."

"This'll be fun." The glimmer in Mia's eyes reminded me

of Penny's most devious expression. "An adventure. I'll grab Brooklyn, and we can head out. Together."

"Fine. Let's just get out of here fast."

We made our way down the front staircase hand in hand. I felt wild, practically tripping my way down the steps, searching for signs of Ben as we reached the halfway point. For a moment, I made eye contact with Sydney Hall, who was standing by the front window in the foyer, staring out at something. I couldn't imagine her posing for Ben's camera. With her poise and confidence, she was the kind of girl who would tell any guy who wanted to take naked pictures of her to go to hell. Then again, Ben Baden had ways of getting what he wanted.

Sydney nodded her head sideways, a small and discreet movement, and I followed her gaze. That's when I saw Nick Rimes, a football player on the JV team, standing on the bottom step with his hands clasped behind his back like a guard. He hadn't seen me yet. I ducked behind Mia's shoulder but lost my balance and knocked into her, tripping us both up so much we stumbled right into him. He looked at me, his eyes wide with surprise, and then leaped toward the front door, yanking it open.

Sydney grabbed my wrist, jerked me up, and pulled me out the door, Mia following close behind. Nick was shouting, "Ben! Ben, get your ass over here, dude!"

It was like time slowed down, Sydney's fingers tightening around my wrist as Mia pressed up against my back. I looked across the street and met Ben's eyes. He was standing next to his car as someone else leaned inside. Something sparkled and flashed at Ben's feet, like fallen stars winking out. As Sydney pulled me around the corner of the house toward the backyard,

I understood I wasn't looking at stars. It was glass—broken glass from the driver's-side window.

I wondered what was so important that Ben would trash his own car to get to it. Especially since a spare set of keys was just a short drive away.

"Go!" Sydney said, releasing my wrist and giving me a little shove.

Mia threw her a look like she was debating which was more important, running or telling Sydney off for pushing me.

"Get out of here," Sydney said. "Now, you two!"

"What's going on?" I tried to catch my breath. Fear rocketed through me.

Sydney shook her head. "I have no idea. But if I were you, I wouldn't wait around to figure it out." She looked over her shoulder. "Hurry! He's coming!"

That's all it took to get me moving: the thought of Ben putting his hands on me, dragging me back up to that bathroom again, or worse.

But then he was there, his hands gripping my arms as they had in the master suite, his eyes wild, chest heaving. I struggled, jerking away just as Mia shoved herself between us.

"Keep your hands off her."

Ben ignored Mia, his eyes flicking over his shoulder, past Sydney to the street, then whipping back to me. "Get out of here, Hadley. I'll try to hold him off as long as I can, but you need to hide."

"Hide?"

"Yes!" Ben said, pulling me to him, squeezing me tight. "I left you upstairs to keep you safe. I wanted to lead him away, but now that he's seen you—"

"Who?" I shoved my forearms against Ben's chest, untangling myself from his grip. "Who's seen me? Why the hell does it matter?"

"There's no time to explain. Just run. As fast as you can. Hide somewhere I won't think to find you. I'll text you when it's safe."

"You have my phone. You took it when you locked me in—"

"Shit." Ben looked back again. "He's coming. I'll text Mia, okay? I'll find a way to reach you. Just remember, you're not safe until I say so." Ben pushed me away. "Now go!"

Mia's fingers were like steel, wrapping around my wrist, pulling me away from the house, through a crowd of people milling around a keg, and down the slope of the backyard.

I heard a voice, scratchy, full of rage, lashing out like a whip. "Where is she?"

"She got away," Ben replied.

"What *the fuck* is going on here, Baden?"

Whoever the guy was, he'd just asked the question spiraling through my mind. I wasn't about to stick around for the answer.

My feet pounded the ground, the thick grass threatening to suck me under. My breath was coming in heaving bursts as Mia and I disappeared into the darkness blanketing the golf course. We twisted into a cluster of trees, seeking the cover of deeper shadows, and raced past the thirteenth hole, our hands fisted tight, swinging wildly as we veered away from the course and into the labyrinth of the woods. We ran as fast as we could possibly go, the night sky sweeping above us, the moon and the stars urging us forward.

14

Cincinnati, Ohio – 11:53 PM
Trip Odometer – 47 Miles

Josh eased the car through the city streets, buildings shooting straight up to the sky, their windows glittering in the bright city lights. The Reds' stadium loomed up ahead, and I wondered if there had been a game earlier.

Josh hadn't spoken since we left the ice-cream shop. I wasn't sure what to do. I had never felt so alone in my life. And with the awkward silence and our history pressing in from all sides, I wondered what might happen—what might be revealed—now that we were alone again after so much time. Suddenly, facing all of that history seemed a million times scarier than facing Ben.

Josh turned his head slightly, meeting my eyes with what felt like a black-hole void. A void I recognized from his first days in the hospital just after Penny's death and from passing him in the halls at school last fall when I was stupid enough to think we still might have a chance.

I looked out the window, catching my reflection in the passenger door's rearview mirror. My vision blurred, and the reflection seemed to fracture into a million different versions of me, rippling from this world into the next and back again. I felt dizzy, trapped, my heart racing in my chest. And then a car turned behind us, its lights flashing into my eyes.

Green interstate signs up ahead indicated routes north and south. The traffic light flipped from green to yellow to red, and Josh eased the car to a stop. Then he looked over at me, raising his eyebrows.

The decision was mine.

"You up for a ride?" I asked.

He shrugged, but his eyes betrayed him.

"South." My voice was steady. Sure.

Josh's lips twitched as he tried not to smile. He reached forward and hit the power button on the GPS. "Don't want your boyfriend following us, now, do we?"

"Good thinking." I tipped my head back against the leather seat.

When the light turned green, I half-expected Josh to go north, to head back home so he could get out of the car and as far away from me as possible. But without hesitation, we veered south, picking up speed as we entered the highway.

Minutes later, as the car settled into a steady pace, perfectly centered in the middle lane, my phone rang. Feeling a renewed sense of hope, a burst of confidence, I reached into my pocket, yanking it free. Ben's face beamed into the space of the car, lighting it up like a tiny sun.

"Is that him?" Josh asked.

"Yeah," I said, noticing the glow of highway lights passing across Josh's face.

"Don't answer it."

I looked down at the phone again, knowing it was about to flip over to voice mail. I'm not sure why I did it—anger or sudden readiness to confront Ben—but I slid my finger across the screen, accepting the call.

"Nice pictures," Ben said. And then he raised his voice: "You drove my car all the way to *Cincinnati*?"

I wondered what he'd say if he knew his car was on a bridge, suspended over the Ohio River, making its way to Kentucky. Or worse, what he'd do if he knew Josh Lane was driving.

"I told you not to answer that," Josh whispered. "Don't say anything. Hang up."

I shook my head and held a hand up in the air to quiet him. Ready. Suddenly ready to deal with Ben.

"You are going to get in my car and drive it back to Oak Grove, you hear me?" Ben's voice was shaking with anger. His anger gave me power. It meant I was winning. "Jesus, Hadley, I know you're there. Say something!"

"You only have yourself to blame. That picture you posted was way worse than me taking your car. For the record, I drove to Circle K. I even bought you a pack of smokes. I was heading back to the party, but that thing with the picture kinda threw me off course. Bottom line: I'm not coming home tonight."

"Excuse me?"

"I need some space. You pull my picture off Facebook, and I'll have your car back to you tomorrow."

I meant it, too. If Ben would just apologize and take down the picture, I'd ask Josh to turn around so I could end this thing for good. All-the-way end it, because no matter how great things had been between us, Ben and I were officially over.

"You think I'm going to take the picture down now? After you stole my car and left town?"

"If you want your car back, you don't have any other

choice."

"I have lots of choices." Ben laughed. "Calling the police is just one of many options."

"The cops, Ben?" I tried to sound bored, but his threat scared me. At least he wouldn't know to alert the Kentucky State Police.

Josh stared at the road, his hands gripping the steering wheel tightly.

"Nah. Not quite yet." Ben chuckled. "I think it'd be way more fun if I found you myself."

"Cincinnati is a pretty big town. . . ."

"I have my ways. You should know that by now."

"Well, good luck," I said, my voice dripping with false cheer.

Ben sucked in a deep breath, then blew it out in a long stream. He started to speak softly, like he was sharing a secret. "Hadley, this is bigger than you can possibly understand. I don't want to fight. But you better get that car back here or else—"

"Or else, what? You don't have anything on me anymore. You're all out of moves."

"Hadley, I swear to God, you're going to regret this."

I looked at Josh and flashed him a nervous smile.

"Maybe," I said into the phone. "But you'll have to catch me first." And then I hung up.

"I told you not to answer," Josh said again, without looking away from the road, the corner of his mouth creased tight.

"You're not in charge of me any more than he is."

"Well, that's rich. But you don't have all the facts."

"What's that supposed to mean?"

Josh shrugged. "Exactly what I said."

"What am I missing?"

"Reach under your seat and find out for yourself."

"Way to be mysterious." I leaned forward, tiptoeing my fingers across the carpeted floorboard. "I don't get it. There's nothing here."

"Keep feeling around," he said as my fingers tripped across the paper ball. That's all I could envision in the first moment my skin made contact. A large, wadded-up paper ball. I stretched my fingers around the item and pulled it out of its hiding space.

"Ben's not just after his car."

"What is this?" I asked, feeling the weight in my hands and realizing it was more than a wad of paper.

"Check it out."

I fumbled with the ball until I found a section of the paper that had been doubled over and realized the ball was actually a brown paper lunch bag. Unfolding the top half, I found the opening and eased my hand inside, feeling a smooth layer of plastic. Pulling the contents out, I saw that it was a large Ziploc bag.

"Pills?" I asked. "I don't understand what this is."

"I checked them out back in the bar district."

"Wait. How did you even know this was here?"

"When I spilled the Skittles back at the Witches' Tower, I reached under the seat to make sure I'd gotten them all. I felt the bag then and was curious, so—"

"So you let me drive *all the way to Cincinnati* with *drugs* in the car? Seriously, Josh?"

"First off, I didn't know it was a bag of drugs until *after* you left me standing outside that bar. It's not like I had anything better to do, so when I had the keys, I figured I'd kill some time snooping."

"What's in here, anyway?" In the flash of highway lights, I could see that there were several different sizes and shapes of pills wrapped up separately within the Ziploc.

"One's Vicodin. I think there's some OxyContin, too."

I turned to face him. "How do you know all that?"

Josh was silent for so long I thought he wasn't going to answer. "The accident," he finally said. "I was pretty messed up. The doctors made me take some stuff. Tried to make me take some other stuff. I learned a thing or two from the experience."

"Oh." I looked back at the road, at the broken white lines leading us farther into the night. I thought of Josh, his broken legs lying beneath the crisp white sheet of a hospital bed. But that made me think of Penny, broken beyond repair, lying against the ruched satin lining of her coffin.

"Now you know what he's really after." Josh's words bounced around us, sizzling in the flashes of light from passing cars and overhead lampposts.

"Right." I shook my head and ran my fingers back and forth across the tiny little pills. "Now I know lots of things."

"Like how you sure chose yourself a real winner?"

I thought about the night I decided to forget about Josh Lane for good. He'd told me to. And it had been time to move on.

I was at a New Year's Eve party, eight months after Penny's death, standing back from the crowd. I'd pressed myself up against the foosball table in the corner of the basement, lying to myself about how Josh meant nothing to me, how I didn't care that he'd gone MIA two weeks before winter break, or where he was as the world rang in the new year. He certainly didn't care about me anymore. And in the spirit of resolutions, I promised myself that I *would* learn to stop thinking about him.

Then, like a wish being granted, Ben walked up to me and started talking, making me feel seen for the first time since Josh had turned me away.

More importantly, Ben made me laugh. When he touched me—his fingertips grazing my hand and my back—it was electric. As the ball dropped and people chanted down from ten to five to one, Ben twisted me toward him, pulling me close, and pressed his lips to mine. Standing there as one year turned into the next, with Ben's arms wrapped around my waist and his lips pressing against my own, I forgot all about Josh Lane.

Ben brought me back to life.

He gave me something to hope for.

So I chose him.

What other choice did I have?

15

The Woods – 11:03 PM

My heart was still racing ten minutes after Mia and I escaped the house and flew from the golf course into the safety of the trees. I looked over my shoulder to make sure we hadn't been followed.

"Where are we going?" Mia's words were a shaky whisper.

"I'm trying to figure out where we are." I hoped we'd turned the right way. Up the hill, toward the trails where Josh and I had once spent so many hours together.

Rotting leaves sighed under our feet, and I shivered. I reached to my side, feeling for my purse, and realized I didn't have it. When I remembered it lying on the floor of the bedroom, I wanted to cry. All I had with me was the phone I'd stolen from Ben and the clear understanding that I had to keep moving or I'd be caught in an even bigger trap.

I took a right, Mia on my heels, and started up a steeper part of the trail, noticing a few familiar-looking trees. I was starting to feel better. Calmer. Like I could actually handle the situation I'd been thrust into. Then Ben's phone rang.

"Holy shit," Mia said, grabbing my arm and squeezing so tightly her fingernails dug into my skin. "That about gave me a heart attack. I thought you didn't have your phone."

"I don't." I yanked Ben's cell from the pocket of my jacket and checked the caller ID. Private—no name, no photo, no number. Absolutely nothing.

That's when the suspicion crept in. It was Ben. Or the guy who had been after me back at the party. Had to be. I swiped a shaky finger across the touch screen, declining the call.

"Whose phone is that?" Mia asked as I shoved it back into my pocket.

"Ben's."

"Any chance that's going to cause issues before we get through tonight?"

"I'm guessing there's a pretty good chance," I said, trying to keep the anxiety out of my voice.

"Perfect." Mia ran a hand through her hair, looking around as if she expected something to jump out and grab her. "That's just perfect."

"There's also a chance that it might give us an advantage."

I looked around, centering myself, remembering exactly where I was and why I was there. When I saw the gnarled sister trees that had been braided together for a century or more, I almost cried with relief.

I rounded the last curve in the trail, Mia right by my side, and stepped from the wood's deepest shadows into a puddle of the moon's light. The tower rose before me, beckoning with the promise of solitude—what I needed if I was going to figure anything out.

"Whoa." Mia grabbed my arm again, tugging me back. "How did we get here?"

"I brought us here. It's safe."

"Didn't we already establish that this place is, like,

overflowing with bad mojo?"

"That's in your head. The tower will give us exactly what we need. Cover. Neither of us can go home—our parents would know something's up. Besides, I'm assuming Ben and the guy he's with will check our houses eventually. Brooklyn's, too. Ben knows her parents are out of town and I'm spending the weekend there."

"Okay. I see your point. But *here*? Do we really have to stop *here*, Hadley?"

"Yes. I have Ben's phone, remember? He might have deleted that picture from Facebook, but I need to wipe it out of existence. Before we do anything else."

"You might want to consider turning off Ben's location services before you worry about the pictures. Unless, of course, you want him to figure out you stole his phone when he comes looking for it."

"Oh my God, you're brilliant!" I swiped through the settings and made sure they were switched to off. "One more thing," I said, back stepping toward the tower and its yawning doorway.

"No, Hadley. No way."

"We have to. What if they followed us? That guy back there—Ben's afraid of him. Ben said to hide somewhere that he won't think to look. He'd never in a million years picture me at the top of this tower."

I didn't wait for her reply. She'd try to stop me. Racing up the spiral staircase, I shoved my way back into the night air. I stood at the top, breathing in and out. Trying to gain control.

I counted to ten and then did what I dreaded most. I wrapped my fingers around Ben's phone and pulled it out of my pocket, waking it up. The bright light flashing into the night hurt my eyes, making me squint. I kept going, intent on facing the truth, no matter how horrible it might be. Ever since the night we'd celebrated Ben's birthday, there'd been a gaping void in my memory.

There were flashes—Ben's smile, the freckles on his hand as he ran his fingers across my skin, how his curtains billowed in the breeze. There were facts—I'd had too much to drink, I'd felt like taking a risk, I'd loved feeling the sweep of my arm as I pulled off my bra. There were the few memories kicked loose by the awful picture. But that was it.

Biting my lip, I pressed the icon and scrolled through the gallery until my folder was there, staring up at me. I sucked in a deep breath, then pressed a shaking fingertip to my name. And waited.

I heard the staircase creak and shudder, and Mia popped through the open doorway, her eyes wild with fear. "Don't you *ever* do that again," she said, shaking her finger at me. "I was scared to death."

"You wouldn't have come up any other way. If I'd waited until you were ready, we'd still be down there."

"Which is a problem because . . . ?"

I ignored her, focusing on the phone. She walked to my side and sucked in a breath as she saw what was on display.

The first picture was me twirling, topless, barefoot, but wearing a pair of skinny jeans. In the next few, I was pulling my jeans down as though I was trying to act sexy but couldn't, wobbling after all the alcohol I'd been stupid enough to drink. Then there were shots where I was posing, leaning on the edge of Ben's bed, one bent knee raised, with my head tipped back, baring it all. And then there were more. Much worse than the rest.

As I scrolled through the images, I realized that my eyes were hazy and confused, and I wasn't looking directly at the camera but behind it, like I couldn't focus, no matter how hard I tried. Just like Penny. My lips were parted, too, as if I was trying to say something but couldn't get it out.

Was I trying to protest?

Had I asked Ben to stop?

"You don't remember anything?" Mia asked.

I shook my head, wanting to melt into the ground. To disappear. Facing the truth was worse than I'd expected.

Mia looked at me, her eyes sad. "How much did you have to drink that night?"

"From the look of it, a lot. But I can't remember."

I swiveled away from Mia, closing my folder, and stared up at the night sky. The stars flickered above, appearing to hide an even deeper secret. I had to know all of it before I moved another inch. I backtracked to the main menu, selected Sydney's folder, and saw more of the same types of shots—starring a gorgeous face and disgustingly perfect body.

"It's not just me," I whispered.

"What do you mean it's not just—"

I showed Mia the phone, the most revealing shot of Sydney. Mia put a hand to her mouth, her eyes crinkling with confusion, which quickly turned to anger.

I went back again, pressing my finger to Treen's name, wanting to finish what I'd started.

"What's Ben doing with these, Hadley? This is seriously—"

The sound of tires racing on the winding road and the

blast of music pulsing through the night cut her off.

I saw headlights and expected the beams to sail by, the car itself a blur, leaving nothing behind but a trickling dance of windswept leaves.

But the car slowed as the driver pulled around the bend.

"Duck!" I reached for Mia's arm, pulling her down with me as I crouched behind the stone wall.

"We have to get out of here." Mia jerked away from me. "Get to the trails and leave."

"No." I tugged her back, pulling her against me. "No one ever comes up here. Just be quiet and we'll be fine."

Mia's body was shaking. She was terrified. I couldn't let her down.

"It could be here, but I wouldn't count on it."

"Seems like you can't count on much tonight, Baden. And I can't count on you. That's why we're going to find her." The second voice. Deeper. Still scratchy. And totally unrecognizable. "She'll help us figure this out."

"I told you already, dude. She doesn't have a clue. We need to get our hands on Josh Lane."

In spite of those pictures, I silently thanked Ben. He was trying to protect me.

"Look, Baden, you're not in charge here. Not since you lost my shit. Trust me, we will find Josh Lane. And we will deal with him. But we're also going after that little bitch you call a girlfriend. Because I don't care what you say. She knows something."

"Bro, chill already. She's harmless. It's not like she's going to—"

"She's not going to do *anything*. Because I'm taking over,

you hear? And I'm not going to *chill*, either, you rich little prick. You think money can solve all your problems? Not this one. This is about more than money. This has to do with respect. And facing consequences. This is about protecting the game."

I expected Ben to explode, to hop into the driver's seat of his BMW and pull away with a squeal of his expensive, high-performance tires, leaving this guy behind. No one talked to Ben Baden that way. Ever.

But all I heard was silence.

The shuffling of feet.

"There's nothing here, Baden."

"I told you it was a slim chance."

"Where did you get your little tip?"

"One of her best friends."

"Because best friends always rat each other out? That was clever." The guy with the scratchy voice had an even scratchier laugh. "And what, exactly, did she tell you?"

"Mia—the chick she ran with—had to pee, so they stopped for a few here at the tower before they headed back to the party."

Brooklyn. Ben had talked to Brooklyn. I wondered what she had spilled. What she was able to keep to herself. How worried she was when she heard about how Mia and I had disappeared.

"There's nothing over by the memorial." Ben's voice was weary. I wondered what he'd gotten himself into. I even felt sorry for him for a sliver of a second. Until I remembered the pictures he had stored on his phone.

"Where'd they pick up Josh Lane?"

The anger that surrounded the question scared me.

"They saw Josh back at Circle K."

"Well, then, that's our next stop. Let's hit it."

"Yeah," Ben said. "Let's hit it."

I pulled away from Mia slowly, creeping my fingers up the wall and grasping tightly onto the edge. My legs were shaky and unstable as I raised myself and peered over the cool ledge of rocks.

I wanted to know exactly who I was up against. Who it was that felt so sure I knew the truth behind whatever big, dark secret I'd tripped into.

But I caught only a flicker as Ben backed away from the pull-off and headed toward town, to the Circle K, where Brooklyn had been smart enough to misdirect them.

As I watched the red taillights of the BMW flow around a sharp curve, I counted the things I had just learned about my new enemy:

He had a voice as rough as sandpaper.

He was wearing a dark pair of jeans and a gray hoodie with the hood up.

He was holding a small, sturdy object in his lap, his fingers curled tightly around the base.

As the sound of the car's engine faded into the night, my mind tried to make sense of what I'd seen.

I felt it was important—something I needed to understand.

But I'd only seen a flash, just bright enough to spark and flare in the light of the moon.

16

Just North of Lexington, Kentucky – 1:27 AM
Trip Odometer – 128 miles

Josh and I had been silent for a long time. I was confused about a lot of things but especially the way he'd mentioned my relationship with Ben. I wondered if Josh had ever cared. About me. About us. Or had it all been a lie?

I pressed my lips shut, not even glancing at Josh's profile while he steered the car around the hilly terrain of northern Kentucky. The quiet darkness of the late-late night and the steady hum of the tires lulled me into a false sense of security. As if we could stay that way, silent but together again, forever.

The thing is, nothing lasts forever.

Just north of Lexington, Kentucky, Josh veered onto a ramp that led to a rest area. He eased into an open space and put the BMW in park, leaned his head back on the headrest, and closed his eyes. I thought he might drift off to sleep, leaving me essentially alone and totally unsure what to do.

He spoke, shattering the silence. "Look, Hadley, I don't like this situation any more than you do. But we're stuck together, so we have to make some decisions."

With his eyes still closed, I took the opportunity to look at him, really look at him, for the first time since Penny died.

Everything felt familiar—the freckles that dotted his nose, the way his lips were slightly parted, the curve of his cheek running into his chin.

"Like what?" I finally managed to ask.

"How about where are we going? What, exactly, is the plan?" Josh opened his eyes and tipped his head toward me, soft wisps of hair falling across his forehead, the lights from the dash illuminating his face. "And then there's that paper bag to consider."

"Right," I said. "The bag."

"It's not smart to have it in the car."

"So, you want to just throw it out?"

"Well, yeah. But I'm not so sure that's the best idea." He yawned. "We *will* have to deal with Ben. Eventually."

"Right," I said. "Ben."

"I have an idea. But I don't know if you're gonna go for it."

"Try me."

"First, we have to figure out what we're doing. Where we're going."

"We're going south," I said, as if that answered everything.

Josh grunted and shook his head. "But what's our final destination? I mean, Kentucky's great—it's not Ohio, specifically not *Oak Grove*, Ohio—but we're just driving around aimlessly."

"We're not driving aimlessly. We're driving—"

"—south. I get that part. And I know what we're running *from*. But we should be running *to* something, shouldn't we?"

"I hadn't thought of that part yet."

"Well, it's time." He sighed. "Where do you want to go?"

"We're almost to Lexington?" I asked.

Josh nodded.

"It doesn't feel like it took too long to get here."

"About an hour and a half."

"Yeah, but it doesn't feel like it. And it *is* spring break." Josh raised his eyebrows. "We could go a little crazy." I laughed, but the sound was dripping with nervousness. The next few minutes would determine everything. "Won't I-75 get us to the ocean?"

"Yeah, but—"

"I vote for a beach," I said, channeling my inner Penny. I had no doubt that she would take this thing all the way. "We could kick off our shoes. Run through the sand."

Josh nodded, slowly. "That does sound pretty tempting."

"We have a car."

"Okay, I'll play along. What about cash? That's a lot of gas money. And food? Not to mention, where would we stay?"

"You think too much. I have one of my mom's credit cards for emergencies. This is an emergency, right?"

"I guess if you kind of squint your eyes until your lashes blur everything together, it might look that way."

"As for the rest, who cares? I'll sleep in the car if I have to."

"What about your mom? Won't she freak if you're not home by curfew?"

I looked at the clock on the dash. 1:33 AM.

"She thinks I'm spending the weekend at Brooklyn's. I can always call and say I'm staying an extra day or two since we're on break. What about your parents?"

"Mom's working the graveyard shift in the ICU now, so I hardly see her anyway." Josh's eyes dropped to the steering wheel. "Dad . . . well, he's around. But kind of *not* at the same time. He won't notice if I don't make it home."

I wondered what he meant but decided not to ask. "So we're good?"

Josh looked out the windshield, his lashes sweeping up and down. When he nodded, I reached across the console and grabbed his arm, squeezing.

"Good." I wanted to thank him. But I couldn't get the words out.

"Right. Because stealing a car and driving it from Ohio to Florida makes so much sense." He looked down at my hand, which was still gripping his arm. I let my fingers melt off his skin and drop away.

"So, what's your idea for Ben's little bag-o-drugs?" I asked.

"We stash them."

"Stash them?"

"Yeah. I'm thinking here."

"At the rest area?" I looked out Josh's window, watching a man with a scruffy face and puffy eyes ease his way out of a red truck and start toward the vending machines standing like soldiers in the bright lights of the welcome center.

"Not on the counter of the ladies' room or anything. We hide them. Back in the woods. Bury them at the base of a tree, mark the trunk, and head out. I don't want them near us. With that load of party favors, if anything goes wrong, we could get busted for distribution."

"It could work. But there's one thing."

Josh looked at me. "What?"

"I want to know what's in that bag. Exactly what every pill is. We're not going to be able to find that out unless we take a few."

"Trust me, you don't want to swallow any of that crap. It'll make you feel like a zombie. And zombies don't make good drivers. There's no way I can get us all the way to Florida, so you're going to have to drive, too."

"Not *taking* as in swallowing. *Taking* as in what we did with this car. Borrowing. There's gotta be someone who can identify them."

"Even that's a risk, especially if we're driving so far." Josh pulled his phone from his pocket. "But we might be able to figure out what everything is without having them in the car."

"How?"

"I know someone who might be able to help." Josh motioned for me to grab the bag from under my seat. "Pull one of each pill out and put them on something flat and dark so they'll be easy to see. Then take a picture."

I leaned down and started unrolling the paper bag, reaching in to pull out the largest plastic bag. My hands were shaking. It might have been the middle of the night, but the rest area's parking lot was brightly lit. The man with the scruffy face and puffy eyes was walking back toward us, a steaming Styrofoam cup in one hand, his keys in the other. He got into his truck, nodding to Josh and me with a lit cigarette dangling from his mouth.

Josh yanked on the driver's-side door handle and shoved his way out of the car just as the man revved his engine and pulled away. The scent of exhaust filled the BMW.

"Where are you going?" I asked.

"Gotta take a leak. While I'm gone, I'll look for a place to bury the package. In the meantime, you might want to think about getting in the backseat so you're not so visible."

Just then, a car pulled into the empty space next to my side of the BMW, a minivan spilling out a weary-looking mother and father and two sleepy-eyed children wearing pj's.

Josh ignored them and walked toward the restrooms. The mother wobbled behind him, pulling her children alongside her, the father trailing them all. I hit the lock and climbed into the backseat.

It didn't take me long to separate the smaller bags. I took one pill from each and lay them a few inches apart on the black leather of the seat. When I finished, I stared down at an oblong white pill, a round yellow one, a deep-blue capsule, and two different sizes of round white discs. They all had some kind of code depressed into or stamped on one side. I'd made sure the number/letter combinations were face-up.

I leaned back to the front of the car and grabbed my phone. It was vibrating, but I didn't care. I'd turned the ringer off after my last chat with Ben. It felt strange to think he was still calling. When the buzzing stopped, I woke up the phone. I had thirteen new voice mails, seventeen texts, and eleven new Facebook notifications. I ignored them all and took a picture, the flash lighting up the whole car.

In the glare, I saw Josh's backpack lying on the floorboard, right beside my foot, shoved halfway under the driver's seat. I glanced through the large windows that fronted the welcome center, toward the entrance to the men's room, and then again to the backpack, wondering what a guy like Josh Lane carried around everywhere he went.

I almost reached down to grab it. To slide the zipper of the main pocket open and dig around for some answers.

But a car eased into the empty space next to the driver's side—some kind of sedan, which was better than a truck or

SUV. Lower to the ground meant less opportunity to peer in and see what I had spread out in front of me.

The front of the car was black.

But then I noticed something strange.

The passenger door was white.

And smack in its center was the decal of a large star.

Parked beside me, stepping out of his car and hiking up his heavy-duty utility belt, was a trooper, a member of the Kentucky State Police.

17

THE WITCHES' TOWER – 11:37 PM

"THIS IS bad, Hadley," Mia said, her voice a shrill whisper.

"This is bad," I agreed.

Mia stood from her crouched-down hiding spot, her hands gripping the ledge of the tower to steady herself. "This is really bad."

"But we can handle it."

"Handle what? The part where you decided to pick up the guy who killed Penny and—"

"Josh didn't *kill* Penny. Not like everyone makes it seem."

"He hit her with his car. She died. Broken down to its simplest form, it goes a little like this: he killed her."

"It was an accident," I said, feeling a need to protect Josh. Finding him at the top of the tower earlier, hearing his voice and looking into his eyes, being so close again after so long—that had all thrown me off balance. But seeing the football team attacking him, hearing Ben and whoever that guy he was with say they were after Josh—made me want to put the past aside.

"You're still defending him? After all this time?" Mia dropped her hands to her sides, curling them into fists as she took in a deep breath.

"You would, too. If you could step back for just a second and see the whole picture."

"You'll have to excuse me. I'm a little out of my element at the moment. Being chased away from a party for God only knows what reason, running through the woods, and then finding myself *here* of all places."

"The tower saved us."

"Yeah, but there are still those pictures. And that guy with the chainsaw voice. And the little fact that *I have to pee*."

"Again?"

"Yes, *again*. If you'll kindly walk down the creep-show staircase with me so I don't die of fright before I can empty my bladder, I'd appreciate it."

I was glad I'd kept the pictures of Penny a secret so Mia couldn't add that item to her list. "We need a plan."

"Obviously." Mia's voice softened. "But where are we supposed to begin?"

"Maybe with a pee break?" I smiled.

Mia rolled her eyes. "You're lucky I love you."

"Obviously." I grabbed her hand and tugged her toward the doorway. The staircase creaked as we raced down the steps, past that old umbrella that belonged to no one and everyone at the same time.

"Come on," I said, leading her to the trails. "Back to the woods? Do we have to?"

"Well, I can think of a million reasons why we can't go traipsing down Old Henderson Road."

Mia groaned, and I wasn't sure if it was from irritation or the pressure on her bladder. We followed a curving trail that took us away from the tower, past the braided sister trees, and down a steep hill.

When Mia and I got to a flat patch, she ducked behind a tree. As I waited for her, I tried to calm myself. I'd made it this far, and I'd get through the rest just fine. Somehow.

"So," Mia said, rounding the tree and making her way back to me. "What do we do next?"

"We have options."

"Do we? Because it kinda feels like we've run out of those."

"There are always options. Shall I list the ones I've come up with?"

"Please."

We walked down the trail, moonlight flickering through the leaves and dancing on the path before us. "The way I look at it, we have a few issues that need to be dealt with."

"I'm thinking you might be right."

"First, there's Josh."

"An issue if there ever was one."

"He took something from Ben."

"I gathered that from the little tête-à-tête we just overheard."

I veered off the main trail, taking a fork that led us down a path shadowed by tightly woven pine trees. The trail would widen as we made our way to the place I knew I needed to be. Mia followed willingly. I took that as a very positive sign.

"We have to find Josh. We need to know what he took from that car. It's the only way to be sure about what we're up against."

"Agreed," Mia said, "but how do we even begin to look for him? He's practically a nonentity. Other than slinking around school, trying to make himself invisible, no one knows what he's been doing the past year."

"You're forgetting that we have history, Josh and I."

"I haven't forgotten," Mia said. "You think you can find him?"

"I hope so. But before we can focus on that, Brooklyn needs to pick us up."

"I like that idea." Mia pulled her phone out of her pocket. "Why the hell didn't I think of it?"

"Little sidetracked, I'm guessing, but before you call her—"

"No." Mia stopped in the middle of the trail, the light from her phone casting a bluish glow on her face as she scrolled through her contact list. "That sounds like stalling, and there will be no stalling when it comes to Brooklyn picking us up. She's texted thirteen times. Total freak-out doesn't begin to describe the tone of these messages."

"We'll text her in a minute. There's just one stop I need to make first."

"One stop *where*? If it's not directly related to us getting into Brooklyn's car—"

"I have to deal with the pictures."

Mia's eyes went wide. "You have his phone. You're covered, right? Brooklyn can take us straight to the police station so you can bust Ben Baden cold."

"I know that's probably what I should do, but the thought of showing those pictures to some crusty cop makes me want to throw up."

Mia shrugged. "I think that's a mistake, but it's your call. You want to go that route, just delete them, end of story."

"What if it's just the beginning of the story?" I bit my lip, listening to the trickle of the creek. "You saw me and Sydney and Treen, but there are more. What if those pictures aren't just on his phone? No matter what I decide to do, I can't risk leaving any trace of them behind."

"What, exactly, are you suggesting?"

"Are you sure you need to know?" I started down the trail again.

"Don't play games with me, Hadley. I'm not just going to blindly follow you around all night."

But she was. Down the dark path. Around the bend. Right to the bank of the creek that twisted through the woods. Our feet pressed into the soft, wet earth, the trickle of water rising around us like thick, heavy smoke.

"He has no idea where we are. Remember that, okay?"

Mia looked down at the silver moonlight flickering along the ripples. "Do *you* even know where we are? I don't have a clue."

I pointed through the trees on the opposite bank. "See that, through there?"

Mia squinted, trying to make out what I was pointing at. "Lawn furniture? A barbecue? Am I supposed to be looking for something specific?"

"You don't recognize that house?"

"Hadley." Mia groaned.

"He said to hide where he wouldn't think to find me."

"So you decided to come here? *Here*, of all places?"

"Ben's house is the best hiding spot."

Mia sighed, her shoulders slumping. "Of course it is."

"We know he's not home."

"We don't really know anything."

"We know they're looking for us. They went to Circle K.

There's no way they'll check here."

"So you want to break into Ben's house?" Mia shook her head.

"I have to. And, if you want to get technical, it's not officially breaking in. Do you know how many times I've been here alone, hanging out after school until weight lifting ended? I know where the key is."

"Not your best idea, Hadley. Remember options? There are always options."

"Yeah, not in this case."

"Hadley Miller, stop and think. Please. You can't just break into his house and, what? Steal—"

"What he stole from me in the first place? What he stole from all those girls? What he did was wrong, Mia." My voice had suddenly gone all shiver-shaky, and I hated the sound. I took a deep breath and steadied myself. "Look, you don't want to come. Fine. Stay here. I'll be back."

I hopped onto a large rock a third of the way across the creek, my foot slipping, splashing in the icy-cold water.

"It's too risky, Hadley," Mia called after me.

I hopped to the next rock and looked over my shoulder. "If we don't take some risks, we'll never get through tonight."

Mia whispered something under her breath.

I hopped to the next rock, relief seeping into my veins when I heard her feet hit a stone behind me.

"You won't regret this," I said.

"Right. Whatever. I really don't have anything to lose. But you do. And God knows you need someone to look after you."

I hopped to the bank, my feet sliding a bit on the damp ground. "I'm glad I have you on my side, Mia Pia."

"You're gonna owe me so freaking big you might not ever be able to pay me back."

"This is the right thing," I said. I thought of the pictures, of all those girls, the image of Penny lying on the blue tile floor of that shower. "Even if it doesn't feel like it, this is the right thing. You'll see."

When Mia jumped to the bank, I grabbed her hand, pulling her along, trying to forget what had happened the last time we'd stood together under those trees. There had been four of us—Mia, Brooklyn, Penny, me—surrounded by the sounds of music and laughter, the thrum of the party's energy vibrating the night air. Penny had been standing right in front of me, a faraway look in her eyes as she told us she was leaving. There had been a shiver in her voice that I'd noticed and ignored, soaking up the warmth of her embrace as we said our final good-bye.

Beneath it all had been my lie to Josh about girls' night and my decision to go to the party. The way the two choices had already collided without our even knowing, setting events in motion that would lead to the death of one of my best friends.

18

Just North of Lexington, Kentucky – 2:03 AM
Trip Odometer – 128 Miles

"You always talk to cops like that?" I asked as Josh opened the driver's-side door and slid into the seat next to me. I was still in shock from watching him stand in the path between the car and the welcome center, chatting with the trooper for the past five minutes. But Josh had bought me enough time to put away the pills and creep back over the console to the passenger seat.

"The thing with cops is, you have to treat them the way they think they deserve to be treated. Lots of eye contact, but not so direct that you seem cocky. Calling them *sir* helps, too." Josh shrugged. "Makes me seem less suspicious, doesn't it?"

"Accosting him at a rest area?"

"It was a diversion." Josh chuckled. "I asked him how many hours until we'd hit Knoxville. Like I was trying to be a cautious driver, weighing how much longer until I'd be too tired to go any farther."

"Did he buy it?"

Josh looked at me and raised his eyebrows. "What do you think?"

I thought it was time—finally—that this was my chance to get answers to the questions that had haunted me for the past year. I heard the echo of Mia's voice ringing through my head, a warning that came from some flickering memory I couldn't quite place.

It's too risky, Hadley.

I wanted to tell her that if I didn't take some risks, I'd never get through tonight.

I swiveled in my seat to face Josh head-on. "I think you've learned a thing or two about how to play the system."

His eyes narrowed. "What's that supposed to mean?"

"After the accident, when you were released from the hospital, there must have been some kind of interrogation."

"Yeah. I'm sure you've heard. The whole thing was ruled an accident."

"But then, back in December, you disappeared a few weeks before winter break. Everyone says you were in juvie. You were gone for at least a month. Maybe that's where you learned how to cozy up to the cops?"

He turned away from me. "You can't believe everything you hear, Hadley."

"So you didn't go to JDC?" I needed to know. Everything. "There were no consequences?"

Josh's eyebrows pulled together in a tight line. "You really think I haven't faced any consequences?"

"Okay. Maybe that wasn't the best word."

"Hadley, you have no idea what you're talking about."

"Then tell me."

"I can't just—"

"I heard you were drinking. The night . . . *that* night. People said all kinds of things . . . that your dad got you out of it by paying someone off. I just want to know what really happened."

"Leave it alone." Josh leaned in so close I could smell chocolaty caramel on his breath from the Twix he'd been eating while he was talking to the trooper. "Please."

"Penny's gone. She was one of my best friends. No one knows what really happened. I have to ask. You're the only one who has answers."

"Trust me, you don't want the answers." Josh's voice was a shaky whisper.

"Try me. Try *something*! You wander around, not standing up for yourself when people accuse you of the worst thing ever. What are people supposed to think when you just take the shit everyone throws your way?"

"What else am I supposed to do?" he asked, his voice cracking.

"I know you, Josh. Knew you, at least, back then. I don't believe you were drinking. I never have. I *know* it was an accident. I just need to hear you say it."

"It doesn't matter." Josh grabbed my hands, squeezing so tight my fingers ached. "Penny's dead. I killed her. And I deserve whatever comes my way because of it."

But that was wrong. It wasn't his fault. It was mine. I reached for the door handle, pushing with all of my weight until I tumbled out of the car.

"Hadley!"

I slammed the door behind me and ran for the sparkling glass door of the welcome center. But then I saw the trooper feeding coins into a vending machine and turned, racing across the grass, wishing I could veer around the corner and disappear. Josh was there before I could escape into the shadows, his hands on my shoulders, forcing me to face him.

"I can't take it back, what I did. If I could make it me instead of her, I would. But that's not how it works. So, yeah, I take everyone's shit. Because I deserve it." Josh's chest heaved, as if he was fighting for control. "But right now, none of that matters. Right now, we have to chill, okay? Because that trooper is going to walk past us in about a minute, and we have to look cool or else he's gonna ask questions."

I shook my head. "I can't answer questions."

"I know. Take a deep breath and think of something easy. Like making a deep hole in the ground so we can hide those pills. Or how we should mark the tree I chose. Two trees, really. Kinda like the sisters at the tower."

My lips parted in a small gasp. "The two that are all twisted together like a braid?"

Josh nodded, his eyes flicking to something over my shoulder then back to me.

"Can you forget everything for a few seconds?" he asked.

"What?"

"Just let it all go. For a few seconds?"

"I don't know how—"

His lips pressed against mine. They were silky soft, gentle, and tasted sweet, taking me back to the woods, the quiet darkness of his basement, the shadowed stoop of my front porch.

I remembered every detail as if it were happening now instead of a year ago—the night we'd escaped the cross-country season-opening picnic together. How he'd held my hand above his head, leading me away from the steady beat of music rising from the iPod dock centered on a table covered with plates of cookies and cupcakes, pulling me into the earthy scent of the woods. Pressing me up against a tree. His breath was a mixture of frosting and spearmint, his lips grazing my collarbone, trailing up the length of my neck to the spot just behind my ear. I remembered the sizzling feeling that trickled up and down my spine, the heat that seemed to flow between and around and through us as his lips found mine.

Standing by that welcome center, I pulled Josh to me, my arms wrapping around his neck, hands clasping together, that old need and exhilaration rushing through my body, and I didn't want to let go.

He held me tight, burying his face in my neck, tickling my ear with his breath. "Not much longer."

None of it made any sense. The kiss, my emotions, his words.

Until I heard the footsteps, thudding along the concrete beside us. Until I tipped my head onto Josh's shoulder and watched the trooper walk past us, place a can of soda on the hood of his car, and open the driver's-side door. He fumbled with something, then grabbed the soda, slid behind the wheel, and pulled his door closed. A minute later, he was backing out of the space, his headlights sweeping across the shadows created by the trees.

And then he was gone.

Josh's hands slipped down my back, freeing me.

Feeling a rush of disappointment, I looked at Josh's feet, almost asking him a million questions—questions that had nothing to do with Penny and everything to do with us—but I couldn't find the words.

Then his phone chimed. He pulled it from his pocket, studying the screen for a few seconds before looking up at me.

"Sorry about the kiss. I just figured it would look natural.

I'd told him I was with my girlfriend and all."

I nodded, still unable to say anything, wondering if he'd felt the energy that had taken over my body.

Josh held up his phone. "It's Sam. You can text that picture and, hopefully, we'll know what those pills are in the next few hours. I'll give you the number after we take care of the package."

More questions tangled in my head as I watched Josh turn and jog back to the car and grab his backpack and the bag from beneath the passenger seat. Those questions twisted as he opened the backpack and stuffed the drugs inside, jogged back to where I was standing, and waved for me to follow. He turned the corner and disappeared into the shadows.

I took a few deep, calming breaths, telling myself it didn't matter. The kiss was nothing. My feelings were nothing more than ripples from the past.

Trailing behind Josh, I stuffed the questions down deep. The answers wouldn't change anything. They wouldn't rewind time or bring Penny back.

I found him kneeling at the base of two twisted trees.

"You're right. They're just like the sisters."

He looked up at me and ran his fingers through his hair. "You gonna help?"

I kneeled beside him, feeling the cool dampness of the ground seeping through the knees of my jeans. Then I pressed my fingers into the ground, pulling at it and tossing handfuls aside.

We worked like that for a while, silent but for our breathing.

Josh pulled the package from his backpack and placed it in the hole we'd created. And then my phone vibrated in the pocket of my jacket, pulling me back to the awkward reality of the moment.

"Is it him?" Josh threw a handful of dirt on top of the brown paper bag, the crinkling sound mixing with the buzz of my phone.

Ben's face smiled up at me from what felt like another place and time.

"Yeah," I said. "I'm answering."

"Hadley, don't—"

"What do you want, Ben?"

He chuckled. "You haven't figured that out yet?"

"Okay, well, lemme guess." I stood and brushed the dirt off my jeans. "You definitely want your car."

"Ding. Ding. Ding. The car, Hadley. Where is it?"

"It's safe with me. Where it's going to stay until I feel like returning it. Have you taken my picture down yet?"

"You're serious?" Ben clicked his tongue. "I said I'm not taking it down until you return my car."

I sighed. "I found your stash."

His breathing hitched on the other end of the line. "Sorry, what?"

"You're sorry? That's deep. But not good enough."

"What did you say you found?"

"Drugs. A bag full of a few hundred pills. I didn't count or anything, but I'm estimating. A blue one, a yellow one, and a couple of—"

"There's a lot riding on that package. Let's cut the crap and—"

"So it's *not* the car you're after? Now I'm confused, because—"

"Hadley!" Ben shouted.

Josh stood up, grabbing for the phone. "Hang up. Just hang up."

I ducked away from Josh's dirt-covered hands and stumbled to the ground, falling in a heap right beside the backpack.

"Did I just hear a guy's voice?" Ben's tone raised a notch or two, his anger rising along with it. I wasn't stupid enough to think he was jealous, at least not in the rational, model-boyfriend sense of the word. It was all about the principle. If he couldn't have me, no one else could. "Who's with you?"

"As if that's any of your business?"

"I got your pictures. The guy in my car isn't the same one you were with at the bar. Call me crazy, but the guy sitting shotgun looks familiar. Like a certain outcast from Oak Grove. And I swear to God, if you're hanging out with that punk—"

Hearing things can sometimes be better than seeing them. I realized this as the phone slipped from my hand and the sound of Ben's accusations fell from my ear.

Lying there, gazing into the depths of Josh's open backpack, I saw something that scared me more than anything had all night: a handgun, its silver barrel smooth enough to spark and flare in the light of the moon.

19

Ben Baden's Backyard – 12:02 AM

"I CANNOT believe I let you talk me into this." Mia had pulled her long brown hair into a ponytail that swished across her back with each step. "I must be losing my mind."

"Did you text Brooklyn?" I whispered as we stalked up to a set of bay windows overlooking the Badens' backyard. "Is she going to meet us?"

"Yes and yes. She'll be at the rendezvous point in fifteen minutes, so let's get in and out as fast as we can."

I stopped walking and looked at Mia. Like me, she was stooped forward at an awkward angle so no one inside the house could possibly see us. Her ponytail had flipped itself over one shoulder, hanging down the length of her neck. Her entire body was rigid, lines drawn tight around her eyes. She was nervous. Scared, even. But she was standing there, right by my side.

"You're a pretty awesome friend," I whispered. She looked at me, surprised, as though she couldn't believe I'd point out something so boring when we were about to break into Ben's house. I'd said it because it was true. But, most of all, because I could. I knew now that moments like this one didn't last forever. That they could be snatched away without warning. That they needed to be appreciated before they were lost.

"I know you don't want to do this. But you're doing it anyway. For me. It means a lot, Mia."

"Yeah, yeah." She gave me a little wink. "What's next, my little sleuth?"

"A quick location scout."

A minute later, we were kneeling on the back patio of the Badens' mini-mansion, staring through the windows into a large room with a cathedral ceiling. In the center of the room, flanked by two oversize chairs, was a black leather couch. Lights flickered, washing the scene in bright blues and greens as someone on the television painted primer on a set of lawn furniture.

In the center of it all sat a woman wrapped in a yellow maxi dress, her rich chestnut hair piled on top of her head, one perfectly manicured hand gripping the stem of an empty, half-tipped wine glass. Her thin frame had sunk into the cushions. In spite of the way her head lolled to one side, and how her eyes drooped closed, she was beautiful.

"We can't go inside," Mia said. "Mrs. Baden's right there, watching TV."

"We don't have to worry about her. She's medicated by now."

"Medicated, how?" Mia asked.

"She has a little thing for pills. It started after her car accident."

"She was on her way to pick up Ben from soccer practice, right? We were in eighth grade. The accident shattered something."

"Her pelvis. She had a few surgeries and recovered okay,

but she never kicked the meds. She's passed out by nine o'clock every night."

"How come you never told me?"

I shrugged. "It's hard on Ben. He doesn't like to talk about it. And I'm not exactly sure that she gets all of her stuff the legal way. . . ."

"So what? She, like, cruises downtown in her Bentley and does a drive-by pickup?"

"There's this guy that stops by every few weeks. One of Ben's father's friends from college or something. I thought it was an affair at first, but they always hang out in the dining room, drinking wine, laughing, catching up. But only for a half hour. Then he leaves, and she's pretty much zoned out for the rest of the day."

"Cozy family," Mia whispered. "What about Mr. Baden?"

"He's away on some business trip this weekend."

"How are we getting in?" Mia asked. "This place has to have a security system."

"State of the art but never used. They think they're untouchable."

I crawled away from the window and stood when I reached the deck, rushing around it and down the slope of the backyard, my feet whispering in the grass. Mia was right behind me, her breath coming in waves, as we stepped to the sliding glass door that led to the finished walk-out basement. Ben's lair—practically his own private apartment—complete with a separate entrance, which, conveniently, was almost always unlocked.

I grabbed the handle and pulled the door open. It gave with only a slight squeak. And then we were inside. A trilogy of blue-black lava lamps bubbled atop a dresser in the back corner, casting an eerie, flowing glow on all of the walls.

"Holy shit, look at that TV." Mia's eyes were locked on an enormous flat-screen mounted across from Ben's bed.

"Don't act so surprised. You've seen his car. Ben gets what he wants, when he wants it. Without fail."

"Except tonight," Mia said with a chuckle.

"You've got that right."

Racing to Ben's desk, I reached for the charging station, yanking the cord for his phone out of the wall and winding it around my knuckles.

"We need a way to carry this stuff out. He's got a few backpacks up on a high shelf in his closet. Grab one, would you?"

Mia's eyes went wide. "I'm here for you, Hadley, but I don't exactly want to take part in this. I'm thinking police and forensic evidence and jail time and—"

"Mia, stop freaking out and think for a second. Think of the pictures. If we go down, he's going down, too. But we're not going to be able to prove anything if we don't have evidence. All of it."

"Oh my God, Hadley, you're killing me." Mia rolled her eyes, but she started moving, flipping the light on and disappearing into the walk-in closet.

I tried to focus. I didn't have long, and I needed to make sure I grabbed everything. Problem was, I wasn't sure what that might include. Tucking the phone charger into the pocket of my jacket, I turned around.

"Think," I said. "Think, think, think. What else do you need?"

My eyes tripped across the bed, halted by the red-striped

comforter. A flash of myself lying there, naked, popped into my head. I'd trusted Ben. Loved him, even. And he had taken all of that and betrayed me.

Suddenly, I questioned every decision I'd made since the start of the night, my mind reeling with thoughts of Josh.

I stumbled over to the bed and sat on the edge, lowering my face into the cup of my hands, squeezing my eyes closed. I felt as if Josh was there, *right there with me*. It was the strangest sensation. I smelled him, too—earth and woods and night—a perfect combination. I sank into the feeling, not caring if it had been brought on by panic or memory, just wanting to lose myself in him.

But then a loud *crash* echoed from the closet, snapping me to my feet.

"Son of a bitch," Mia whisper-shouted.

"What happened?" I rushed toward the closet, reaching out for the door frame to steady myself because I was dizzy, still feeling the heat of Josh, even though it didn't make any sense.

"I found the backpacks," Mia said, blowing a strand of hair from her eyes. Three backpacks were piled around her feet. One of them was open, its front flap gaping like a wound. Inside was a wooden box, the lid carved with an intricate design.

"What's that?" My fingers gripped the door frame tighter. Something about that box felt familiar but wrong, like a puzzle piece that didn't quite fit. I closed my eyes, feeling there should be trees swaying above me. Like I was standing at the edge of a deep, dark hole. Like the box wasn't a box at all but something cold and shiny and cruel.

Mia leaned down and scooped up the backpacks, stuffing two away on the shelf, clutching the other to her chest as she peered in at the box. "Looks like a little jewelry box, don't you think?"

I nodded, that light-headed feeling sweeping over me again.

Mia bit her lower lip. "Kind of strange. Ben probably doesn't have a whole lot of jewelry."

I took a deep breath, letting the tension slide away as logic set in. It was just a backpack. Just a wooden box.

"We need to stay focused. We're here for a reason, Mia."

I stepped away from the closet door—and the strange sense that something was off balance—with Mia close on my heels. I pushed a thumb into the front pocket of my skinny jeans, my skin grazing the silver band I'd tucked away earlier, making me think of that picture. Oh, God, that picture. I *hated* that picture.

"Hadley?" Mia reached out for my arm as she slung the now-closed backpack across her shoulder. "Are you okay? You look really pale and—"

She stopped mid-sentence. I didn't have a chance to tell her that I was not okay, that I might never be okay again after that picture ruined my life. I certainly didn't have the chance to grab Ben's computer—the reason we'd come here in the first place.

The voices just outside the sliding glass door stopped everything.

"We *will* find them," a very scratchy voice said. The same voice from the tower. "*Both* of them."

"Can't you just give it a rest?"

"No. We can't give it a rest." Ben. That voice was definitely Ben. But who had spoken just before him?

There was a pause. A shuffling of feet.

"Sounds like you're not up for this," the scratchy voice said. "You should probably go home."

I looked at Mia, my eyes wide. She mouthed something that looked a lot like *We are fucked*.

I shook my head, pointing toward the dark opening that led to Ben's bathroom. Scurrying toward it, I heard the swish of the backpack against Mia's shirt as she followed.

The sliding glass door opened as we made it to the bathroom tiles, cool and blue like the ocean. I swung around, nearly knocking heads with Mia, and whispered, "Shower," just as the voices started again, louder this time.

"I'm not going home," the new voice said. It was familiar, but I couldn't place it. The whoosh of blood rushing through my head threatened to block everything out.

"Well, if you're not with us," the scratchy voice said, "you're against us."

"Right," the familiar one said. "You've made your point."

I crept to the shower and Mia followed me inside, pulling the beveled glass door closed behind her. I tugged her to the far wall, as deep into the shadows as possible.

Standing there, trying to steady my breathing, I hoped my heart wasn't beating so loudly that Ben would hear it and come running. I grabbed Mia's hand and gave it a squeeze. She squeezed back.

I wanted to tell her I was sorry. That I'd been wrong about every single choice I had made on this crazy night.

I wanted to say a million things in that moment.
But all I could do was stand there.
Silent.
Waiting.

20

Knoxville, Tennessee – 4:57 AM
Trip Odometer – 297 miles

"I NEED to ask you a question." My voice was shaky, almost overtaken by the hum of the tires treading on the highway.

Since leaving the rest area nearly three hours ago, I'd slipped in and out of sleep, my unconscious mind replaying that rest-stop kiss over and over again—the feel of Josh's lips pressed against mine, the warmth of his breath on my neck, the heat of his hands touching me.

And then the vision of the gun would take over.

Josh glanced at me, his eyebrows raised. "Shoot."

The word almost stopped me. But I had to ask. "Why do you have a gun?"

Josh took in a slow breath. "You went through my backpack?"

"That's not an answer, Josh."

"The gun isn't your concern."

"How can you say that? It's in this car right now. With us. I want to know why."

"You afraid or something?" There was a teasing note to his voice. It should have freaked me out. Instead, it reminded me of the old Josh.

"Of you?" I shook my head. Josh wouldn't hurt me. No matter what happened between us, I knew he would never hurt me. Physically, at least. "No."

"Good. That should be the end of the discussion."

"After you tell me one thing. What are *you* afraid of?"

Josh laughed, but the sound was not a happy one.

"Tyler, maybe? His friends? Have they been making threats or—"

My questions were cut off by the sharp sound of a ringing phone—a phone that couldn't have been mine because I'd powered it down after my last call with Ben.

"Forget what you saw, Hadley. Just drop it."

The discussion was over. I wanted to keep pushing but knew it wasn't the time. Instead, I leaned my head back and closed my eyes, the ringing of the phone crashing into me as flickering streetlights raced across my eyelids.

"Why are you calling me?" Josh's tense greeting put me on alert.

"Yeah, that's right. I dealt with that already, so you can—" Josh's eyes darted to me. Through a muffled garble of rushed words from the other end of the line, I knew one thing. The person Josh was speaking to was male.

"Shit." Josh sighed. "Definitely not. I understand. Look . . . Thanks, okay? You didn't have to—"

More from the other end of the line, the staccato sound of words pouring through the phone.

"Sure. I appreciate it."

As Josh pulled the phone from his ear, I saw a glimpse of someone's picture—the flash of a red shirt and short blond hair. But that was all, nothing more.

"Who was that?"

Josh sped up and passed a car in the left lane, then flicked on the blinker, cutting in front of it. He didn't glance my way or acknowledge my question.

"I thought it was Ben," I said. "At first, I mean."

"Ben wouldn't call me. Ever."

"He might." I wondered, with Josh's past year, who *would* call him? And why? "He figured out you're in on this, Josh. Mia took a picture from the back of—"

"I don't care what he's figured out." Josh yawned. "The guy's a class A jerk-off."

"No argument there. Was it your friend . . . whoever you sent the picture of the pills to?"

"Sam?" Josh asked.

I wondered if Josh's drug expert was male or female. And then I got scared—the fluttering in my stomach meant that I cared.

"So, did *Sam* tell you what they are?"

"That wasn't Sam."

"You won't tell me about the gun. You won't tell me who just called. Why won't you tell me anything?"

Josh was silent, his teeth raking across his lower lip.

"Jesus, Josh. I'm just trying to figure out what's going on."

"You're pumping me for information. Back at the rest stop. Now."

"Can you blame me?" I asked. "I still have no idea what happened last year. And then there's the gun in your backpack. I'm worried that—"

"Worried?" Josh shook his head. "You're not worried. You don't give a shit about anything that has to do with me unless it affects you."

"Josh, I—How can you think that?"

"Oh, give it up. You're just like everybody else. Stop acting like you care."

"I'm *not* like everybody else. And I'm not *pumping you for information.* I have questions, sure. Not just about the accident, but about everything that's happened since. I want to know what your life is like now. The reason I don't ask is because it's . . ."

"It's what?"

"I don't know. Awkward?"

"Awkward because after what I did, I shouldn't have a life, right? Because I'm not allowed to have friends?"

"No, Josh. Because I'm afraid of offending you. Or bringing up something that might really suck for you to think about. Or having you take my head off, like you're doing right now. So Sam should be a safe topic, right? I don't know anyone named Sam—I'm guessing he's a new friend. How did you meet him?" I paused, waiting to see if Josh would correct me. Was *he* a *she*? Was the *him* actually a *her*? Like, a *girlfriend* kind of *her*?

Josh sighed. "Look, I'm sorry, okay? It's just hard sometimes."

"Yeah. Trust me. I get that."

"I met Sam at the hospital."

"Oh." I wavered between feeling guilty for bringing up yet another reminder of Penny and ticked that I still had no idea if Sam was male or female.

"Your attempt at avoiding shitty topics, it's a novel idea." Josh's voice sounded as tired as he looked. "But it's not very realistic these days."

"What was it like? At the hospital?"

"Which time? After the accident, it's a long, drug-induced blur. Doctors, nurses, physical and occupational therapists, IV drips, and—"

"What do you mean *which time*? You were there for weeks."

"Forty-seven days, if you count rehab after the hospital. But I had to go back." Josh paused, taking in a deep breath. "I went back a few weeks before winter break."

"You were in the hospital then?" I thought back to the empty desk in English class, the rumors floating through the halls about Josh being in juvie, pictured myself at that New Year's Eve party leaning against the foosball table, wondering where Josh was and lying to myself about how I didn't care.

"It sure as hell wasn't juvie. I bet there were lots of rumors after they sent me away, but I'm guessing none of them were true."

"Someone sent you away?"

"My parents." Josh paused. "There's a reason I didn't want to answer your questions, okay? It's embarrassing. Mortifying."

"Josh, you don't have to be embarrassed about anything with me. I know you. Have known you for—"

"You don't anymore, though. You don't know anything."

"Then tell me. Please."

"Don't say I didn't warn you." Josh tapped his thumb on the wheel, stopped, then started tapping again. "They sent me to a psych ward. They were worried I was going to kill myself. Or go crazy. Whatever. I wouldn't have done the first part. But I'm not so sure I haven't avoided the second."

"Oh, God, Josh, I didn't—"

"And that's where I met Sam. We bonded over hours of group therapy, warm fuzzy moments with our fucked-up peers, an endless supply of pills clinking together in little paper cups, and—"

"Josh." I looked at him then. Really looked at him. And in the flash of lights from a car passing on the other side of the freeway, I saw him fade from his current tortured self into the guy I'd once known. The guy I'd fallen so hard for I had to erase him completely from my mind and heart. "I tried to be there for you. I wanted to help. But every time I came close, you pushed me away. Do you even remember the day I went to see you in the hospital?"

I reached out, my fingers stretching across the space between us, a million tiny moments from our past boiling to the surface. But, like that day in the hospital, Josh pulled away, jerking his arm from my hand just before I could touch him.

"I remember," he said. "I meant what I said then. I wanted you to walk away. To leave me alone. I *still* want you to leave me alone."

"Josh, please."

He shook his head. "Next subject."

"Look, I need you to understand—"

"What? That this whole thing is as random as it gets? That you never in a million years would have spoken to me on top of that tower if your asshole boyfriend hadn't posted that picture of you on Facebook?" Josh laughed. "Trust me, I understand why we're here. You found me at just the right moment, and you decided to use me."

I twisted sideways in my seat. "And you weren't using me?"

Josh narrowed his eyes.

"When I invited you to the party, it was the first opportunity you've had in the last year to do something normal."

"As if we even made it to any party?"

"I'm just saying *if*—if we'd made it, you would have needed me."

"That's an interesting theory." Josh shook his head. "False. But interesting."

"What, you think you could have just waltzed through the front door? Grabbed yourself a cup and headed for the keg?"

"If you must know, I'd planned to go before I ever saw you. The entire senior class was invited, right? Ryan Peterson said so himself, *I heard him*, two days before break. He stood up on a table in the central commons and announced it. I knew tonight was my night. The tower was just a stop, a place to center myself before doing what I had to do."

I saw it again, the moonlight flashing off the smooth surface of that gun.

"What were you going there to do?" I asked.

"Fix things. I wanted to talk to Tyler." Josh tightened his grip on the steering wheel. His jaw muscles flexed.

"Talk to Tyler? No offense or anything, but that doesn't sound very—Oh, God, Josh. Is that why you have the gun? You were going to *make* Tyler talk to you?"

"Please, Hadley. Give me a little more credit than that." Josh stared straight ahead. The lines of his face were as hard as the tone of his voice. "It doesn't matter."

I knew that wasn't true. But I didn't have any idea what to say next, so I pressed my lips together and stared out the passenger-side window.

The steady thrum of the tires rolling along the pavement was the only sound until Josh flicked the blinker. He eased into the far right lane of the highway and onto a sloped exit ramp. I knew we were in Tennessee—we had just passed a sign placing us thirteen miles from Knoxville—but I didn't know much else. It was hard to tell anything other than that we were on a two-lane country road.

"We're running on empty," Josh said, tipping his chin up, the anger drained from his voice. "Sign said there's a gas station this way. I need a snack. And a nap. Those Jell-O shots should have worn off by now. Your turn behind the wheel."

"Josh, you have to tell me. Why did you want to talk to Tyler? What was so important that you'd risk going to that party by yourself? Tyler's friends, if they'd seen you, there's no telling what—"

"Enough, Hadley. Please. Just stop."

My mind tripped backward, starting with the first kiss at the tower and slipping through to the time after Josh had turned me away at the hospital, when I'd texted and called and emailed him, when he'd ignored me and ignored me and ignored me. Until that day in the library: I'd forced the issue by walking straight to his table and sitting down. He'd looked right at me, shook his head, and leaned forward, his voice a whisper as he told me to stop, *just stop*. It was over and he wanted me to leave him alone. His eyes had been hard, cold. And as he stood and walked out the door, everything I'd been hanging on to since the hospital—all my hope that he hadn't known what he was saying when he turned me away—slipped out of my grasp.

In that moment, I'd believed him.

But in this one, with the admission that he wanted to fix things with Tyler, I had to wonder—if I'd fought a little harder, if I'd held on, if I'd just told the whole truth—where might we be now?

21

Ben Baden's Bathroom – 12:57 AM

"We're dead," Mia whispered, her words bouncing off the glass walls of the shower. "He's going to find us. And then he's going to kill us."

"Quiet," I said.

"I don't get it, man. What the fuck are we doing here? I told you the plan. You're getting in my way. Not to mention that you lost my—"

"I know the plan," Ben said. "Trust me. We're not going to stop until we find it."

"What's the big deal?" the third person asked, irritation creeping into his words. "Whatever you're looking for, Hadley can't keep it forever. Just catch up with her tomorrow when she's not so pissed about the picture."

"We're on my timeline now." The scratchy words raked across my skin. "That means we find her tonight."

"I already told you," Ben said. "Hadley doesn't know anything. We need to find Josh Lane."

"Ben's trying to protect you," Mia whispered. "But he's scared. Whoever he's with, he's afraid of the guy."

I heard it, too. The fear in Ben's voice. The hesitation. It's as if he was calculating every word before he spoke.

"Your girlfriend brought Josh Lane to the party, which means she's our best shot at finding him. Call her. Find out where he is."

"That's the problem," Ben said. "I can't."

"Why the hell not?" Scratchy Voice Guy was pissed.

"I kinda stole her phone. And then I threw it into the ravine when we were back at the Witches' Tower."

"I thought *your* phone was missing," the third voice said, his irritation still evident.

"It is. I lost it back at the party," Ben said. "It must have fallen out when we were searching the car. But it's under control. We'll go back to find it just as soon as—" He cut off mid-sentence, and all I could hear was the rustling of feet on the carpet.

"Holy shit," Mia whispered. "He's coming."

"Shhh." I squeezed her hand tight. I could feel my blood pumping through my fingers. "We'll be fine."

"Someone's been here." Ben's voice had moved from one side of the room to the other. He was closer to the bathroom. To us.

"Don't tell me something else is missing."

"No," Ben said. "But the light from the closet's on. I turned it off before I left."

"Seriously? I don't know what you've gotten yourself into, Ben, but that sounds like paranoia has set in. Let's just go back to the party and—"

"Enough!" Scratchy Voice Guy yelled. "The party is *not* an option. Someone was here, so we search the place before we do anything else. If we don't find her, we think about how to contact her since Ben took away her phone. Great thinking, by the way, douche bag."

Footsteps came closer. My entire body stiffened. Mia held her breath.

"Where the hell are you going?" Scratchy Voice Guy asked.

"Take it easy, bro." He laughed, but the irritation was still there. "I just gotta take a leak. While I'm in there, I'll check the linen closet to make sure Hadley's not hiding out. Don't forget to look under the bed."

I knew the voice. Who it belonged to. It was the laugh, the way it rose at the end. Just like Penny's. And the sarcasm, the dry humor Penny had been famous for.

"Tyler," I whispered. "It's Tyler."

Mia sucked in a breath just as the light flipped on, the flash of bright white so harsh against my eyes that I squeezed them tight.

The door clicked shut, and all that was left was a deafening silence.

But then came Tyler's release echoing against the walls, so loud I thought I wouldn't be heard moving my foot just an inch, to slide away from Mia and give us both a bit more space. When I did, I tipped sideways, throwing Mia off balance. The movement was slight. Only an inch or two. But a large mirror hung over the sink and toilet, and in its reflection, Tyler had the perfect view of the shower behind him—of the shadowy figures hiding on the other side of the beveled glass doors.

A few last drips plopped into the water.

"You have got to be kidding me," Tyler whispered.

The sound of the zipper split the night in half—into the moments before Tyler knew we were there and the moments just after.

Mia's hand gripped mine tighter.

Tyler whipped around and yanked the shower door open, his face pulled tight with so much anger I thought he would give us away for sure.

"How *stupid* are you two?" he whispered.

Mia shifted her weight from one foot to the other. I hoped she didn't have to pee.

"You made it out of that party alive and you come *here*? Do you have any idea who's out there with Ben right now?" Tyler asked, stabbing his thumb over his shoulder. *"Roller Haughton."* He paused to let his words sink in.

"Roller Haughton?" I asked, my voice a whisper. "Isn't he some kind of small-time drug dealer?"

"I'm not sure he's small-time anymore. He supplies most of the high school and then some," Tyler said. "They lost something tonight. Something important. Won't tell me what, but I'm guessing it's not exactly legal."

"Roller graduated with Brooklyn's brother," Mia said. "Every time Eddie comes back to Oak Grove, Roller tries to meet up with him, but Eddie does whatever he can to avoid the guy. Says he's nothing but trouble."

"Interesting. That's exactly what my mom always said about Eddie." Tyler looked at me, his eyebrows arched. "News flash: Roller's not just trouble, he's pissed. *Really* pissed. And for some reason, Hadley, he's blaming you. I'm only tagging along to make sure things don't get out of hand. You were like a sister to Penny. She'd kill me if I didn't watch out for you."

I took a deep breath. "I can handle Roller. But only if you get Mia out of here. You have to—"

"I'm not leaving you," Mia said, jerking her hand from

mine and crossing her arms over her chest. "No freaking way."

"Roller Haughton, Mia. I don't want to get you mixed up with him."

"Yeah, well, I don't want *either of you* mixed up with him," Tyler said. "I don't know what he's looking for—drugs, or money, or something even worse—but if you tell me where it is, I'll take him to it. End of story."

"I don't know *what* it is, so I have no idea *where* it is."

"We don't." Mia sighed. "But Josh does."

"Technically," I said, "we don't know that for sure."

"Do you know where Josh is?" Tyler asked, worry creeping into his words.

"No. Last time I saw him, he was racing out of Ryan's party."

"You need to find Josh." Tyler looked me right in the eyes. "You need to warn him, okay?"

"We'll get right on that," Mia said. "If we make it out of here alive."

"I'll make sure you have the chance to escape. But you gotta lay low tonight. Don't let them find you."

"Why?" I asked.

"Because they've both *freaking lost it*, that's why," Tyler said.

"I wasn't asking why we should stay away from Roller and Ben. Why are you trying to save Josh? I figured you'd want to help them destroy him."

Knuckles rapped on the other side of the door. "What's taking so long, man?"

"I'm in here talking to Hadley and Mia," Tyler said.

I almost hit him, my hand balling into a fist as his words registered in my brain. I was stupid to think he would help.

But then Tyler laughed. "Gotcha, Baden. I'm taking a dump. A little privacy, please?"

"Oh, now he's the funny man." Ben laughed. It was his I've-had-too-much-to-drink laugh. I'd heard the same one the night of his birthday. Its echo reached up from the depths of my memory, a new flash making me feel dizzy and weak, and I needed to know . . . What had Ben done to me?

"Hurry the fuck up, dude," he said.

"If you want me to hurry, leave me alone."

I expected Ben to charge through the door, to know through some sixth sense that I was just a few small steps away. But then I wondered: if he knew we were here, would he lead Roller to us? Or away?

"Spray some of that flowery shit my mom left in there when you're finished," Ben said, his footsteps fading.

Tyler looked at me, his mouth turned down. "You asked why I'm trying to help Josh? Let's just say I owe him."

I wanted to ask what that meant, how Tyler could possibly owe Josh anything, but he kept talking, and I had to struggle to keep up.

"My parents are out of town this week. With the anniversary of Penny's . . . They had to get away. You can hide out at my house until this blows over. Remember where the spare key is?"

"Yeah, but—"

Tyler turned and flushed the toilet, glancing at us from the reflection in the mirror. "You'll go? As soon as we leave?"

I nodded. At the very same time, Mia shook her head. The movement was slight, but I caught it.

"Don't forget to find Josh."

"I won't." Tyler was right. Finding Josh was critical. He knew what Ben was after and could either hand it to me or, if he'd hidden it, take me to it. More importantly, I had to warn Josh that he was in serious danger.

"You don't have your phone." Tyler pulled his from the back pocket of his jeans and started scrolling through his contacts. "Here's Josh's number."

I stared at the numbers, willing myself to remember, glad that Mia was staring, too, her lips moving as she whispered them aloud.

"Find him. Then all of you, lay low." Tyler tucked his phone away and flipped the light switch, plunging us back into darkness. A murky glow filled the room when he opened the door, but he pulled it almost closed right behind him.

"You're not gonna want to go in there," Tyler said as he moved steadily away from us.

"You couldn't have done that back at Circle K?" Ben asked.

"Sorry, dude." Tyler laughed. "Now, what's the plan? Where are we headed next?"

"That's on a need-to-know basis," Roller said. "And right now, you don't need to know."

"Whatever," Tyler said. "Let's hit it."

I sighed and yanked my bangs out of my eyes, feeling a cool sheen of sweat on my forehead. Relief coursed through me. They were leaving, and we would have a chance to get what we had come for.

There was a shuffling of feet. The squeak of the sliding glass door. And then nothing but silence.

"Hadley," Mia whispered, her voice cracking.

"Yeah?"

"I can't. Penny's house? Not tonight."

"Mia, it's the best place for us to hide."

"Promise, Hadley. Promise you won't make me go there."

My mind was reeling. The only thing I could focus on with any certainty was the list of items that I needed to take from Ben's room. So I did the only thing I could to keep Mia going.

"I promise."

"Oh, thank God," Mia said. "Now, let me pee, and then let's get the hell out of here."

22

Atlanta, Georgia – 8:43 AM
Trip Odometer – 507 Miles

Hours had passed, but I couldn't get it out of my mind: the conversation we'd had just before turning on to the Tennessee backcountry road. The feeling I had that maybe, if I'd just tried a little harder, Josh wouldn't have been able to push me away. And the gun, every time I blinked, I saw it, and every time I saw it, I wondered.

Why, exactly, did Josh have a gun in his backpack? What had he been planning as he stood at the top of the Witches' Tower, his mind set on heading to Ryan Peterson's party?

A million questions had spiraled through my mind as Josh pulled into the run-down gas station, as he swung Ben's BMW alongside one of the three pumps and unfolded himself from the car, stretching his arms high up in the air. I had almost asked again. But then, as the gas flowed into the tank, he leaned down by my open window.

"You're up," Josh had said, tossing the keys into my lap. His eyes had been droopy, his chin covered in caramel-colored stubble. He'd looked so tired, so *normal* for once, that I'd kept quiet. "I'm beat. You've got to pay attention, though. We're taking I-85 south. It's faster."

I'd gone inside for a restroom break and a drink, and when I'd returned to the car, he was stretched out in the passenger seat. He was asleep before I even made it back to the highway, and he hadn't stirred once since, not as the sky turned from a deep bluish-purple into a swirling mixture of oranges and pinks. Not as we'd crossed the state line from Tennessee into Georgia, the rising sun casting its rays on the world, making everything around us shine with promise.

Nearly four hours later, I steered the car around a bend, glancing over at Josh. So still and quiet, so vulnerable as he lay there with one arm slung above his head, with his mouth open slightly, I thought about the simple truth that I knew deep down—the truth I had always known but couldn't bear to face.

I'd done this to Josh. Ruined his life. And there was only one way to make it right.

It was time to stop holding back. Keeping my eyes on the road, I slipped my hand from the steering wheel and touched him, grazing my fingers across the smooth skin of his arm. When I glanced over again, he was looking up at me, his eyes sleepy but more alive than I'd seen them since the night of the accident.

"We should talk," I said, my hand falling away from his arm.

"We should." Josh cleared his throat. "I want to start."

"There are things you need to know. Things I never—"

"I wasn't drinking." His voice was a hoarse whisper. "I know you said you never believed it. But I wanted you to hear me say the words. *I. Wasn't. Drinking.*"

I felt a surge of relief. I hadn't ever thought the rumors were true, not all the way, but there were times when doubt settled in, and confusion mixed up the details. I pressed my foot on the accelerator, hoping that each passing mile would make our past clearer.

"I went over to Joe's that night. The night Penny . . ." Josh sighed. "I still hate to say it, you know?"

I nodded, keeping my eyes focused on the broken white lines stretching in front of the car.

"After you called to cancel on me for your girls' night, Ricky texted that he'd just gotten a new video game. So, I met him over at Joe's house—we'd all agreed to avoid Baden's party." I tightened my grip on the steering wheel. "We hung out for a while, and then, when I could hardly keep my eyes open, I said I had to go. Ricky needed a ride—he was blasted from some concoction they'd made raiding Joe's parents' liquor cabinet—so I took him home."

"That's why you were on Old Henderson Road? You were the designated driver?"

"I guess you could call it that, but I'm hardly innocent. After taking Ricky home, I decided I wanted to see you. I couldn't stop thinking about you—how I wanted a kiss. Just one kiss. I was close to Brooklyn's, and even though it was *movies and pizza, no boys allowed*, I figured it was worth a shot. So when I hit Old Henderson, I pulled out my phone and—"

"Oh, Josh, no."

"I started texting you. Just one letter at a time, right? Then I'd look up to the road to make sure I was still on course. I thought I was being safe and—"

"Josh."

"I didn't see her, Hadley. She was standing right there in the middle of the road, but I didn't see her until it was too late."

I wanted to ask a million things at once. But my brain wasn't working well enough to form the words, let alone voice the questions.

Josh sighed, dropping his face into his hands and rubbing his eyes.

"It wasn't your fault," I whispered. I had to come clean, even if it ruined the last chance we might have. A chance I wasn't sure I wanted but was sure I didn't want to lose. "The accident. Penny. It was my fault."

"God, Hadley, no. I didn't tell you that to make you feel guilty. I just wanted you to know that I was thinking of you. That even though you probably don't believe me, you meant something to me."

"I lied, Josh." I bit my lower lip. I had never said it out loud before. But I had to now. "We didn't do movies and pizza at Brooklyn's. We went to Ben's party. And if I hadn't lied, if I'd gone to dinner with you like we'd planned, you never would have been on Old Henderson Road. You and Penny never would have crossed paths. She'd be alive. And you . . . you'd be—"

"You think I don't know where you went that night?" Josh's words charged the air between us. "That I haven't known all along?"

"You knew?"

"I'm not stupid, Hadley. I figured it out pretty fast."

"How?"

"First of all, when you called to tell me about girls' night, there were car keys jingling in the background. Someone was pretty anxious to get a move on. Penny Rawlins never missed a blowout party in her entire life. Toss Brooklyn into the mix, and you can double that last point."

"But you didn't say anything." And he was wrong. We'd dragged Penny to that party. "Why didn't you—"

"Because I didn't care. I didn't want to make you feel like shit for wanting to do something that would have been torture for me. I wanted you to go. To have fun. To bust you later and make you tell me all the gory details, and laugh with you as you described Ben strutting around like some kind of player."

"But we never got that chance."

"No. We didn't."

"Because you pushed me away. I was there for you, Josh. I tried."

"Your best friend was dead, Hadley. I killed her. I didn't deserve your help."

"That's why you ended things?"

"That's the heart of it, I guess."

Suddenly, I was pissed. I knew I shouldn't be—that Josh didn't deserve my anger. But when I thought of that day in the library I couldn't help myself. "I didn't want to lose both of you. You made me feel like I'd meant nothing to you."

"It was the only way."

"No. You could have given me a choice. You could have been honest."

"Honest, huh?" He propped his elbow on the door, running a hand through his hair. "Like you were about your girls' night? I don't know, Hadley. If I had, I'd never have found out the truth about you. That you could so easily replace someone like me with someone like Ben Baden."

I knew it was over then. Not just the discussion. Us. All the history had sizzled away any thread of hope that we might actually be finding our way back to each other.

My focus skated from the road. Josh was resting his head in his palm.

As my eyes traced the angle of his arm, sliding down the slope of his wrist and across the ridges of his muscles, I saw it.

And it made me even angrier. I knew without asking—it was a constant reminder, a way for him to punish himself every single day.

A small circular tattoo, centered on his inner biceps.

One single penny.

Heads.

Up.

23

BEN BADEN'S BEDROOM – 1:43 AM

"WE HAVE to hurry," Mia said, letting the nearly-empty backpack slide down one arm, plopping it onto Ben's bed.

"We have to finish what we started first." My eyes flicked around the room, stopping on the black computer desk tucked away in the far corner, taking in the laptop, the charging station, all the wires.

"We almost died and you're still thinking about stealing?"

"I'm not *thinking* about stealing," I said, walking across the plush carpet, pulling the laptop forward, and tugging wires up from the back of the desk. "I'm stealing. Actively."

"Fine." Mia clapped her hands two times, super-fast. "Give me what you want to take, and I'll pack it away. Three minutes, Hadley. Then I'm dragging you out of here."

I looked over my shoulder, flashing Mia a smile. "You're the best."

"I won't be anything if you get me killed tonight. Just remember that."

"You want to get us out of here faster? Grab the external hard drive." I nodded my head toward the side of the computer desk where a black box that contained a backup of Ben's entire computer sat.

Mia dropped the backpack on the floor beside me and unplugged the drive, pulling it free from the tangle of wires. When I kneeled down and stuffed the laptop in the largest pocket of the backpack, it hit something solid. The wooden box. I had forgotten all about it. With no time to spare, I slipped the laptop behind it, yanking the charger from the wall and twisting it around my knuckles before dropping it in the opening. Mia packed away the hard drive, and I breathed a sigh of relief.

Ben's phone. Ben's laptop. Ben's external hard drive.

I walked across the room, trying to focus. I had to be sure. I would never get this chance again, and I couldn't leave anything behind. I stood next to Ben's bed—the one where we'd snuggled and whispered and laughed together on so many winter nights—stone-still, thinking.

Ben's phone. Ben's laptop. Ben's external hard drive.

"It's time," Mia said. "I don't care what you say. We have to get out of here." She pulled her phone from the back pocket of her jeans, waking it up. The screen cast a blue glow on her face as she sliced her finger across its surface, her eyes intensely focused. "Brooklyn's waiting. I'm texting her that we'll be there in five."

I turned in a slow circle, eyes roaming, thoughts churning. One last search. Nothing jumped out at me, nothing was screaming to be taken or searched or destroyed. Except the picture on Ben's nightstand.

I walked to it, staring at myself, remembering the moment but feeling very far away from that girl who'd once sat in a booth at Edie's Diner, eyes squeezed shut, head tipped back mid-laugh. Ben sat just behind me, his arm draped lazily over my shoulder, chin resting against the side of my cheek. His eyes were bright, the thin line of his lips pulled back in a quiet smile. It had been a snow day, no school, fat flakes churning through the sky beyond the window just behind us. He'd insisted on picking me up, taking me for hot cocoa. He even asked for extra whipped cream because he knew that was the way I liked it. The tip of his nose had been red from the cold, his hands big and warm as they held mine. I had felt safe. I had trusted him.

I closed my eyes for a moment, then raised the picture frame in the air, crashing it down against the corner of the nightstand, the shatter cracking the silence.

"Holy shit, Hadley." I heard Mia's footsteps, then felt her grab my hand, tugging me away from the splinters of glass that littered Ben's carpet.

"Sorry," I said, shaking my head. "I—"

"No time for any of that. We've gotta go."

Her ponytail slipped over her shoulder as she leaned down and zipped the backpack closed, tossing it over one shoulder as she stood, shoving her arm through the other strap, and tucking her thumbs underneath to keep the straps in place.

The whole thing reminded me of Josh—the backpack and the straps, the thumbs tucked for extra security—and I wondered where he could be. My heart suddenly ached for him as it had in the weeks and months after the accident.

"I have to call Josh."

Mia grabbed my hand, pulling me to the sliding glass door. "Not now, you don't."

"I need to find him." The need was strong. Overpowering.

It stayed with me as Mia pulled me through the door,

over the cool grass of the Badens' backyard, and across the creek, Ben's backpack slap-slap-slapping with each step. The need was there when we spilled out of the woods and onto Sycamore Street, as we raced to the corner of Sycamore and Gum, where Brooklyn was parked and waiting. The need stopped me dead as Mia pulled open the passenger door and yanked the seat forward, folding herself inside the car before resting the backpack on her lap.

"Took you guys long enough." Brooklyn looked up at me from the driver's seat of her VW Bug.

"Sorry," Mia said, her breath coming in bursts. "Long story."

"I expect full details." Brooklyn eyed Mia in the backseat, then me still standing just outside the car. "I feel totally out of the loop, you know? You two leaving me back there at the party? Very unsettling."

"That was all out of our control. We'll fill you in." Mia pulled the passenger seat back into place and yanked her rubber band out of her hair, spilling it around her shoulders. "Hadley, hop in so we can get out of here."

I slid into the passenger seat and pulled the door closed, feeling strangely lost, like something was missing.

Brooklyn drove away, and Mia launched into a breathless play-by-play, starting with how I'd dragged her through the woods and up to the top of the tower, detailing the pictures on Ben's phone, and then telling about the events that had taken place once we'd gotten to Ben's house.

I listened, but I couldn't focus. Not really. Because Josh was out there, and it was up to me to warn him about the danger he was in. Brooklyn nearly swerved off the road when Mia told her about Roller, which just made the need burn brighter. Josh was in real trouble. There was no telling what could happen to him if I didn't act fast.

"Give me your phone," I said as Mia finished explaining how Tyler had saved us, how cool he'd been under pressure, how he'd kept Ben and Roller from our hiding spot.

"For what?" Brooklyn asked.

"Oh," Mia said. I could almost hear her eyes roll behind me. "That."

"What *that*?" Brooklyn stopped at a red light in the center of town. Her car was perched on the overpass to I-75, the green signs illuminated by her headlights, offering us an escape either north or south. An escape that was too late to take, even if we'd wanted to. And *God* how I wanted to. How I wished that after the tower I'd taken Ben's car, driven us to this very spot, and turned one way or the other. We'd be safe. Far beyond the reach of this twisted version of Ben. Free from the threat of Roller.

But I couldn't go anywhere now.

"Josh," I said. "Tyler told us to find him. To warn him. Besides that, Josh has whatever it is Ben needs, and I need to get it from him."

But I wanted to do this because it was the only way to keep him safe. I didn't blame him. There were too many reasons for me to blame myself.

"Fine," Brooklyn said. "Use mine if you have to. It's in my purse. But before you call Josh, tell me where I should drive. Are we heading somewhere specific?"

"For now, we're safer on the move." I felt my nerves settle as I pulled out Brooklyn's phone. "As soon as I get ahold of

Josh, I want to make a plan to meet up with him."

"Of course you do," Mia said. "That's the worst idea I've ever heard. You seem determined to play out all of your worst ideas tonight."

"I'm sorry for pulling you into this. I won't be mad if you want to bail. You can just—"

"No way we're bailing," Brooklyn said.

"Yeah," Mia agreed. "Give us a little credit."

And then she launched into an explanation of how we'd stripped Ben's computer desk. I heard the zipper of the backpack, her hands rifling through the contents as she ticked off the items we'd taken.

Holding my breath, I dialed Josh, knowing without a doubt that I had the order of the numbers right. As the phone began to ring, I realized that I had no idea what to say or how I'd convince him to meet up with me.

It didn't matter. Josh didn't answer. I debated leaving a message, then decided against it, ending the call as Mia said something about how she'd forgotten about the wooden box.

"Why do you need a box?" Brooklyn asked.

"We didn't need it," Mia said. "It just kind of got swept up in the shuffle."

I tuned them out, texting Josh.

> Me: Need to see you. ASAP. This thing is way bigger than you know. Call me at this number so we can make a plan. PLEASE. —Hadley

My heart raced as I hit SEND, watching to make sure the

message had been delivered. I thought of Josh reading my words and wondered what he would think. What he might do.

And then I heard Mia behind me. Or rather, I *didn't* hear her. She'd stopped whatever she was saying, mid-sentence—sucked in a breath and held it tight for one second, two, and then three.

When I looked back over the seat, my heart stopped dead.

In one hand, she held the wooden box. The lid was missing, the dark belly of the box nothing but shadow.

Mia's other hand held a small wooden turtle with a bobbly head.

Purple. With tiny green polka dots. And a delicate set of bright blue wings.

"That's one of Penny's turtles," I said. "How did you—"

"It's her favorite," Mia said, her face drained of all color. "The one she lost."

"But she didn't *lose* it," Brooklyn said. "Remember how pissed she was when she found it missing? There was a note on the shelf. She got all quiet and red-faced when she read it, then crinkled the paper into a little ball."

"She told us Tyler was holding the turtle ransom. I thought it was one of their stupid feuds, but—"

"The turtle was in the box," Mia said.

"That means the whole thing with Tyler wasn't the real story." I felt it was all connected. I just had to figure out how.

"Hadley." Mia squeezed her eyes tight. "We promised. After the funeral, we said we'd leave it alone, that we'd stop trying to figure out why Penny had seemed so—"

"But that ransom note was the start of everything. She wasn't herself for at least two weeks before she died." I thought of the pictures, of Penny crumpled on the blue tile floor of Ben's shower where I had just been standing. *God* how I wished time were a thing I could manipulate. That simply being in that space would have allowed me to flip back to the night Penny had been lying there, so I could have stopped things and taken her home. Maybe none of this would be happening now. "Whatever had been going on with her started the day she realized that turtle was missing. We were there, we all saw her face. She was upset about something bigger than losing a silly little knick-knack."

"There was the party, too." Brooklyn's voice was low. Nervous. Like she didn't want to discuss this any more than Mia did but knew we had to.

"*Ben's* party," I said, one more piece clicking into place.

"She didn't want to go," Brooklyn said. "We practically had to drag her there. As if Penny Rawlins ever missed a chance to party."

"She didn't agree until I called Josh and canceled on him," I said, remembering how horrible I'd felt for lying but how good it had felt to pull Penny out of her funk. "I thought the party would help."

"We all thought the party would help," Brooklyn said.

Mia sighed. "But then she decided to leave."

"Yeah. And we just let her."

My final moments with Penny swept in as if they had happened only minutes ago.

There had been a spilled drink, an angry voice calling out.

The flutter of her lashes as she caught me staring, the tight set of her lips as she insisted that she needed time alone.

How she'd given each of us a hug, then turned without

saying good-bye, shoving her way through the crowd.

Penny's sandaled feet running.

Long legs—so strong, so *alive*—hopping across the rocks that spanned the creek in Ben's backyard.

Silky hair swooshing across her back.

And Penny disappearing among the swaying trees, vanishing into the darkness without a glance over her shoulder.

24

Columbus, Georgia – 10:53 AM
Trip Odometer – 610 Miles

Sunlight flashed off the rear window of the car in front of me, causing me to squint and wish I had a pair of sunglasses as I tried reading the interstate signs. We'd made it to US 27. The Georgia-Florida border was just a few short hours away. Looking at the clock, I felt a twinge of guilt. Brooklyn and Mia were probably so worried they were ready to kill me.

I'd turned my phone off after my last call with Ben, but shutting him out meant I'd been ignoring my best friends, too. And I missed them—needed them. Josh was asleep—he had been for nearly two hours. I felt more alone than I had in all my life.

I slipped my hand into the small pocket of space under the stereo and grabbed my phone, powering it on. The battery was only half drained. Purposely avoiding any updates, I called Brooklyn. It didn't even ring twice.

"Hadley! Are you okay? We've been trying to reach you and—"

"I'm fine," I said.

"Well, we're not! We've been freaking crazy worried. *Where the hell are you?*"

I smiled. "You really want to know?"

"I think that's the least you could share."

"Georgia."

I imagined Brooklyn's face, her eyes popping wide, her perfectly pink lips falling open. "I'm sorry, what?"

"*Georgia.*" I giggled. I couldn't help myself. Saying it out loud, sharing how far I'd decided to go, felt too good. There was a twinge of sadness when I thought of Penny. She would have *loved* this crazy night. "I'm closing in on Florida."

"Florida?!" Brooklyn shouted. "You're almost to Florida?"

"Well," I said. "It *is* spring break."

I heard Mia's voice, a squeal ringing out from the other end of the line. And then something else, the deeper tone of a guy's voice.

"Who's there with you?" I asked.

"That's not important right now. You have to listen. Very carefully. Ben came to Cincinnati just like you expected. We tried to send him on the scavenger hunt, but he caught on after, like, the first two stops."

"Yeah? And then what?"

"Okay, this is going to sting. Like, really sting. Just know that you're smarter than him, and you can outplay any move he—"

"Just say it!"

"He has a GPS tracking device on his BMW. Apparently, it comes standard these days when you blow enough cash on a car. Anyway, he's been following you, and I don't think he's too far behind. So, please—"

"I'm sorry, what?"

"What to which part? You have got to keep up!"

"What to all of it. We turned the GPS *off* before we even left Cincinnati."

"You might have turned off the GPS in the dash, but there's still a tracker. Some Internet site he can access or something. I have no idea how it works. Just that it does and he knows exactly where you are. Like, *exactly* exactly. He's probably only an hour behind you, depending on how many stops you've made and how fast he's going. I should have paid more attention to those stupid story problems sophomore year about two cars traveling at different speeds, but they made me feel dizzy and—"

"Holy shit."

"Just breathe, okay? I have more to tell you."

My stomach turned on itself. "I'm not sure I can handle more."

"Knowledge equals safety."

"Jesus, Brooklyn, you're scaring me." Ben was after me. Right behind me? I knew we didn't have time to waste, but I couldn't keep driving—not with the total freak-out feeling that was pressing in on my chest, making it hard to breathe. I veered across two lanes of light traffic, barely making the exit ramp for some little town that probably wasn't even on a map.

"Are you ready?" Brooklyn asked.

Pulling the car to a stop at the end of the exit ramp, I closed my eyes. "Shoot."

"Ben's not alone."

"Okay, that's not so bad. Is it?"

"He's with that Roller guy. Roller Haughton? The one everyone hits up for party favors."

I leaned forward, tapping my forehead on the steering

wheel.

"You catch me when I say *party favors*?" Brooklyn asked. "I did some checking, and this guy is big-time in Oak Grove these days."

The package Josh and I had buried was starting to make sense. "That's bad."

"Just remember, you're smarter than both of them combined. You'll think of a way out of this."

"I'm going to have to face them," I said, glancing over at Josh. His head was tilted toward the door. It looked like he was still sleeping, but I couldn't be sure.

"You will definitely have to face them," Brooklyn said. "But not before you know one last thing."

"No. Not unless it's good news, B."

"It's kinda good and bad at the same time. . . . It started when Mia snagged his phone. He realized it later, so we had to give it back, but not before—"

"Ben's phone?" A wave of relief washed over me. If they had his phone for even a few minutes, then they had wiped the picture of me out of existence.

"Yeah. Mia played like she was wasted when they first got to the bar, all sloppy and leaning up against him, and slipped it out of his pocket as we were telling him we thought you'd gone to Graeter's."

"You deleted the picture, right?" I asked. "Please tell me you deleted it from Facebook *and* his phone."

"The Facebook administrators responded to our message and did that part themselves. As for his phone, we had planned on it. Obviously. But this whole thing with your picture, Hadley, it's bigger than we first thought."

"Bigger how?"

"Bigger, as in there's more than one picture of you. And some of them are a little more, um, *revealing* than the one Ben posted."

I squeezed my eyes shut. "Please tell me you deleted them. Every last one."

"We thought about it," Brooklyn said.

"*Thought* about it? Oh my God, Brook—"

"Yours weren't the only pictures. There were other girls."

I held my breath as Brooklyn told me what she'd seen, listening as she listed the string of names, feeling an oddly familiar connection.

"We didn't delete anything because we're going to bust Ben. Anyone twisted enough to do what he has deserves to go down."

I felt like I was going to throw up.

"We thought you needed to see them. All of them. We emailed the files to you. And to Tyler."

"Rawlins? Have you lost your mind? He's on Ben's side!"

"No. He's not."

A horn blared behind me. I jumped, my breath catching as I looked in the rearview mirror, sure that Ben was there—right there—behind me.

"Tyler was with Ben when they got to Cinci, but he stayed behind when Ben and Roller left. *Penny* is one of the girls on Ben's phone. The pictures of her are bad. Tyler's here with us now. Totally behind our plan."

"Plan? What plan?"

"The plan to bust Ben. Keep. Up."

"If those pictures are as bad as you say, I don't want them

getting out."

"You're the victim here. Remember that."

"But I don't want to be." The horn blared again, and I flicked on the blinker, turning right onto the cracked pavement of a street lined with fast-food restaurants. "Brooklyn, I'm sorry, but I have to go."

"What? You can't just—"

"I'll call soon. I need to figure out what we're going to do."

"We? As in you and who else?"

I turned into a McDonald's. "Josh."

"Josh *Lane*? You're still with Josh Lane? I thought we ditched him back at—"

"I couldn't very well drive after all those Jell-O shots, so I found him. He's been . . . *good*." I pulled into an empty space and put the car in park, leaning back against the seat and closing my eyes. Josh had been a lot more than *good*. He'd been helpful and supportive and motivating. And then there was the kiss. I felt dizzy just thinking about it. "Brooklyn. Are you still there?"

"I'm trying to process the combined use of 'Josh Lane' and 'good.'" Brooklyn sighed. "I guess one positive is that you're not alone."

"He's helping." I watched the rise and fall of his chest. "Trust me."

"You do need someone strong on your side right now. And after the past year, Josh Lane has proven that he's stronger than most of us."

"That's true."

"You'll call soon? You swear?"

"Yes. And I'll keep my phone on for now in case you need

me."

"Good. Be careful, okay? Ben's pissed. Out-of-his-mind pissed. And so is Roller. With those pictures, you have the upper hand. But you still have to be safe."

"Promise. I love you. Mia Pia, too. You'll tell her?"

"On it. And remember, Hadley, you can do this."

"Right," I said, not so sure that was true.

I slipped the phone back into the console, then turned to Josh and shook his arm, wondering if he was really sleeping.

Wondering what he was thinking if he'd heard everything I'd just said.

25

MAIN STREET – 2:11 AM

"HAS JOSH texted you yet?" Brooklyn asked as she turned onto Main Street.

"No." I checked her phone to be sure, but I knew I hadn't missed anything.

"Maybe you should leave it alone?" She sounded hopeful.

"Was that a question?" Mia asked. "Because the answer is pretty clear. Not that she's going to listen with this Choose-the-Worst-Option game we seem to be playing."

"I can't leave it alone, guys. I started this."

Mia huffed. "You didn't start anything. Ben did by posting that picture. He totally baited you."

I was angry. Getting back at Ben wasn't just for me anymore; it was for all the girls on Ben's phone. Most of all, it was for Penny. But I needed Brooklyn and Mia on my side. And there was only one way to keep them from trying to stop me every step of the way. I had to make them care as much as I did.

"Pull over." I looked out the window, the neon sign for Edie's Diner shining brightly in the darkness of the night. It reminded me of something just out of reach. I thought of Josh and was hit with the crazy notion that, somehow, the sign could lead me to him.

"Pull over?" Brooklyn asked as we passed the sign, the blue-tinted light washing through the car. "I thought you said we were safer on the move."

"We are."

"Then—"

"Just do it." I slipped Ben's phone from the pocket of my jacket.

Brooklyn pulled into the diner's back lot and looked at me with soft, sad eyes. "What's going on, Hadley? What aren't you telling us?"

I swiped my finger across the screen of Ben's phone, navigating to the pictures, not stopping, not thinking. I turned the phone around and heard a double gasp of recognition.

"Penny?" Brooklyn grabbed the phone. "You didn't tell me—"

"She didn't tell me, either." Mia leaned forward, her shoulders pressing against the front seats, her eyes following Brooklyn's finger swiping through the stream of photos, ending with the shot of Penny, dripping wet, curled on a sea of ocean-blue tiles.

"Hadley?" Brooklyn looked up at me, her eyes shining with tears and rage.

"Don't get emotional. I can't handle emotional. Not tonight."

"I'm going to be sick." Mia pushed against my seat with so much force, I didn't ask, I simply moved—fingers pulling the door handle, forearm pushing the door, feet sweeping out and across the pavement.

Mia followed, bending at the waist, heaving up the contents

of her stomach, which, I knew, included a few swigs of gin and a handful of Skittles.

"Do you think she knew?" Brooklyn asked, her words quiet and hard, as if she was hoping no one would hear because she didn't really want to face the answer.

"I don't know."

"*You* didn't." Brooklyn leaned over the console so she could look into my eyes. "He did the same thing to you, and, for whatever reason, you didn't remember any of it."

Mia heaved again. The sound made my own stomach churn.

"But I remembered that I didn't remember. The gaps scared me."

"Gaps are one thing," Brooklyn said. "But remembering—that has to be worse."

"I wouldn't know. I still don't remember. Even with the pictures."

"So, unless she saw the pictures, chances are she never knew," Brooklyn said. "And there's no way she could have seen the pictures, right? Which means she never had to face this. God, I hope she never had to face this."

Mia grabbed my hand, squeezing tight, as though I was the only thing keeping her from floating away.

"But we all know something was going on. She wasn't herself. She was jumpy. Angry. She was pulling away."

"Guys," Mia said. "Can we please not do this?"

"Hadley's right," Brooklyn said. "It wasn't just the party she didn't want to go to. She skipped girls' night the weekend before."

Mia dropped my hand. "I can't do this."

"We have to. We owe it to Penny to figure this out. To make Ben pay for what he's done."

"What about what we've done?" Mia asked, her voice trembling. "We forced her to go to that party, even though we knew something was wrong."

"We thought the party was going to make things better. We tried."

"But the party made it worse."

"We don't know that," I said. "We don't know why she left, why she walked into those woods and—"

"I know." Mia's lips trembled. Tears gleamed in her eyes.

"What are you talking about? You never said—"

"I never said anything because I didn't want you to hate me."

I tried to steady my breathing and stay calm, but I wanted to shake her. "You have to tell us," I whispered.

Mia dropped her chin to her chest, covering her face with her hands. I walked to her, folded her into my arms, and gave her a good squeeze.

"It's going to be okay. We'll deal with this. Together. But we need to be honest. To tell each other everything."

Mia nodded, tears streaming down her cheeks. "I hated keeping this secret."

"Then it's time to let it go." I led her back to the car. Taking a deep breath, I settled myself in the passenger seat and closed the door.

"I was dancing in the backyard," Mia said. "Remember the music? It was so loud it felt like a second heart beating in my chest. But I couldn't go on forever, because I had to pee."

Brooklyn laughed. It came out quiet at first, stifled, but

then broke free. That got us all going, the stress of the moment released.

"I went inside, right through the sliding glass door into Ben's bedroom. I'd seen Penny walk in a few minutes before me, and I remember thinking our timing was perfect. Nothing's better than a bathroom catch-up during a party, right?"

"But she wasn't in the bathroom?" I asked.

"She wasn't anywhere. At least that's what I thought at first. But then I heard her voice. She was angry. About to blow."

"You found her?" Brooklyn asked.

"Not exactly. She was behind a closed door. I didn't know where the door led—thought maybe it was the laundry room, or a utility room, or something. Tonight, when I had to look for that backpack, I figured out she'd been in Ben's closet. Arguing. With Ben."

"About what?" I asked.

"I couldn't tell. I heard her say that she wanted something back."

"The turtle?" Brooklyn asked.

"It could have been the pictures," I said. "If she knew what he'd done, she'd have been all over him for those pictures."

"I don't know. But Ben laughed, mentioning something about a safety measure. And then I heard them moving, so I busted ass to the bathroom."

"So, she might have known?" I asked. "Why didn't she tell us?"

"I should have asked her what the fight was about. I should have made her tell me. But she was so pissed, and I was trying to give her space, to wait for her to open up in her own time. Except she was all out of time. And I had no idea."

"None of us could have stopped her from leaving that party," I said. "She'd made up her mind."

"We should have tried," Mia said. "We could have followed her. And then, maybe . . ."

"Guys," Brooklyn said. "Mia was right. This isn't helping."

I shook my head. "It is. It might not feel like it right now, but we're on the right track. We might actually be able to figure things out."

"Haven't we already?" Brooklyn asked. "Ben got her wasted. He took some horrible pictures. Penny remembered or figured it out some other way. And she was pissed. She *died* pissed. That's the horrible, awful end of the story."

"It's not," I said. "We're not going to let it be. We don't know anything. Not for sure. But we need to."

"What if knowing makes it worse?" Mia asked. "This feels worse. We tried to help Penny, but instead, we set up her death."

"What if it wasn't us?" I asked. "This whole thing is connected to Ben. There's got to be more to it."

"Not likely," Brooklyn said.

"Okay, so say you're right. I still want Ben to pay for what he's done. As much as it hurts to face this, I know you guys do, too. But we have to know everything, or at least as much as we possibly can. And there's only one way to make that happen for sure."

I paused then, the silence unfolding like broken lines painted on a lonely stretch of highway.

"No," Mia said. "I can't go there, Hadley. You promised."

"I did. You don't have to go. But I do."

"Oh my God. Seriously? You sound just like her, you know?

Right before she walked into those woods and disappeared forever."

Brooklyn sighed, looking back at Mia. "We can't let her go alone."

"Fine. But just so you know, I am going to be *such* a bitch about this."

26

COLUMBUS, GEORGIA – 11:07 AM
TRIP ODOMETER – 613 MILES

"WAKE UP!" I smacked Josh on the leg again. I was now sure he wasn't faking his nap, that he hadn't heard any of the positive things I'd said about him to Brooklyn, which made me feel both disappointed and sad.

I kept my eyes trained on the looping arches of the big yellow *M* sign just in front of the parked car, trying to steady myself.

Josh stirred, twisting in his seat until he was facing me, wincing from the sun's glare. "McDonald's?"

"I'm hungry." That part was true. But there was so much more.

"I could eat." He stretched his arms over his head.

"Before that, I have an update."

"That sounds ominous." Josh started rubbing his eyes with his knuckles.

"Ben knows where we are."

Josh stopped rubbing.

"He's been following us all night. He has some kind of tracking device that works even after the GPS has been turned off."

Josh blinked, then nodded his head a few times.

"You don't seem surprised."

"Figures, I guess. I mean, this is a state-of-the-art car, right? Don't they all come standard with state-of-the-art security these days?" Josh shrugged, then yawned. "Doesn't matter. We're still ahead of him."

"*Them*. That's the other thing. Ben's with Roller Haughton."

"The drug dealer?"

"That's the one."

I pictured him then—Roller Haughton—his frame skinny and tall, his stubble-shadowed face nothing but sharp angles, his eyes deep set and lifeless. He was the kind of guy who was always there in the background. I wondered how many times I'd passed him without realizing—in the doorway of Circle K, pulling into the gas station, leaving Edie's Diner.

"I suppose I shouldn't be surprised," Josh said. "I can't exactly picture Ben and Roller as business partners, though."

"That bag of pills is all the proof I need. They're partners, all right. And they're coming after us. What if we've stopped more times than them? For longer? What if—"

"No way they've caught up. But you can't keep running forever. You know you have to face this eventually."

"I don't want to face it," I said. "Not Ben or the picture or the drugs."

"What other choice do you have? Just try to think of the bright side."

"There's a bright side?"

"You're not going to have to face them alone." Josh smiled. "And since we're ahead, we can pick the final destination and then get our bearings before they catch up."

"We can't stop until we hit a beach," I said. "I need to see the ocean."

"Deal," Josh said. "But the first thing we're going to do is eat. Then I'll take the wheel so you can sleep until we find the right spot."

"And then we just wait for them?"

Josh tipped his head toward me, his hair falling across his eyes. "If we do it this way, we're in control. We'll have the upper hand."

I sighed. "I don't like this."

"Then don't think about it. Not yet. For now, think about food." Josh opened the passenger door.

"I need a minute." My hands shook at the thought of pulling up those pictures. I had to see them to know what I was using against Ben, and I had to do it without Josh nearby. But I was afraid to face the worst parts of Ben's birthday—the parts I couldn't remember.

Josh sighed, running a hand through his messy hair, and turned to look at me. "I'll go in and order. What do you want?"

"Hamburger. Fries. Coke." I suddenly realized how hungry I was. "And maybe some cookies. They have chocolate chip, don't they? Like, fresh baked."

Josh rolled his eyes, but his lips curled up with the hint of a smile. "I'll check." He stepped out of the car and leaned down, meeting my eyes again. "Things are pretty messed up, Hadley, but for now, all you have to think about is food and sleep. They're coming, but I promise we'll be ready."

"You think?"

Josh smiled then. For real. It was a beautiful thing.

"I promise. I won't let you down."

He closed the door, leaving me alone in Ben's car, telling myself that Josh was right. He had to be right. That I was ready to pull up my email and face the night I couldn't remember. But then something caught my eye—Josh's phone, resting between the floor mat and a track of the passenger seat. I wondered if Sam had called or texted while Josh was asleep. I needed as much information as I could get before a face-off with Ben.

Looking out the rear window, I saw Josh through the big windows of the restaurant, three people standing in front of him in line. Then I grabbed his phone.

There were no text messages, so I looked at the incoming call log. That's when I saw the last name I'd ever expect to find in Josh Lane's phone, and I knew the identity of the mystery caller who had woken me up all the way back in Tennessee. But no matter how I twisted it, the information didn't make sense.

And then there was a click-swoosh, a change in the air pressure cocooning me in the car.

"My wallet must have slipped out of my pock—What are you doing?"

I turned the phone around. "Why did Tyler Rawlins call you at five o'clock in the morning?"

Josh took the phone from my hand. "It's complicated."

"I gathered that much. Care to share?"

"I want to. But I can't."

"I told you everything, Josh. Everything."

"This thing with Tyler, it's not mine to tell."

"I was actually starting to trust you again. . . ." I shoved my way out of the car, slamming the door behind me before I walked across the parking lot.

I wanted to run. Away from Josh. Away from everything that had been following me since I'd left Oak Grove.

But I steadied myself and stood strong.

That was the only thing left for me to do.

27

THE RAWLINS'S BACKYARD – 2:39 AM

WE STOOD under the shelter of the sweet gum tree where Mrs. Rawlins had once taken a picture of the four of us hanging upside down, our knees hooked around the scratchy bark of the lowest limbs. We had been laughing, all of us, as if the joyful world we lived in would never cease to exist.

I read the text I'd sent to Josh nearly an hour ago.

"Nothing yet?" Brooklyn asked.

"Nada."

"Of course," Mia said. "I finally want him around to distract us from going inside that house, and he's not available."

"I haven't stopped by since the day of the funeral," Brooklyn said. "Being around all of her stuff was torture. I knew she was gone, but I still expected her to turn the corner and walk into the room."

I ignored them, typing the only thing I could think of to get Josh's attention.

> Me: You are in danger. I have to see
> you. Please.

I hit SEND.

The ceramic frog was right where I always remembered it sitting—tucked next to the base of a weeping cherry tree, the umbrella of branches blooming with pink flowers.

"B and E is not the most productive pastime," Mia said as I grabbed the frog and pulled the house key from inside his belly.

"We're not breaking in," I said, swinging the back door open and stepping into the kitchen, where I was assaulted by the familiar scent of lemon Pledge mixed with vanilla. "Tyler told us to come."

"It smells exactly the same." Mia stepped up behind me. "How is that possible?"

Memories flooded me as I made my way down the hall and up the stairs to the second floor: Penny making me a midnight batch of chocolate chip pancakes, dancing the entire time; bouncing on her brother's bed, singing into a hairbrush microphone just to piss him off; smiling mischievously as she formulated a new plan for devious adventure. The way she walked with such confidence, the way she laughed with such ease, the way she lived every moment of her life with no fear or regret.

Stopping just outside the door to Penny's room, I took a deep breath. I needed the truth, but that didn't make me excited to search the bedroom of the girl I'd spent the last year mourning.

Brooklyn and Mia walked up behind me, so quiet I didn't hear them so much as feel their presence. I reached out and grabbed the doorknob, twisting. The room was pitch-black, the curtains drawn tight in a way that Penny would have hated. I walked around the bed, one hand trailing the smooth lip of the footboard, and pulled the curtains open, letting a stream of moonlight wash through the room.

"It's exactly the same," Brooklyn said.

Mia let out a groan. "Her clothes are still out." She pointed to a padded chair in the corner where a T-shirt, hoodie, and jeans lay heaped across one arm. "She wore that the morning she died. We went for breakfast at Edie's and . . . that's what she was wearing."

"I'm not going to be able to handle being here for very long," Brooklyn said. "What are we looking for?"

"I don't know." I took a deep breath, hoping Penny would show me the way. "It would be easier if she'd kept some kind of journal."

"One thing we all know for sure about Penny—she never journaled a day in her life." Mia sighed.

"What about her phone?" Brooklyn asked. "We could try to find it. Check her texts or—"

"I'm sure her parents went through her phone," I said. "Or the police. If they'd found anything off, we'd know by now. They would have asked questions."

"So what's the point?" Mia asked. "We don't know what we're looking for, and we don't have a clue how to find it. What are we doing here?"

"I'm still figuring that out, so hush," I said, turning in a slow circle. "Let me think."

I took in Penny's lavender bedspread, the starburst pattern she'd painted on the headboard, the silver tree she'd made out of twisted wire where her jewelry was still hanging, her bookshelf stuffed with sketch pads and paperbacks, the gaggle of bobblehead turtles she'd collected and arranged on the shelf just above her drafting table. It was her favorite thing, that drafting table, the only gift she'd asked for when she turned thirteen. My eyes settled on the table's slanted surface, taking in a large sketch pad open to a charcoal picture of a girl wearing a white dress.

She was planted in the earth, the ground encasing her body from just below the line of her breasts. Her waist and legs were visible through a cross-section view of the world below ground, a tangle of roots, bare feet kicking for freedom. Her arms sheltered a face that was turned up to the sky, eyes closed, hair tossing in a wild wind.

"She may not have journaled, but her art always told a story."

Brooklyn's gaze found the picture, and her eyes went wide.

Mia stepped forward, one hand extended, fingers stopping just short of touching the page.

I moved before either of them could try to stop me, my fingers gripping the silver handle just below the drawing board, pulling the drawer out until the moonlight spilled across the contents.

"Isn't this stuff off-limits?" Mia said. "She never let us see her art. Not until it was finished."

"She would kill us," Brooklyn said. "But I'm not sure that matters now."

I had already dug in, my hands shuffling through the loose pieces of paper. I stopped, captivated by a girl standing in the middle of a downpour, a sheer dress clinging to her body. Her arms were spread wide, as if she was trying to reach out from the page. Her haunted eyes stared right at me, silver in the moonlight.

"There's no mouth," Mia said. "She drew raindrops and eyelashes and fingernails, but she forgot the mouth?"

"She didn't forget." I shuffled to the next image. "There's another. And another. They're all dated a few weeks before she died."

I took in each image. A girl sitting at the base of a fence, legs pulled to her chest, arms wrapped around her knees, eyes pleading. Another standing on a high-up tree branch, one arm slung around a thick trunk, the other tucked behind her body, her face turned away from the sky. And the worst, a girl standing at the top of the tower. *Our tower*. She'd drawn it perfectly, the bricks gleaming, giving the illusion of starlight. The pictures were intricate, detailed, complete. Except each and every girl was missing her mouth.

"She drew the tower," Mia said. And then, "She drew the tower?"

"Forget the tower," Brooklyn said. "It's eerie, sure, but what about those missing mouths?"

It seemed obvious what those missing mouths represented, but when I flipped to the next image, I lost my train of thought.

"Oh my God," Brooklyn said.

Mia didn't make a sound. She just backed to the chair and fell onto the soft cushion.

"She knew," I said, my heart pounding, my entire body tingling. We'd found proof: a girl, naked and curled on a patchwork of teal-colored tiles, a swirl of water encircling her body. "That's one of Ben's pictures. There's no doubt she saw it. No doubt that she knew."

My fingers grazed something on the back of the picture.

An envelope taped in place.

I yanked it free.

Penny's handwriting, deep grooves pressed into the paper.

For After.

I didn't stop to think what it meant. Setting the picture on the drawing board, I slipped a finger beneath the seal of the envelope, ripping it open. The words were blurry. I swiped at my eyes and found tears covering my lashes and cheeks. Walking to the window, I held the paper in a stream of silver moonlight, noticing that the note had been crinkled and flattened before being folded. And then I read:

> **Let the turtle be a reminder:**
> **The things you think are safe are not.**
> **If you talk, the pictures go public.**
> **And then they'll go after Tyler.**
> **You'll go down.**
> **He'll go down, too.**
> **But you will not take me with you.**

"That's Ben's handwriting," I said, finding it hard to breathe, leaning against the windowsill.

"What does it mean?" Mia asked.

"He threatened her. Ben taking that turtle, it was a threat."

"It was a promise," Brooklyn said. "She knew. And she was going to talk. But he couldn't let her."

"So he raided her room. Took something she loved. That empty space was a constant reminder of how close he was and that he was always watching."

"He was always here," Mia said. "He's been Tyler's best friend since, what, second grade?"

"He knew her well enough to play on her fears," I said. "He used the only thing he could to keep her quiet. Tyler."

I remembered the bathroom, my promise to Tyler. Josh.

I yanked Brooklyn's phone out of my pocket, waking it and

pulling up my one-sided text thread. If any part of the old Josh existed, I had just figured out the only way I could lure him to me:

Me: You're not the only one in danger.
I am, too. I need you. We need
each other.

I hit SEND and stared at the screen, willing him to respond.

The girls huddled around the letter, the envelope at their feet, Penny's *For After* staring up through the window at the night sky. I wondered what it meant, those two words. After what? But then Brooklyn's phone buzzed in my hand.

My finger shook as I swiped it across the screen.

Josh: Where are you?

I started to type and got through the first three letters before I realized I couldn't very well have Josh meet us at the Rawlins's house. Tyler might have told us to warn Josh, but that didn't mean he wanted Josh in his home.

Brooklyn's parents were out of town. It was a risk—Ben was still on the hunt, but if he was going to search there, he probably already had.

Me: I'll be at Brooklyn's in 10.

A minute passed. Then another. Just when I was starting to lose hope, the phone buzzed again.

Josh: I'll see you there.

28

Just South of the Florida State Line – 2:33 PM
Trip Odometer – 793 Miles

"Hadley!"

The voice came to me through a foggy haze, as if I was underwater.

"Hadley!"

The pitch was familiar. I couldn't place why, but I knew I liked the sound—the way the deep tone rolled across the two syllables of my name.

"You have to wake up."

I felt a hand on my leg. Shaking. Shaking. I opened my eyes. Groaned at the light. Squeezing my eyes closed again, I tried to place myself, noticing only red starbursts popping on the insides of my eyelids. It took a minute—figuring out that the steady hum surrounding me was from tires gripping the ground, that the rocking movement lulling me back to sleep was a car racing forward. And then I remembered.

Florida.

Josh Lane.

Ben Baden. Drugs. The stolen car.

The pictures. My burning shame.

"What time is it?" I asked, rubbing my eyes.

"It's time for you to wake up and read this text," Josh said. "It's from Sam. We have an ID on the pills."

The words snapped me upright. I shielded my eyes with one hand as I studied the phone. I'd looked at Ben's pictures back at McDonald's, locked in a stall in the bathroom so Josh wouldn't see them or my reaction. I hoped, more than anything, that the pills would explain not only how Ben had been able to photograph all of us, but why no one seemed to remember. Maybe we did all remember, on one level or another, but were too ashamed to do anything about it.

"OxyContin and Vicodin." I squinted Josh. "You nailed those on the first try."

"The accident gave me a crash course in the wonders of pharmaceuticals."

"What's Kadian?"

"A brand of morphine."

"Morphine? Why would Ben need morphine?"

"With a supply like that, he's gotta be trying to sell it, right?"

"It's not like Ben needs the cash."

Josh shrugged. "Some people just like the rush that comes with breaking rules."

My eyes tripped to the last two drugs listed in the text. "Percocet and Xanax? What do those do?"

"Those are downers. They'll make you feel slow, like you're floating through life. Like nothing really matters because it's all just kind of happening around you. You're watching but not really participating."

Josh's words barely registered. I felt a strange mixture of relief and horror as I read the four short sentences that followed Sam's list.

Sam: Whoever you snagged these pills from is a twisted fuck. In the wrong hands they could do major damage. The term "rape culture" comes to mind. Be careful.

I read the text over and over and over again. My hands began to shake.

"Hadley. Are you okay?"

"The picture of me, the one on Facebook?"

Josh nodded. "I thought we weren't talking about that anymore."

"There are others. Worse than the one Ben posted. I don't remember him taking any of them. I hardly remember anything from that night."

Josh was staring at the road, his jaw clenching and unclenching, his hands gripping the steering wheel so tightly his knuckles had turned white.

"Sam's text, it says . . ." I couldn't say the words out loud. And I had to be very careful. I couldn't trust Josh with everything. There was no way I could tell him about the pictures of the rest of the girls. Especially of Penny.

But me. He already knew about me. . . . "He drugged me. I trusted him and . . . God, I don't even know what to think right now."

"Then don't." Josh glanced at me, his eyes soft. "Just don't think about it."

"How can I not?" I asked, holding the phone in the air. "It's the only thing I'll be able to think about."

"You're stronger than that, Hadley. You can't let it throw you off balance. We're about to face him. You have to be ready. You need to find a way to use your anger to your advantage. Use it against him. Don't allow him to turn it against you."

I sighed and leaned forward, propping my elbows on my knees, dropping my face into my hands. "This is too much."

And then I felt Josh's hand resting on the back of my head, the heat from his skin racing down my spine, spreading through every inch of me.

"You can do this, Hadley."

I shook my head, trying to steady the shivering that had overtaken my body.

"I don't think I can."

"You're in control," Josh said, his fingers massaging my neck. "You have his car. You know where his drugs are. You—"

"He can't have them back!" I turned my face up to Josh, roughly swiping tears away with the back of my hand. "I'm not telling him where we buried the pills. Not if he's using them like I think he is."

"Okay." Josh nodded. "That's good. Focus on that right now."

"But what about Roller? Shit, Josh, what did I get us into?"

Josh laughed, the sound rolling through the car. "I won't lie, it's a mess. But we've made it this far. Nothing's going to stop us now."

"Where are we, anyway?"

"We passed through Tallahassee about fifteen minutes ago."

"Holy shit, we're finally in Florida?"

Josh smiled.

"We're really going to make it to a beach."

"You got that right." Josh pressed his foot on the gas pedal and looked over his shoulder, switching to the fast lane. "And just so you have something to look forward to, I'll tell you a secret. We're closing in on our final destination."

"So you picked the spot?" I asked, feeling a sliver of my stress slip away. We might actually get one thing right. "Where are we headed?"

"Can't tell." Josh shrugged, his smile reaching all the way to his eyes, taking me back to the time before anything bad had ever happened in either of our lives. "This part needs to be a surprise."

"No fair. You have to tell me where we're—"

Josh's eyes darted to the rearview mirror, narrowing as a swelling sound broke its way into the car.

"Shit." Josh slammed his palm on the steering wheel. "We're screwed. We made it this fucking far, and now it's over."

The steady waves of a siren spiraled around me. I turned in my seat, hoping to see the shiny grille of an ambulance that needed to pass. Instead, I saw the glinting black paint and flashing lights of a Florida state trooper's car, looking very much like a hungry shark hunting its next victim.

29

Brooklyn Simpson's House – 3:03 AM

"He's here," I said, my voice a whisper as we turned into Brooklyn's driveway.

The headlights exposed the shadowy figure standing on her front porch.

I jumped out of the car as soon as she parked. Rounding the corner as the garage door rolled open, I hopped onto the front walkway and ran right into his chest. It was harder than I remembered, his hands stronger as they reached out, grabbing my shoulders to keep me steady.

"Josh," I said, breathlessly, looking up into his eyes. The moonlight and starlight framed his face. "Finally. I didn't think—"

"We going in the front?" a voice asked from behind him. "Or through the garage? From what I understand, hanging out in the open isn't the best idea. . . ."

Josh moved aside to make room for whoever he had brought with him. A *girl.* Petite but in an all-legs kind of way that was accentuated by her super-short shorts. The baggy T-shirt falling off one shoulder, paired with a messy bun, told me she wasn't the type to try too hard. But even so, there was no denying she was gorgeous.

"Hadley," Josh said, looking from me to the girl and back again. "This is Sam."

"Nice to meet you." But it wasn't. My chest had gone tight, and my cheeks were burning. There was nothing nice at all about seeing Josh with this beautiful creature whom he obviously trusted more than he trusted me.

"Pleasantries inside, perhaps?" Sam asked, brushing past Josh and me, her black combat-style boots clomping on the brick path.

Josh followed her without a word. I wanted to scream.

Instead, I trailed him, closing the garage behind me as I made my way inside the house, hearing the rumble of the door motor and chain as I swept through the mudroom and into the kitchen.

"Nice of you to join us, Josh Lane." Brooklyn leaned her hip against the kitchen table. Ben's backpack was beside her, perched on a red-orange-yellow-striped placemat. Her arms were crossed over her chest, one foot kicked out to the side. "Now, spill it. What'd you take from Ben?"

"Not even a hint of foreplay?" Sam asked, mirroring Brooklyn's stance. "Just going in for the kill, huh?"

"And you are?" Brooklyn raised her eyebrows.

"Sam." She gave a curtsy, which looked strangely precise, even with the boots.

"Well, *Sam*, this isn't exactly a social call."

"I'm quite aware of that. Josh is risking his ass to be here, so show a little respect, why don't you."

Brooklyn gave Josh a death glare. "Who is *she*, anyway?"

Josh shrugged. "A friend."

I had to wonder what kind of friend.

"We met at the hospital." Sam winked, lowering her voice to a whisper. "The psych ward, to be precise. So play nice, or I might just go ape on you."

At first, I figured she was lying, trying to be dramatic, but when I saw the color drain from Josh's face, I knew it was true.

"Shit, Josh." Sam's face fell. "I'm sorry. I thought they knew. You said there were rumors. I assumed the secret was out."

Josh shook his head. "It's not like it matters. Psych ward, juvie, whatever."

"Wait," Mia said. "When everyone thought you were in juvie, you were really in the psych ward?"

"He started in the hospital," Sam said. "One of your precious football players decided to rearrange his face. But Josh wouldn't give the asshole up, so his parents—"

"Enough," Josh said, shrugging out of his backpack and dropping it on a kitchen chair with a dull clunk. "Can we get to the point here?"

I tried to remember the point. *Josh was in the hospital? The* psychiatric *unit?*

"What did you take from Ben?" Brooklyn asked.

"Back off, Barbie," Sam said.

"What did you just call me?"

"Barbie. And I told you to back off." Wisps of Sam's hair fell from her bun into her face as she talked. "You have no proof that Josh took anything from this Ben guy."

"Oh my God, seriously?" Mia snapped her fingers. "Look, we don't have time for this. Josh is in danger. Hadley, too. We're all on the same side here."

Brooklyn snorted at that. So did Sam.

"We know you have it," Mia said. "Whatever it is that Ben and Roller are looking for, so you might as well just show us."

"Roller?" Josh asked. "Roller Haughton?"

"This is bad," I said. "I can't make a plan until I know everything."

Josh paused for a moment, his eyes locking on mine, then he sighed and muttered something under his breath. Grabbing his backpack, he tugged the zipper open, but not all the way, reaching inside as if the space was full of secrets. My vision blurred as the darkness swallowed his hands, a rogue shadow giving the illusion that his fingers were encrusted in dirt, and I wondered what he might have buried inside. What he might be hiding from me.

His hands emerged from the space seconds later, fingers clamped around a brown paper bag. It was lumpy, the top section wrapped back down and around, making a ball. He tossed it on the kitchen table. The *thunk* as it hit the wood vibrated in the air. Seeing the package unnerved me, as though I should have known what Ben had been hiding. That maybe somewhere, deep inside, I did know and could remember the shape and texture of the contents as they slipped between my fingertips, but I'd hidden it from myself.

"That's it?" Mia asked. "You're *sure* that's what Ben's looking for?"

Sam smiled. "No doubt about it."

"Can I assume that we're dealing with a controlled substance?" Brooklyn asked.

"Several," Sam said. "It's a treasure trove of prescription meds. In the wrong hands, they could do major damage. The term *rape culture* comes to mind."

Suddenly, it made sense. How Ben had done what he'd done—to me, to Penny, to all the others—without any of us remembering.

"We've got OxyContin, Vicodin, Kadian, Percocet, Xanax." Sam ticked off the items from memory. "This Ben guy is a twisted fuck. Which one of you lucky ladies is dating him?"

"I *was* dating him. Past tense." I flashed Sam a perky smile, thinking how nice it would feel to grab her shiny, chestnut-colored bun and give it a good yank. "How did you figure out what those pills actually were?"

Sam's face flushed with pride. "A few hours of online research. It was nothing."

"We have to figure out how to get this back to them," Josh said.

"Wait a minute." I threw a hand up in the air.

At the same time, Sam slapped Josh on the shoulder. "You cannot be serious!"

Josh looked from Sam to me.

"No way in hell you're giving anything back," she said. "With all they've put you through after that accident, you're not bending over just because some idiot with a stupid name like Roller lost his drugs."

"Technically, I stole them. And if I'd known Roller Haughton was involved, I wouldn't have gone anywhere near that bag."

"But you did," I said. "And there's a lot more going on here than just that package of pills."

"What does that mean?" Josh asked.

I sighed, then looked at Brooklyn and Mia.

Brooklyn shrugged.

Mia gave a little nod.

After everything, Josh deserved to know about Penny. What had happened to her. The state of mind she'd been in when she walked up to the tower the night she died. "It's kind of a long story."

"I've got time."

Sam rolled her eyes.

"What about you?" I asked her. "Do you have time to help with a project?"

"Maybe," she said, defensive but curious.

"How good are you with computers?" I didn't need a genius. Just someone more tech-savvy than Brooklyn or Mia. Better yet, someone more tech-savvy than Brooklyn and Mia combined.

Sam gave a noncommittal shrug.

"Don't be so modest," Josh said. "Sam here's a computer whiz."

I looked at Josh. "You trust her?"

His eyes were tight. Serious. "She wouldn't be here if I didn't."

"I mean with your life." I paused. "You trust her with your life?"

My mind wanted him to say yes.

We needed her.

But my heart was dying for him to say no.

Josh looked me right in the eye. "I trust her completely."

Sighing, I walked over to the table, gripped the zipper of Ben's backpack, and gave it a tug.

The front panel fell away, revealing the laptop, the external hard drive, and a tangle of wires that looked almost as messy as I felt.

30

Just South of the Florida State Line – 2:47 PM
Trip Odometer – 793 Miles

"License, registration, and proof of insurance, please," the trooper said, leaning the brim of his hat into the open window, his eyes scanning the front and back of the car.

Josh looked at me, his eyes wide. I wondered if he was thinking the same thing I was: that we were minutes away from being hauled off to jail.

I took a deep breath and leaned forward. "There might be a little problem with that," I said, forcing what I hoped was an innocent giggle from my lips.

The trooper's eyes snapped up to meet mine. "And what would that be, miss?"

"Well, as I'm sure you've noticed, we're from Ohio. We're on our way to the beach for spring break, and we've been driving all night, taking turns, of course, to be safe, getting sleep when we needed it. And on one of our stops, we got separated from the other car in our group. Which isn't a big deal. We have permission to be driving this car. But neither of us actually *owns* this BMW. The guy on the registration is in the other car."

The trooper narrowed his eyes, then pulled a radio from his

belt, reciting a code to the dispatcher on the other end before replacing it in the cradle at his hip.

He looked at Josh. "License, registration, and proof of insurance, please."

Josh leaned forward, his chest bumping the steering wheel. I watched his steady hands as he pulled his wallet from the back pocket of his cargo shorts, opened it, slid his license out, and handed it to the trooper.

"Registration?" the trooper said for a third time.

"I guess it'd be in here," I said, pulling the glove compartment open, praying with everything in me that Ben didn't have another bag of pills stuffed inside, ready to drop out onto my lap. I breathed a sigh of relief when I saw only packets of catsup and a wad of paper napkins. I reached in and grabbed a stack of papers rubber-banded together and rifled through them.

"Registration," I said, handing a paper to Josh, who passed it through his open window. "And proof of insurance," I added, pulling another paper from the top of the stack. I silently thanked Ben for keeping his beloved car in order.

"Do you know why I pulled you over?" the trooper asked, his mouth chomping away on a slice of neon blue gum.

"No, sir," Josh said. "I've been careful to follow the speed limit."

"You weren't speeding," the trooper said between chomps. "You forgot your turn signal back there when you changed lanes."

"I did?" Josh looked over his shoulder as though he could see into the past if he tried hard enough. Like he could watch himself break the law. "I didn't realize. I apologize."

"It's not a major infraction," the trooper said. "But since you've driven such a long way, I wanted to be sure you're alert. We lose kids every year during spring break—drugs, speeding, lack of sleep. You name it, I've seen it. And it's never pretty."

I looked down at my hands, reminded of what we had lost during last year's spring break.

"You would have gotten off with a warning," the trooper said. "If everything checked out."

"Well, sir," Josh said, not missing a beat, "just let us know what we can do to make sure everything does check out."

"Any chance the owner of this vehicle could meet us out here?" the trooper asked.

"He won't be driving by, if that's what you mean," I said. "They're ahead of us."

"If I can't get proof that you have permission to drive this car, I'll have to—"

"We could call him," Josh said. "Would that be enough proof?"

I almost laughed. The thought was reckless. Not to mention, I'd rather spend the rest of my life in jail for grand theft auto than try to get Ben's help with anything ever again. But Josh had left me with no other choice.

"This is my boyfriend's car." I gave a little head tilt, shrugging, as if it was nothing. "I could call him. No problem."

The trooper sighed, looking across the convertible top, appearing to contemplate his options, his teeth grinding that slice of gum.

Josh widened his eyes, trying to tell me he was sorry.

Ben won't help, I mouthed.

He will, Josh replied. *He thinks we have his drugs.*

I tipped my head back on the headrest, closing my eyes, wishing I was anywhere but in this place, in this moment.

But then I remembered Josh's backpack, slumped in the small space behind his seat, and the gun inside. I felt a trickle of sweat drip down my back. We *had* to count on Ben. He was our only chance. A stolen car might be bad, but throw a concealed weapon into the mix, and I started to wonder if I'd even graduate high school. And then I thought of what charges like those could do to Josh's future, considering his less than flawless history.

The trooper leaned down again. I could tell because the gum-chomping suddenly became louder. My eyes snapped open, and I turned to face him, holding my hands together because they had started shaking again.

"Should I make the call?" I asked.

"I suppose that would work," the trooper said with a nod. "You get this boyfriend of yours on the line, and tell him the situation. Then pass the phone to me."

I smiled at the officer.

Nodded.

Tried to say thanks.

But nothing came out.

As I reached into the space that held my phone, pulled it free, and powered it on, I hoped that my voice would sound strong by the time Ben answered my call. That he would listen. And that he would tell the trooper exactly what he wanted to hear.

31

Brooklyn Simpson's Backyard – 3:52 AM

"Ben Baden." Josh shook his head. Moonlight streamed through the clouds overhead, painting him a silvery blue. "I can't believe what a bastard that guy is."

I backed out of the photo album on Ben's phone, scanning the folders one last time—Sydney, Jules, Becky, Treen. Hadley. And, of course, Penny.

"He's the worst," I said, still feeling a tiny pang of guilt. As horrible as Ben was, I knew he was trying to keep me safe in his own twisted way.

Josh and I were sitting on a trampoline in the middle of Brooklyn's backyard, legs crossed, facing each other with our knees touching. I'd explained everything, starting with my year-old lie about girls' night, not stopping until I'd gotten through the threat Ben had left for Penny and how it tied into the pictures on his phone. I expected the earth to tilt with my confession—for the stars to fade away. But the planetary alignment remained steady, and the stars continued to wink above us in the blue-black sky.

And Josh didn't get angry. He just listened, taking it all in.

"Ben drugged her," I said. I couldn't understand why. Then again, there was nothing in the world that could make sense of the things Ben had done.

"That night, when Penny walked up to the tower, it was because of the pictures. Because Ben had threatened her and Tyler. Because of their argument. But it all started with me lying to you."

Josh's eyes narrowed. "I don't follow."

"It's not your fault." I took a deep breath. "Penny. The accident. It's Ben's fault. And my fault. But not yours."

"Hadley, you can't blame yourself." Josh reached out, brushing his fingertips across my chin, making my entire body tingle. I had a flickering thought of Sam, but I pushed it away.

"But you were in the wrong place at the wrong time because I ditched you. If it hadn't been for me, *neither* of you would have been on Old Henderson Road. You'd both be living normal lives right now."

"There's more to it than that." Josh tipped his face to the sky, closing his eyes. "There's so much more, and I probably shouldn't tell you the worst part. But if you've been blaming yourself all this time, you deserve to know."

"Know what?" My voice was whisper soft. I didn't want to scare him away.

Josh touched his forehead against mine, his breath washing over me. "I'm going to show you something. Something I haven't shown anyone. Ever."

"What is it?"

Josh pressed his lips tight and shifted, pulling his wallet from the back pocket of his cargo shorts, shaking the trampoline and me and the whole night sky. I watched as he opened the leather wallet and pulled out a folded piece of paper.

He reached for my hands, placing the sheet between my

palms, squeezing tightly.

"This changes everything. And at the same time, it changes nothing. Do you understand?"

"No."

"You can't tell. Anyone. This is a secret, Hadley. You have to help me protect it."

A sick feeling churned through my stomach. I didn't want to read it. Yet I wanted to know.

But what I wanted didn't matter when I saw the look in Josh's eyes—he *needed* me to read this note, whatever it was. I took a deep breath and unfolded the paper, slowly, carefully.

Josh pulled his phone out of his pocket and powered it on, a bluish light illuminating the looping script that swept across the unlined page. I was sure it had been torn from one of Penny's sketchbooks.

It wasn't addressed to anyone. The words just started, as if she had grabbed the purple pen and began writing mid-thought:

> Sleep. I need sleep. But I can't seem to. Not ever. Not anymore.
>
> I've done something I'm ashamed of. I tried to fix it—really, I did—but that only made it worse. I hope you never find out. If you do, you'll be ashamed, too. I just hope you don't hate me. Not for anything.
>
> This seems bad, I know, what I'm about to do.

But it's my only way out.

I've picked the most beautiful spot. And the best part—before I go, I'll know what it feels like to fly.

So if you think of me, picture this—my arms spread wide, the starlight and the moonlight my backdrop, as I soar through the sky.

Goodnight, goodnight. A million times goodnight.

P

Tears streamed down my cheeks as I stared at that *P*, a looping purple letter that seemed irrelevant but meant so much.

Penny.

The girl who loved to party almost as much as she loved to draw. The girl who had the foulest mouth of anyone I'd known in all my life. The girl who had felt like an extension of me for as long as I could remember.

Josh reached out and ran his fingers along my cheek, swiping a strand of hair away from my eyes. "You okay?"

I nodded, then shook my head. I scanned the letter again, seeing for the first time two numbers in the top right-hand corner of the tattered page.

4/13

"Four thirteen?" I asked, my voice cracking. "As in April thirteenth?"

Josh nodded.

"Exactly one year ago. She planned it? The whole thing?"

"That's what the police think," Josh said. "That she either hadn't made it to the top of the tower yet, or had and couldn't follow through, so she opted for a different way out."

I tried to keep up but was having trouble. I saw a trooper wearing a wide-brimmed hat, chomping on a slice of neon-blue gum. The vision was so real, I would have sworn that he was actually there. "The police have seen this? That means the Rawlinses have, too."

Josh sighed. "They gave it to me. So I would know the truth. So I wouldn't spend the rest of my life blaming myself." He ducked his head, running his fingers over the paper shaking in my hand.

"But everyone else blames you. And they don't have to. If they saw the letter—"

"Like I said, the letter doesn't change anything."

"But if people knew the truth—"

"That's the thing. No one can know the truth. Not with all the secrets. Secrets I agreed to keep safe."

"But you're sacrificing yourself, Josh. For what?"

"She was real," he whispered. "And she hurt. Her family is still here. Hurting. They asked me to honor her memory by keeping this secret. They don't want her to be defined by the fact that she decided to take her own life. I'm the only one who can protect her. The only one who can protect them all."

I shook my head. "That doesn't make any sense."

"It does, though. It's the only thing that's made sense since the accident." Josh reached for the note, lying half on his lap, half on mine, a wisp of paper so thin it looked as if it might tear in a soft breeze. I wondered how it was strong enough to hold all of that pain. Watching Josh fold Penny's words back into hiding, sliding them into the darkness of his wallet, a wave of anger burst through me.

"It's not fair."

"Fair or not"—Josh shook his head—"it's the least I can do. I can't change what happened. I owe her family whatever they ask of me."

He wouldn't meet my eyes. He just kept staring at the shadows our bodies created on the trampoline as we hovered over the ground.

"You *can* change it. Don't you see? *We* can change it."

"How?" he asked, his voice cracking. "I *killed* her. Not like you with your lie. Not like Ben with those pictures. I ran a car right into her. I wasn't paying attention, Hadley. I was texting you. I wanted to meet up, it's all I could think about, and I wasn't watching the road like I should have been. No matter what you say, the whole thing was my fault."

Josh tried to pull his hands free from mine, but I squeezed tight and wouldn't let go. His words funneled into my consciousness, falling into place where they belonged. As if they had been there already and I just had to discover them again. Strangely, it was the same way I felt about Josh himself. It felt like we had spent the entire night together sorting things out, not just an hour.

"The Penny I knew wouldn't want you to live trapped by her choices."

Josh stopped trying to pull his hands from mine.

"You know I'm right. She would hate what she's done to you." I pressed my forehead to his. He looked up, his nose grazing mine. "You want to honor Penny? Help me do the one thing she couldn't."

Josh's eyes crinkled with confusion.

"Expose Ben. We don't have to use *her* pictures to nail his ass to the wall. We can keep her out of it and still take him down."

The corners of Josh's mouth trembled, as if he wanted to smile but had forgotten how.

"After we get through tonight, we'll go talk to Penny's family about the pictures. Together."

"Hadley, I can't—"

"They deserve to know the truth, Josh. The whole truth. It'll be hard, but at least they'll have answers. And once they do—once they face what actually happened—they'll set you free."

"You think?"

"I don't just think. I know."

Tipping my face up, my lips met his, soft at first, but more insistent as his hands slid their way up my arms, his fingers trailing their way to my neck, twining in my hair.

I fell back slowly, Josh moving with me, until we were lying together, tangled in each other, the strength of our kiss shivering the canvas of the trampoline and rippling out to the silver glow of the night beyond.

32

Just South of the Florida State Line – 2:56 PM
Trip Odometer – 793 Miles

"Had-ley Miller." Ben's voice caused goose bumps to break out all over my skin. "Fascinating that you decided to call."

"Hey, Ben," I said, trying to sound casual, to send him a warning that he had to listen and play along.

"I've been trying to reach you, but you know that already, don't you?"

"Yeah, sorry I missed your calls." My eyes darted to the trooper and away just as quickly. "I was sleeping, and Josh didn't want to answer the phone since he was driving."

"What the hell is going on?" Ben asked. "You sound almost . . . normal."

"There's a little problem. Nothing to worry about, your car is just fine." I reached down deep and found a small giggle.

"Hadley, don't fuck around with me."

"Yes, I'm fine, too," I said, waving a hand in the air. "You don't need to turn around and find us or anything." I paused.

"Hadley, have you lost touch with reality, because—"

"I know you're like an hour ahead, and I swear you can keep going. You just have to talk to the state trooper that pulled Josh over a few minutes ago."

"State trooper? You're kidding, right?"

"He needs you to tell him that we have your permission to drive your car. And maybe confirm that our little spring break caravan got separated on our way down to the condo."

Ben started laughing—the deep kind of belly laugh that can quickly turn out of control.

"We showed him your registration and proof of insurance already." I looked up at the trooper and could tell from the way he was chomping at his gum that he was losing patience. I flashed him a smile and held a finger in the air—*one second.*

"I'm going to pass the phone over to the trooper now, okay, Ben?"

His laughter stopped abruptly. "You have my shit?"

"Only one way to find out," I said, my voice singsong sweet as I slipped the phone away from my face and leaned into Josh, moving my hand toward the open window.

The trooper swept the phone from me and, in one swift movement, pressed it against his puffy cheek. "Benjamin Baden?" he asked, his eyes on the insurance card.

After a beat, the trooper nodded, then turned to look out across several lanes of interstate traffic. "And they *both* have your permission to drive?"

Josh sat frozen in the driver's seat. I wondered what was running through his mind, with that gun tucked into his backpack. The consequences would be disastrous if the cop decided to search the car. But Josh didn't seem to care. His hands were steady, parked at five and seven o'clock on the steering wheel, his legs and feet also entirely still. Nothing indicated even the slightest bit of anxiety.

"Right," the trooper said, nodding. "I see."

I sucked in a deep breath, looking out at the yellow-brown grass that bordered the shoulder. I debated shoving the passenger-side door open and running as fast as I could, up the steep hill and across the exit ramp, into the labyrinth of outlet mall walkways tucked just behind a tall sign that reached up toward the sunny Florida sky.

At least we'd made it to Florida. No matter what he did, Ben couldn't change that fact.

"To verify that I'm actually speaking with Benjamin Baden, I'll need to check the system for your home address and social security number," the trooper said. He turned and walked back to his car, leaving Josh and me alone again.

I looked at Josh, watching his eyelashes sweep steadily up and down. "You're not freaking out?"

Josh slowly turned his head to face me. "What's the point?"

"Um, we could both go to jail. If he decides to search—"

Josh placed a finger against his lips. "Everything is going to be fine."

"How do you know?" I twisted so I could look out the rear window. The trooper was sitting in his front seat, looking at a computer monitor perched on the dash of his car, still holding my phone to his face.

Josh shrugged. "If Ben was going to bust us, we'd already know it."

"He could be talking right now. Telling that trooper how we stole his car and left town. That we crossed a million state lines and—"

"Relax, Hadley. Ben thinks we have his stash." Josh smirked. "And I'm sure Roller's riding his ass. No way that guy is tagging along just for the fun of the chase. If Ben turns us in, he turns himself in. And I'm guessing that part would be easier than facing what Roller will hand down if he doesn't get what he's after."

"Ben might sacrifice himself to make a point." I looked back at the trooper and saw that he was twisting in his seat, his legs stretching out to the road as he stood. "It'd be some major payback if he got us busted for his bag of drugs."

"You're forgetting one thing, Hadley. We buried the pills in Kentucky."

"But Ben doesn't know that." My words were a streaming rush, my eyes locked on the trooper as he walked along the driver's side of the car, advancing on Josh's still-open window. "If Ben spills the whole story, that cop is going to search this car. And when he does, he'll find your gun."

Josh's head whipped up, his lips parted in surprise. "Don't, Hadley. Don't talk about that."

I wanted to ask a million *why*s, but the trooper was there—right there—standing at the door. Bending down. Leaning in, the wide brim of his hat bumping the convertible top.

That's when I finally saw the signs of fear that had been missing all along, evidence that Josh was aware the situation with the gun was crazy-bad.

It was in his eyes, the sizzling shade of green like an electric current. I could barely breathe.

And then there was the trooper, his own eyes ticking from me to Josh and back again, growing more curious by the moment.

He knew something was off.

All I could do was sit there, the echo of that word—*gun—gun—gun*—pinging through the car, threatening to take back every inch we had gained on Ben Baden.

33

Brooklyn Simpson's Bedroom – 4:37 AM

"You guys aren't going to believe this." Brooklyn looked over her shoulder as she walked down the hall from the kitchen, three bowls of ice cream balanced in her hands, bare feet slapping the wood floor.

"So, tell us." I wished she hadn't interrupted Josh and me. We'd been lying together, alternating between talking about our current mess, talking about our past mess, and not talking at all. I wasn't so sure Sam would appreciate the not-talking parts. But sliding off the trampoline, I faced reality, realizing how slim the chances were that *Josh and me* would ever again be *Josh and me.*

"Can't tell you," Brooklyn said, starting up the staircase. "It's something you have to see to believe. Fair warning: brace yourselves."

"I'm not sure I like the sound of that," I said.

"Just know that you can deal with this." Brooklyn topped the landing and made her way to her room. "You're smarter than Ben. Stronger, too."

"You have to start with a pep talk? It's that bad?"

As she entered her room, Brooklyn gave me a pained look

confirming my fears.

"Finally," Mia said from the center of the white four-poster bed. She flipped a magazine closed and tossed it on the bedspread before grabbing a bowl of ice cream from Brooklyn.

"If you'd peeled yourself away from that magazine and come downstairs to help me, it might have gone faster." Brooklyn set a bowl on the computer desk for Sam, whose fingers were working the keyboard of Ben's laptop.

"This Sam chick is on fire," Mia said, taking a bite of ice cream and pointing her spoon at Sam's back.

"It's true." Brooklyn plopped herself into a beanbag chair in the corner. "You brought us a keeper, Josh-Man."

Sam laughed. "And here I thought you two were nothing but haters."

"You're too brilliant to hate," Mia said. "For seriously real. You're almost as good as this ice cream."

Sam looked at Josh, then me, and back again. "Everything okay?"

Josh smiled. "Pretty much."

Sam rolled her eyes. "Thank God," she said, looking directly at me. "He talks about you all the time. It borders on obsessive. I've been telling him to call you for months, to man up and—"

"Okay," Josh said, his cheeks flushed. "I think we get the point. More importantly, what'd you find?"

"Something that'll knock your ass into next week." Sam swiveled the laptop so we could see the screen, where a website was displayed.

"The Free Agents?" Josh asked. "What's that?'

"It's an online club."

"But it's a whole lot worse than it sounds," Mia added. "Show them the main page."

"What's a website have to do with Ben?" I asked as Sam started clicking links. "I thought you were going to search for the pictures and figure out a way to—"

"I dealt with the pictures. I emailed the files to you, Brooklyn, and Mia so the police can track them back to Ben. Just a precaution while we figure out the next step. But after that, I did a little nosing around."

"And she hit the freaking mother lode," Brooklyn said.

"So . . ." Sam pointed to a screen listing several options—announcements, messages, chat room, images, challenges. "This isn't so much a website as some kind of group networking site. I'm not familiar with this server, but it's similar to Google or Yahoo Groups, where content is private and only official members can access the information."

"What's the point?" I asked.

"There are all kinds of groups out there," Sam said. "Artists, business professionals, gamers, moms, you name it. Groups are typically set up so people can network online. But this one—"

"*The Free Agents*," Mia interjected.

"—the Free Agents is interesting because Ben's a member." Sam shook her head. "He's a sick one, your Ben."

"He's not *my* Ben."

Josh took a step closer to the computer. "What's this group all about?"

"In a word," Brooklyn said, wrinkling her nose, "porn."

It took a moment before I let the news fully sink in.

"You don't want visual proof," Mia said. "Trust. Me."

"Am I on the site?" I asked. "The pictures Ben took of me?

Are they here?"

Sam looked me right in the eyes. "Yes. They were uploaded a few weeks ago. The others have been uploaded, too. Looks like he's been an active member for just over a year."

"Since right before Penny died," I said.

"There are over a hundred members," Mia said. "Most of them from colleges around here. Looks like they have to perform some kind of challenge to join."

"Let me guess," I said. "The challenges have to do with pictures. Pictures like the ones we found on Ben's phone?"

"As sick as that is . . . some of the challenges are specific, listing names for a member to target," Sam said. "Like a race to see who gets her first. There's a point system and a penalty board, all kinds of crazy shit to track the progress of the members."

"It's a pyramid scheme," Brooklyn said. "Once you join, you have to recruit other members. You face penalties if you don't. And penalties if you try and fail."

"Roller's ranked pretty high," Mia said, eyes wide as she took another bite of ice cream. "He has more points than most of the other members and is listed as one of the top ten Free Agents."

My mind was spinning. An online porn ring? One that my boyfriend belonged to? I was frozen with fear. The fear of what might happen if this all made it out in the open. Fear of what might happen if it didn't. But the thought of Ben, or one of the other members, hurting someone else like Penny outweighed everything else.

"How'd you even get access?" Josh asked.

Sam chuckled. "Dumbass saved the login password so

the site would remember him. It's like he was begging to get caught."

"Speaking of caught," Brooklyn said, "Ben's life won't ever be the same after we turn this in."

"He's going down," Mia said. "Hard. We're going to make sure of it."

"We are?"

Everyone in the room looked at me as if I'd lost my mind.

"Hey, I'm not questioning the *turn this in* part. It's the *we* that threw me off. This information came from a stolen computer. That's a big risk when you think about involving police."

"Oh, we're in," Brooklyn said.

Mia nodded. "We're definitely in."

"Nothing would give me more pleasure than being part of this takedown," Sam said. "This is going to be huge."

34

Just South of the Florida State Line – 3:09 PM
Trip Odometer – 793 Miles

"You two are free to go." The trooper stood just outside Josh's open window, the steady flow of traffic whipping hot air around him and into the car. He shifted the weight of his utility belt, sunlight glinting off the gun tucked into the holster at his waist. "But first you need to sign this."

A yellow sheet of paper fluttered in the backdraft of a passing car as the trooper thrust a clipboard through the window.

"What is it?" I asked as Josh leaned the clipboard against the steering wheel.

"A warning citation," the trooper said, reaching into the car again. "Here. Your boyfriend is still on the line. He wants to say good-bye."

Of course he does, I thought as I placed the phone to my ear.

"Ben?" I asked, my voice bubble-gum sweet. "You still there?"

"Listen, Hadley. You fucked with the wrong person last night."

"Right," I said. "Of course I'll be safe."

"I found your little note on the bulletin board at Graeter's. And I *can*, Hadley, I *can* catch you. I'm very close to you now—and to that son of a bitch Josh Lane."

I wanted to scream a thousand things at Ben, but that would have to wait. "Josh is taking good care of me, just like he promised."

"You can run," Ben said, "but you can't hide."

"I'll see you soon," I said, blowing a kiss into the phone. "Can't wait."

I ended the call and placed the cell in my lap, a smile creeping to my lips. I wasn't afraid anymore. I was ready.

Josh passed the clipboard back through the open window. The trooper tore the duplicate off and handed it to Josh with a nod.

"You two drive safe," the trooper said. Then he turned, walked back to his car, and slid behind the steering wheel.

"I cannot believe that worked." My voice was low even though the trooper was gone. "We got Ben Baden to vouch for us, and that freaking cop bought the whole thing."

Josh closed his eyes, as if he was trying to block me out.

"Oh, come on, Josh." I smacked him on the leg, and his eyes popped open, but he didn't look my way. "You have to be at least a little excited."

He checked the rearview mirror, flipped on the blinker, and veered into a break in the traffic, his eyes focused on the road, his foot pressing the gas pedal until we'd reached the speed limit.

"Are you waiting for props?" I asked. "I wasn't behind your idea at first, but I'll admit, it was brilliant."

Josh stared out at the road, his thumb tapping the wheel.

"I don't get it. Why aren't you talking to me? You want me to grovel or something?" I rolled my eyes. "Fine. Here goes:

you were *totally* right. That was some *seriously* smooth thinking. I'm *completely* in awe of your ability to remain calm and focused under pressure. How's that work for you?"

Josh glanced at me, just for a second.

"Josh? What's wrong?"

"Nothing." He bit his lip. Paused. And then, "Everything. God, Hadley, I don't know anymore."

"I don't under—"

"You're wrong, you know? I don't always think well under pressure. Not since Penny."

"Is this about the gun?"

I watched him, taking in his clenched jaw and the way his face had tilted away from me. The silence stretching between us was as empty as the year we'd spent apart. "I know you're not a bad person. I know you wouldn't be carrying a gun around if you didn't think you needed it."

"I wouldn't. And maybe I don't, but I was nervous, and—"

"Nervous about what?"

"Talking to Tyler. I was going to Peterson's party to ask for Tyler's forgiveness."

"Forgiveness?" I asked as though I had never heard the word before.

"I know it sounds crazy, but—"

"I don't understand. What did you hope to accomplish confronting Tyler? Especially *last night*?"

"I wasn't planning on *confronting* him exactly. It was more like asking for a pardon."

"With a gun in your hand?"

"No! I wasn't going to use the gun. Not unless I needed to. I grabbed it last minute, okay? I know it was stupid, but those guys—Tyler's friends—I was afraid they'd try to stop me."

"I'm guessing they would have. Not the *try* part. The *stop* part, for sure. It would've been brutal."

"I've had run-ins with them before. With Mike Yates, specifically."

"He's a total hothead. I'm not surprised."

"Would you be surprised if I told you he's the reason I went to the hospital just before Christmas?"

"What do you mean? I thought your parents made you go because they were worried about you."

"That was only part of the story. It started with Yates."

"How?" I asked, my stomach flipping.

"He was cruising around town with a few guys a couple weeks after Thanksgiving. Long story short, I was on my bike, and they ran me off the road, then parked, and got out of the car. I don't remember much after the first couple of swings."

"Josh, that's horrible!"

"The worst part was my mom finding me on the front lawn the next morning and taking me straight to the ER. The cops showed up and asked all kinds of questions, but I couldn't turn Mike in without making everything worse. So, I played the memory-loss card. My parents didn't believe me. When I was released, they took me straight up to the psych ward for an evaluation. They thought I was depressed, maybe suicidal. I was stuck there for thirty days."

"Holy shit, Josh. But I still don't understand. Why the gun?"

"It was supposed to be a safety measure." Josh shook his head. "I know it was stupid. I wasn't really thinking when I grabbed it from my dad's closet on my way out."

"I don't get it. Why walk into a death trap just for an apology?" My words shivered in the air between us. "It doesn't make any sense. Unless . . . I still don't know the whole story."

Josh sighed. "People are right to hate me. I killed her. But there's more. So much more."

"Tell me. I want to help."

"You can't help me," Josh said. "You have yourself to worry about. You have to focus on tonight."

"I *can* help, Josh. Give me a chance. Start by telling one person the truth. The whole truth. And then go from there."

Josh pressed his lips together, appearing as if he didn't trust himself to keep his own secret. "We're less than two hours from our final stop. I'll think about it, okay? For now, you need to focus on how you're going to handle Ben."

"Right. I know that."

"You can do this," he said. "You're stronger than you think."

"You are, too."

Josh's lips pulled back with the hint of a smile. "I'm starting to think that maybe I am."

As we barreled down the highway, I wanted to tell him that he was one of the strongest people I knew. He'd survived so much since Penny's death. More than I'd ever imagined.

The problem was, the more I learned about Josh, the more I began to doubt my own strength.

If I was so strong, why had I let him push me away?

Why hadn't I held on longer?

35

Brooklyn Simpson's Bedroom – 5:17 AM

"We can't mess this up." I was sitting at the head of Brooklyn's bed, pressing myself into a stack of pillows. Josh was beside me. "If we're going to bust Ben, this plan has to be flawless."

"Flawless will be pretty tough to pull off with so many variables to consider." Sam scrunched her loose bun with one hand. The computer screen behind her was still displaying the home page of the Free Agents.

"But the plan we came up with *is* flawless." Brooklyn leaned back in the beanbag chair, her arms propped behind her head. "We call the police right now and have them come over so we can show them what we found. Voilà! Ben's busted, and the Free Agents are, like, no more."

"I've been thinking about that." Mia propped her head on her hand and sighed. "Will it matter that the computer is stolen? On those true crime shows, little details can screw a case over. I don't want Ben to get off on a technicality."

Sam waved a hand in the air. "There are ways around that. Hadley can say her computer died, and she borrowed Ben's to work on a paper or something. Have you ever been inside his house without him there?"

"Yeah, a bunch of times."

"Okay, so the computer's not stolen, just borrowed." Mia swayed her feet in the air. "Makes sense since you guys have been dating for a few months. What else do we need to figure out before we call?"

"I'm still stuck on the calling part," I said, inching closer to Josh. Being close to him made me feel stronger.

"What?" Mia asked. "We have to call the police. It's the only way—"

"It's not the only way."

Brooklyn groaned. "Hadley, can you please just *not* make this more complicated than it already is?"

Josh looked at me. "What do you want to do?" he asked.

"I'm not sure." I shrugged. "I just don't want Ben to get off too easy."

"Trust me," Sam said. "The police aren't going to go easy on any of these guys once they see this site. Forget the computer; these Free Agents are all going down. Each and every one of them."

"Maybe I want Ben to know I'm behind it." *This* was the only way. My way. I had to do it. For Penny. "I want a little time alone with Ben. Enough that he thinks he's going to get away with it. I want to hear what he has to say. And then I want him to know I'm the reason he's getting busted."

"Sounds dangerous," Mia said.

"It's only dangerous if I make a stupid move."

"It's dangerous even if you make all the right moves," Mia insisted. "Consider who you're dealing with, Hadley. Ben and Roller are both desperate."

"Maybe we can set it up so the police are there, then. I just need to see Ben's face, you guys. Roller's, too. I want to see the look in their eyes when they realize it's over, all because of me."

"So, what?" Brooklyn asked. "You just call a meeting and expect Ben to show?"

"Exactly. If he thinks I'm going to give up his drugs, he'll tell Roller, and they'll both be there in a heartbeat. If we pick the right spot, the police could monitor the entire scene."

"I don't like it," Mia said. "It's way too dangerous."

"Not if I go," Josh said.

"No!" Sam said. "You've been through enough."

"What I've been through is a result of all this." Josh stood and started pacing. "I want exactly what Hadley wants. To see the look on their faces when they realize they're going down because of something I did."

The doorbell rang, echoing through the house.

We all froze.

One second passed.

Two.

Three.

I wondered if I'd imagined the sound. If we all had. But then it rang again, shattering the silence.

This time the ringing didn't stop, as if the button was stuck or someone was pressing without letting up.

Brooklyn swept her curtains aside, peering out the window to the front yard. "Ben's car's in the driveway. I can see the shadow of a guy standing on the front walkway, hoodie, jeans—"

"Roller." I jumped off the bed. "Holy shit, what are we going to do?"

"Relax." Josh reached out and grabbed my hand. "We're in control here."

"Come out, come out, wherever you are." The voice drifted up from the front porch, muffled by the windows, deep, quiet, and scratchy.

The doorbell kept ringing.

Roller. Ben. They were there on the front porch, standing beside the rocking chairs where Brooklyn, Mia, and I had sat earlier in the week, painting our nails, listening to music, and drinking pink lemonade.

My skin broke out in a cold sweat. My eyes burned with frustration. We had been so close.

"You have to cover for us," Josh said, looking from Brooklyn to Mia, his eyes stopping on Sam. "You need to buy us enough time so we can sneak out the back."

"Sneak out?" Mia asked. "To go where?"

Josh looked at me, eyebrows raised. He didn't have to say a word.

"The tower. I'll use Josh's phone to text Brooklyn when we get there. You show Ben my text so he knows it's for real."

"And then what?" Mia asked. "What the hell comes next?"

"He follows us." Josh's voice was confident. Sure. "We'll have enough time to set things up if you can keep them here until we text you."

"What about the police?" Sam asked. "We're not letting you do this without backup."

"Then call them with an anonymous tip as soon as Ben and Roller take off." Josh smiled. It really was the most beautiful thing. "Nothing's going to go wrong. Trust me."

He lifted his arm, running a hand through his hair. I took him in, memorizing every detail, my eyes trailing the slope of his wrist, sliding up the length of his arm, thinking how very much I did trust him, even after all this time. How much I had missed him and how wrong I had been to ever let him push me away.

Which made what I saw next even harder to bear.

A permanent reminder of what had happened one year ago.

A symbol of his guilt and shame.

A small circular tattoo, centered on his inner biceps.

One single Penny.

Heads.

Up.

36

Grant Island, Florida – 5:17 PM
Trip Odometer – 873 miles

I STOOD at the top of the lighthouse, the salty sea air whipping through my hair, looking out at the ocean. The deep blue water stretched all the way to the horizon, which was dotted with a few ships that looked teeny-tiny so far off in the distance. I wished I could keep going, riding Ben's BMW across the surface of the water until I met the sky and could spin with the stars.

But after crossing the causeway, reaching the island, and driving past a twisted, dancing tree, Josh had turned right, away from civilization, along a street lined with deserted beach houses, until we'd reached the end of the road. Now there was nowhere left for me to run.

I'd smiled when I first realized where he'd taken me, my gaze fixed on the tall white structure scraping the sky. I'd wanted to say something about it being just like our place at home. But Josh's stiff posture kept me from breaking the silence.

After parking in a deserted lot, Josh looked at me, a sad smile pulling at the corners of his mouth.

"I'll tell you everything, Hadley. I promise. I just need a little more time."

I'd nodded. My chest burned from holding my breath; I

was terrified that the slightest current of air could blow his promise away.

He stepped out of the car, grabbed his backpack, and made his way down a short path that led to a ribbon of silky white beach. I watched as he kicked off his Converse shoes, snatching them up with a spray of sand, and walked toward the edge of the water. It seemed to breathe—the whole ocean—in and out.

I walked toward the lighthouse, which was perched on a mountain of stones, shoving my way through the little door with a sign that said CLOSED FOR RENOVATION and up a set of spiral steps, my hand sliding along the gritty surface of the banister. At the top, I made my way out of the lantern room, to the wraparound platform, and sat, threading my legs through a rickety railing.

The white crests of the waves swelled like rolling thunder, racing toward Josh as he sat on the beach, his knees bent toward the sun. My eyes soaked in all the details that I'd spent the last year trying to forget—all the ways he'd changed. The lazy curl of his hair was longer now. The hunch of his shoulders was more pronounced, as if he was caving in on himself. And though I couldn't see them, I knew that his eyes had dimmed.

I sat there, wishing for strength. First with Josh. And then with Ben.

Pulling myself up, the wind tore through me as I slipped back into the lantern room. I had to make things right. Before another moment passed.

I spun myself down the steps and onto the beach, kicking off my shoes at the foot of a dune, and noticed for the first time the piece of paper clutched in Josh's hands, flapping in the wind.

I walked up behind him, stopping just a few feet short,

glad that the angle of the sun cast my shadow behind me. I could see over his shoulder and could just make out the looping script that swept across the tattered page. The purple pen. The words that pummeled me.

Sleep. I need sleep.

I knew Josh hadn't written them.

I'm ashamed . . . it's my only way out.

I was dizzy. The wind twisted around me, insisting—I had to read on.

I'll know what it feels like to fly.

I saw her hopping across the creek behind the Badens' backyard, disappearing as she rounded a tree, racing away from the party. In that moment, Penny Rawlins had fewer than two hours to live.

Goodnight, goodnight. A million times goodnight.

P

Josh turned, sensing me. He folded the note in half and then folded it once more.

I sat next to him, placing my hand on his, leaning against him as I slipped the note through his fingers and let it unfold and flutter in the billowing air. "I know why she did it."

37

Simpsons' Kitchen – 5:33 AM

I raced down the staircase, Josh behind me, ducking as we passed the front door. The only barrier between them and us was a thick slab of wood. Thankfully, the three windows in the entry were above eye level, recessed into the door itself, small and beveled and nearly impossible to see through.

"Hurry," Brooklyn whispered, killing the lights, trailing behind Josh, Mia on her heels, Sam at the back of the pack.

The doorbell stopped.

"Hadley." Ben's voice was muffled. I pictured his cheek, scratchy with stubble, pressed up against the door. "Hadley, I know you're in there."

Someone behind me whispered, "Asshole."

Brooklyn brushed past me, bumping the foyer table and toppling a vase, which crashed to the floor. She jumped back. "Shit!"

"We can hear you in there." Roller. His fist pounding on the door. "You can't hide forever."

That damn doorbell started again, drowning out the sound of our footsteps, washing away every thought that tried to take hold in my mind.

Making our way into the kitchen, Josh grabbed his

backpack, swinging it onto one shoulder, thrusting his other arm through the empty strap, that penny tattoo flashing out as he grabbed hold of my hand.

"What do you want, Ben?" Mia's voice, loud, solid, pissed. She was standing at the front door, her palms pressed up against the dark wood.

"What the hell is she doing?" I whispered.

"Stalling so you can get out," Brooklyn said. "Duh."

"You know what I want," Ben said. "Hadley. We just need to talk to her."

"Talk, huh?" Mia shouted through the dark panel of wood. "Feels like you're about to break the door down."

"We can settle this easy. No problems at all."

"Who's with you?" Mia asked.

"Let's cut the shit," Roller said. "You know who I am."

"Yeah, well, sorry to disappoint, but Hadley's not here."

"No way I believe that," Ben said. "Hadley was supposed to spend the entire weekend here. With Brooklyn's parents out of town, this is the only place for her to hide. Open the door and let me inside."

"She's not here."

There was a pause. An angry murmur from the other side of the door. And then Ben's voice again. "Let us in so we can see for ourselves."

"I don't know," Mia said. "We'd have to negotiate terms."

"She's got them," Brooklyn whispered, nodding her head toward the mudroom. "I'll make sure she keeps them by the door. Get out of here, fast."

"Hey, Josh," Sam said. "Don't screw this up."

Josh shook his head. "No chance of that."

Then it was just us, rushing across the tile floor of the mudroom, past a blur of coats and shoes, through the doorway, and into the cool darkness of the garage.

Josh's arm slipped around my waist, his other hand squeezing mine tight. I tugged him slowly past Brooklyn's car, toward the workbench and tool cabinet in the back corner. I was nervous—my legs were tingly, numb—and I wondered if I would be able to make it all the way to the tower. Then I thought of Josh, his legs nearly destroyed in the accident. He wasn't strong enough to run that far.

If we couldn't run, it would take us forever to get to the tower.

We didn't have that kind of time.

I searched the darkness, trying to find something, anything, that would help us move faster. When I saw four bikes hanging from the ceiling, I nearly cried with relief.

"We need to move fast. Can you handle riding on the trails?"

"Yeah, but they might be a little dangerous before the sun's up."

"We don't have a choice."

I grabbed two helmets off a shelf as Josh unhooked the bikes, then raced back to the corner, feeling the wall with my hand, fingers stretching until I found what I was looking for.

The door handle. Our escape.

Yanking the door open, the hinges screamed out to the night. I wanted to scream, too. I was sure that door had just given us away.

Josh shoved Brooklyn's bike outside, pulling her brother's along with him. Propping his helmet on his head, he snapped the strap under his chin. I did the same, watching as he swung one leg over the seat of Eddie's bike, shifting the backpack on his shoulders. He looked back at me.

"Ready?"

I nodded. "Let's get out of here."

Josh pedaled slowly at first, past a line of blossoming crab apple trees. He led us through the grass, around the trampoline, and toward the woods bordering Brooklyn's backyard. When we hit the trailhead and the shelter of the trees, we gained speed. By the time we reached the first big hill, Josh was standing on the pedals, air whipping through the fabric of his T-shirt and the mesh of the backpack, giving him the illusion of wings.

I followed, my pulse thundering in my ears.

Behind me, I heard voices.

Rising.

Falling.

Staccato.

Full of rage.

Racing me—chasing me.

38

Grant Island, Florida – 5:33 PM
Trip Odometer – 873 miles

"I told you I needed to be alone."

"But you didn't mean it." I swept a strand of hair from my eyes. "Did you?"

I ran my thumb along the ridges of his knuckles, feeling his hands shaking beneath mine. He hadn't meant it a year ago, either.

Josh grunted and looked out over the blanket of blue stretching before us.

"Penny killed herself." I said the words softly. Then again, louder, more sure. "Penny killed herself. And you've known all this time. But you haven't told anyone."

Josh shook his head, his hair brushing against my cheek. "You weren't supposed to see the note."

"But I did." The paper flapped in the wind. "It changes everything."

My chest rose and fell, threatening to explode with all the emotion rushing through me. Anger and sorrow about Penny's choice. Frustration and regret over how Josh had been treated in the wake of her death. But mostly, a fierce sense of protection. And hope. It scared me more than anything, but it was there. Hope for Josh and me. Together.

"I don't understand everything that happened." I leaned into Josh, my face inches from his, my lips grazing his ear. "But people should know the truth."

Josh tipped his head against mine. "It's too late," he said. "I have to keep her secret. I made a promise."

"But I didn't." He wouldn't meet my eyes. "Now that I know, I'm going to make it right. Tyler's my friend. I can talk to him. Make him see that what this is doing to you isn't . . . Wait a minute. *Tyler* called you. Tell me what he said."

Josh shook his head. "It isn't important." He still wouldn't meet my eyes.

"Tell me."

Josh sighed. "He called to warn me that Ben was on our trail. That he was tracking the GPS. It's why I changed our route. I thought we'd at least have a chance—"

"Tyler *warned* you? He actually—"

"Don't be angry. I didn't want you to worry. And I had no idea how to tell you that he called without telling you everything else."

"I'm not mad. Don't you see? It means he's trying to protect you."

"Actually, he wanted to be sure I would keep *you* safe. Maybe he told me to watch my back, too. But it doesn't mean things will ever go back to the way they were." Josh ducked his head, trailing his fingers through the sand.

"You never know. Penny would never have wished this—your life, the way you've been treated—on anyone. Tyler has to know that."

Josh took a few deep breaths, his shoulders shaking, and

then finally looked at me, the sea-glass green of his eyes glinting with tears, swirling with sorrow and loss.

"It's why I had to end things. With that lie between us, I couldn't be with you. Couldn't let you get caught up in my mess. I still can't—"

"Oh, no. You're not pushing me away again. First we deal with my mess. Then we deal with yours. Together."

"Hadley, I can't let you—"

"Oh my God." It finally clicked. All of it. Right into place.

"What?"

"I didn't know everything. But you don't, either."

Penny had seen the pictures. She had to have. And the pictures are the reason she wrote that note. The reason she did what she did. I *knew* it.

Pulling my phone free, I navigated to the slide show Brooklyn and Mia had sent. Josh deserved to know that Penny's choice was based on more than he'd ever suspected.

I'd seen her that night, alone, near the creek in the Badens' backyard. People streamed between us, partially blocking my view, but she had been staring into the woods as though they were calling to her. She moved toward the trees but backed away just before crossing the creek, walking into a guy with a plastic cup. Beer spilled, the guy shouted, and Penny's eyes squeezed tight, as if she were making the most important wish of her life. When her lashes fluttered open, she caught me staring. Brooklyn and Mia were debating the finer points of some guy's ass, and I pulled them away, tugging them through the crowd until we were right by Penny's side. She'd smiled, then said the party was lame and she was out.

I wanted to leave with her—something was wrong, and I

knew it—but she insisted on going alone. Brooklyn and Mia tried, too, but she stopped us all.

I need to think, Penny had said. *A walk in the woods will solve everything.*

I made her promise to call me. Because after thinking, there's always talking. With us, at least. Now I realized she hadn't promised. She'd simply nodded before turning away.

Penny must have been afraid of people finding out, ashamed of what she had done. Confused about how it had happened. Just as I had been feeling since I first saw the picture Ben posted on Facebook.

"You see?" I asked as Josh's eyes moved from the pictures to the waves. "It wasn't your fault."

I reached my hand up, my fingers sliding over the scruffy stubble on his face, running across the smooth skin of his lips. Leaning forward—slowly, so very slowly—my mouth grazed his. And then his hands slipped free of mine, reaching around to the small of my back, pulling me to him, down to the sand.

I drank him in, the salty taste of the air and his heat burning everything away. And I made a million silent promises to myself and to him, to the waves and the wind and the sugary pink sky. I would find a way to keep him safe, to take every bad thing and make it right.

39

THE WITCHES' TOWER – 5:51 AM

WE WERE panting when we arrived at the tower, gasping for air as we leaned the bikes against the shadowed side of the sister trees.

And then we scrambled.

Josh pacing off steps in the woods.

Me ducking through the door of the tower, spiraling my way up the staircase to leave the clue, and racing my way back down again.

Ten breathless minutes after we arrived, we stepped into the clearing, Josh behind me, his arms wrapped around my waist. The tower stood before us, shrouded by a hazy mist.

Running my hand up the length of his arm, I saw it again.

"The tattoo," I said, my voice scratchy with exhaustion. "Why'd you get it?"

"To remember her. So I would never forget why I was keeping her secret."

"That's sad." The sky had broken into a fiery pink glow that stretched as far as I could see, wisps of clouds hanging from the streaks of light like sugary beads of cotton candy. "And sweet."

Breathing Josh in, the scent of boy and earth and night all mixed together, gave me strength.

"We're ready?" I asked.

Josh nodded. "As ready as we'll ever be."

I held my hand between us, palm up.

Josh dropped his phone onto the tangled map of lines creasing my palm and smiled. "Almost over now."

"Sure is," I said. I typed Brooklyn's number, hoping that Ben was still there so she could pass my message along, just as we'd planned.

Me: I'm in the woods
I'm way up high.
Come and find me.
Dare you to try.

I hit SEND and watched as the text went through.

"Done," I said. "He should be here soon."

40

Grant Island, Florida – 5:51 PM
Trip Odometer – 873 Miles

"You're sure you want to wait here?" Josh asked, swinging his sandy feet into the car and pulling the passenger-side door closed before tossing his backpack into the back.

I drummed my fingers on the steering wheel. "I'm sure." I tucked my hands in the front pockets of my jeans to control my nerves. "You're okay?"

"I think I am." Josh smiled. "Or at least I will be."

"Good." I smiled back as my fingers grazed the surface of my favorite ring, the one I'd tucked away in my pocket when this crazy night had only just begun.

"I appreciate what you want to do, but you can't have any expectations. Penny's family might have given me that note so I wouldn't spend the rest of my life blaming myself, but there's no guarantee they'll be ready to tell the world what really happened. Not even if we do decide to show them what Ben did to her. I have to be okay with that."

"No *ifs*. They're going to see those pictures." I pulled the ring from my pocket and slid it on my finger, back where it belonged. I wasn't going to let Ben Baden take one more thing away from me. "Tyler's already seen them. According to

Brooklyn, he's up for helping bust Ben, so he must be planning to tell his parents. You see? It's all falling into place. Without you even trying."

Josh sighed. "It's scary to hope."

I leaned toward him, tracing the outline of the penny tattoo with the tip of my finger. "I'm sorry I let you push me away. God, you must have hated me."

"I hated Ben Baden a whole lot more."

"You know why I started dating him, right?"

"To spite me?"

"To forget you. No matter how hard I tried, I couldn't forget you."

Josh smiled. "Looks like your plan failed pretty miserably."

"I'm glad." I laughed.

Josh looked at me, his eyes drooping. "Me, too."

"You must be tired. Why don't you try to get some sleep. I'll keep watch. They're bound to be here soon."

"Wake me as soon as you see Roller's car?"

I looked in the rearview mirror, angling it so I could see the road behind us.

"You think we made the right decision?"

"It's your call. . . . But when you throw Roller Haughton into the mix, I think it's our best bet."

"So, we're ready?" I asked.

"As ready as we'll ever be." Josh closed his eyes, nestling his head into the curve of the seat. "And once this is over, we'll be free."

His breathing slowed, deepened. I watched the clock tick away the minutes. Counted each as it passed, shifting in my seat when I hit the number five. Josh stirred, his mouth parting slightly. I focused more on him than on the rearview mirror. Finally, his breathing steadied. It had been seven minutes.

And then I reached, slowly and carefully, into the backseat.

Eased the zipper of the backpack open.

Dropped my hand inside.

And clasped my fingers around the cool, slick surface of the gun.

41

The Witches' Tower – 6:23 AM

Josh stood at the edge of the woods, the sister trees behind him, sunlight burning away a gauzy haze that circled their twining legs.

"You hid the package?"

Josh nodded. "He won't find it. Not without the clues."

"Which we won't offer up until he admits what he did. To me. To Penny. To all those girls. By then the police should be here."

"You're good by the tower? You're sure you don't want me right by your side?"

"I'm fine." I shoved my hands into the front pockets of my jeans. "You need to stay hidden. If they see you, this won't work. They need to think they're in control."

Josh shook his head. "When this is over—"

"When this is over, the police will have both of them, and we'll be free." I smiled, my fingers grazing the surface of my favorite ring, the one I'd tucked away in my pocket when this crazy night had only just begun. "And then we are going to go talk to Tyler Rawlins. We're going to tell him everything. You and me. Together."

"Not today, Hadley. It's too—"

"Do you hear that?" I pulled the ring from my pocket and slid it on my finger, back where it belonged. I wasn't going to let Ben Baden take one more thing away from me.

The whoosh of wind racing up the hill was faint at first, then grew louder, accompanied by the sound of tires squealing around a bend.

"We're on," I said.

Josh winked at me, his lips parting in a smile. "You got this," he said. "Don't let them scare you."

"Me?" I asked. "Never."

Josh raced toward me, crossing the space between us in a few steps. He slipped his arms around my waist and kissed me, his lips smiling, his heart beating against mine.

I watched him disappear behind the sister trees, so grateful to finally have him back. There wasn't any room for fear.

Until the BMW skidded to a stop in the pull-off.

Until Ben and Roller swung open their doors at the exact same time, stepped out of the car, and started walking toward me.

42

Grant Island, Florida – 6:23 PM
Trip Odometer – 873 Miles

It sounded far away at first, the tapping that made me feel off balance. There was something I needed to remember. The sound continued, louder, threatening to split my head right open.

Then it was there, all of it rushing me. The jagged pieces of a thousand dreams.

The picture of me on Facebook.

The tower, the moon, and the glittering green of Josh's eyes.

The drugs and the girls and Penny with her million good-nights.

The rest seemed mixed up—a tunnel of mirrors and a phone, a teal tile mosaic, beautiful girls with no mouths, and two bikes leaning up against the braided sister trees back at the tower.

Eyes opening, hand clenching tight around the heavy lump I'd stuffed into the pocket of my jacket, I faced him.

"Caught you!" Ben stood at the window, lips curled back in a nervous kind of smile.

I reached across the console for Josh, grabbed his arm. He stirred, sitting up before he was fully awake.

"What?" But I didn't have to answer. Josh's eyes pulled tight as they focused on Ben and, just behind him, the tall, skinny frame of Roller.

"Sorry," I whispered. "I must have fallen asleep."

"It's okay," Josh said.

I shook my head. "I was supposed to be on watch."

"It's going to be okay. Just follow the plan, and we'll be fine."

I unlocked the car and reached for the handle, but Ben beat me to it, yanking the door open and sweeping an arm out to one side.

"Hadley," he said, his eyes swimming with a mix of emotions. He was pissed. But there seemed to be something else swirling around the edges. Regret. Or maybe even fear. "It's time for us to talk."

I stepped onto the pavement, a fine layer of sand scratching under my feet, and looked him right in the eyes. "Yes. It's time."

Behind me, I heard Josh open his door, his feet planting hard on the pavement.

Ben looked at him from over the convertible top, then back at me. "Alone, Hadley. We talk alone."

"I'll watch this one." Roller jutted his chin toward Josh. "Make sure he doesn't get away."

I glared at Roller, taking in the crooked set of his nose, the coal black of his eyes. I was suddenly afraid of leaving Josh alone. Terrified that splitting up was the worst thing we could do. But it was too late to turn back now. I had to stay focused, to follow the plan. I started toward the lighthouse, the wind tossing my hair, ripping through my clothes, crashing the heavy weight in my pocket against my hip.

43

The Witches' Tower – 6:26 AM

"Caught you!" Ben stalked toward me, crossing the last few feet separating us.

Roller stopped just behind him, legs spread wide, arms crossed over his chest.

"Who's this?" I asked. "Your new bestie?"

"Hadley, please." Ben looked so tired, circles cutting a deep purple swath just beneath his eyes. "Just give me the package."

I smiled. It was shaky and forced, but I hoped it looked strong. "Not so fast."

"Game's over," Ben said. "Just give it up."

"Funny that you mention games." I tipped my head to the side, letting my words sink in.

"What's she talking about?" Roller asked, his eyes cutting from me to Ben and back again.

"Should I not call it a game? Do you prefer the official title?"

"Dude," Roller said, "she'd better not be talking about—"

"Relax," Ben said. Roller opened his mouth, about to say more, but then pressed his lips together. "She doesn't know a thing."

"I don't know a thing about what?" I asked. "The pictures

on your phone? Or your twisted little club? The Free Agen—"

"You said she didn't know," Roller lashed out at Ben. "You said there was *no way* she'd figure things out."

Ben ignored him, looking at me, eyes pleading.

"I tried to keep you out of it."

44

Grant Island, Florida – 6:26 PM
Trip Odometer – 873 Miles

"You tried to keep me out of it?" I asked as I crossed from the pavement of the parking lot onto the flowing sand, my feet sinking in.

"I had it all figured out," Ben said, catching up. "I was almost free and clear, but you had to go and steal my car."

"And your drugs. Don't forget about the drugs."

"There's more to this than you know. So much more, Hadley."

"More?" I didn't stop. Didn't even look at him. "You mean that naked picture of me that you posted on Facebook?"

"I had to," Ben said, his voice insistent. "I didn't have a choice. He made me. It was supposed to get you back to the party. I never thought you'd—"

"Because he wanted the drugs?"

"Yes. Everything was about the pills."

"What about all the others?"

Ben grabbed my wrist, stopping me from taking another step.

"Others?"

"On your phone, Ben. Sydney. Jules. Becky. Treen."

"God, Hadley, stop." His eyes were wild as my words registered.

"I can't stop." Jerking free of his grip, the wind tossed my hair around my face. "There's one more."

"Please—"

"Penny." The name unfurled in the wind, tossed into the sky.

"Don't do this." Ben looked over his shoulder, his eyes finding Roller and then flitting back to me. "You need to leave this alone."

"I bet you'd like that."

"Believe it or not, I'm trying to keep you safe. I'm trying to keep all of you safe."

45

The Witches' Tower – 6:31 AM

"Safe? By drugging us?"

"I wanted to make sure nobody remembered." Ben squeezed his eyes shut, clenching his hands into fists. "Wait. That came out wrong. I didn't mean it like—"

"You're sick." I took a step back, my heart racing. Ben was admitting it—everything he had done—and Josh was tucked away behind the sister trees, recording the entire confession. The police would know the whole twisted story as soon as they arrived.

"The not remembering, it wasn't about me. It was about the girls. I didn't want them to remember because I knew they would hate what they had done."

"What you *made* them do."

"I didn't force anyone to do anything," Ben said. "You have to believe me. All the girls, what they did, they were on board."

"Except for the drugs? I'm guessing none of us just agreed to the part where we were drugged."

"Hadley—"

"But even then, your plan failed, didn't it? At least once."

"Enough with this shit," Roller said, rocking on his heels, a coil about to spring. "Where's the package?"

Ben stood there looking at me with those tired eyes.

"You messed up with Penny. She remembered. She *knew* what you had done to her."

Ben sighed. "She wasn't sure, but she was relentless. She wouldn't leave me alone, so I showed her a picture. One picture. I thought it would keep her quiet. But it just made things worse."

"So, after Penny, you figured out how to get it right. A trial-and-error kind of thing? Tell me, how many pills does it take to erase a memory?"

"I didn't want to hurt anyone," Ben said. "I swear. Least of all Penny."

46

Grant Island, Florida – 6:31 PM
Trip Odometer – 873 Miles

"If you didn't want to hurt them, why did you take the pictures? The truth, Ben. Tell me the truth."

"It's a game." Ben's voice was weary, defeated. "An online club called The Free Agents. Lots of guys are involved. I got sucked in for reasons you don't even want to know."

"A game? Where you drug girls and take their pictures?"

"Yeah." Ben's eyes dropped to the sand. "I hated it, okay? And Penny, I didn't *want* to start with her. I had to."

"*Had* to?"

"There are rules. Challenges. And penalties if you don't follow through. I was supposed to bring someone in. But my first recruit wasn't interested. As a precaution, I had to ensure his silence."

"Tyler?" The realization made me feel ill.

"Penny was insurance—a way to keep Tyler quiet if he ever decided to talk. It's how they protect the club—using people you love against you."

"But he's still friends with you. He knows about all of this, and he's still friends with you?"

"He knows general stuff about the Free Agents, but he has no idea about the pictures of Penny. And I'd like to keep it that way. It's what she would have wanted."

"You can't use her memory like that." I started walking again, crossing the sand with even strides. "Besides, Tyler does know. You're going to have to explain to him yourself."

"I didn't think there was any other way out," Ben said, chasing after me. "Not at first. But then I found one. Roller wanted players, but he wanted something else even more."

"This should be good."

"He liked what I did with the pills. I was the first one to try it. I swear I only did it for the girls, but Roller thought it would be good for the club, said it would prolong the life of the game, that it was the strongest safeguard of all. Blocking the memories of the girls would ensure the safety of the members and help increase participation."

"Because more Free Agents is exactly what the world needs. . . ."

"With each new member bringing someone else in, participation was soaring. There was even a way for members to gamble on challenges. But Roller needed an in with a dealer who could supply the pills. Enough so that any member who wanted to place an order could."

"I don't get it. What does that have to do with you?"

"It doesn't. It has more to do with my mom."

"Your mom?" But I didn't need him to explain. I already knew.

"Her thing with pills . . . it's not exactly legit. Neither is the guy who supplies her. Roller said he'd let me go—dismiss me, no consequences—if I hooked him up with my mom's guy."

"And the package?"

"It's a trial run. If Roller can move it in less than a week, he's in. And I'm no longer a Free Agent. Just like that. A full pardon."

47

The Witches' Tower – 6:39 AM

"A FULL pardon? I bet Penny would have enjoyed a pardon from you and your twisted game. *She* never got the chance."

"Well, I never had a chance, either." Ben made fists of his hands. "This whole thing has been out of my control from the start."

"*You're* the one who joined. You dragged *all of us* into this. How can you say you're not in control?"

"Because I'm not!" Ben's face twisted with shame. "I never have been. Roller targeted me as a new member. I refused him at first, but he's relentless, one of the top recruiters, earning major points for each guy he brings in. He doesn't take no for an answer."

"You're telling me the reason behind all of this is that Roller was so relentless, you just caved? Give me a break! I can't believe—"

"I joined to protect my mom, Hadley. Roller knows about her thing for pills. He's her backup supplier when her guy isn't available, and he threatened to turn her in if I didn't join. So I did. But I negotiated a release when I promised to make the connection with her dealer."

"So, you're in pretty deep," I said, looking into Roller's flat, black eyes. "Which means you're going down with Ben."

"I thought you said this chick wasn't going to give us any trouble. She's been nothing but, Baden."

"She's off-limits," Ben said, his voice a low growl.

"Nothing is off-limits."

"I did everything you asked. You can't—"

"I can, and I will, and you know it."

"Just to be clear," I interrupted, "you want your package?"

"Yes." Roller's word was tight, angry.

My body wavered as if I was caught in a strong gust of wind. But I focused, centering my mind on the only thing that mattered—getting Josh and me out of there, away from Ben and Roller for good.

"Okay," I said with a shrug. "Here's how this is going to go."

48

Grant Island, Florida – 6:39 PM
Trip Odometer – 873 miles

"You will agree to ending this on my terms." I moved carefully as we made our way up the uneven rocks to the lighthouse, one step at a time.

"You're not in charge, Hadley," Ben said.

"Roller seems pretty pissed off. And very motivated, driving you all the way to Florida. I'm not sure he'd like it if I told him you declined my offer."

"What, exactly, are you offering?" Ben stopped and looked up at the tall structure erupting from the rocky ground. "And where are you taking me?"

"Josh and I need a way to get home. So, you're going to leave your car for us to drive back to Oak Grove." I fought the wind, twining my hair away from my face, wrapping it into one long strand in my grip. "Consider it the least you can do."

"No fucking way, Hadley."

I bit my lip, tilting my head to the side. "If you don't agree to my terms, you'll never find what you're after."

Ben narrowed his eyes at me.

"The pills, Ben," I whispered, unclasping my fingers, letting my hair fly wild. "I'm talking about the pills. They're not in the car. They're not anywhere near here. But I'll give you a clue to where we hid them, *if* you agree to leave us the BMW."

49

The Witches' Tower – 6:43 AM

"You hid the package?" Ben's eyes went wide.

"Yes. I'm not sure giving it up now is the best option."

"It's your only option, little girl," Roller said, stepping forward, the rising sun catching on the crooked set of his nose, extinguished in the coal black of his eyes.

"Actually, I still have a few others. And if you want a clue that'll lead you to what you've been looking for, you're going to agree to some things first."

"Jesus Christ, Ben. Who is this chick?"

"I'm the chick who can reunite you with your precious package," I said, my cheeks on fire.

"Oh, yeah?" Roller asked. "How's this going to work?"

"I'm in charge. And right now, I'm offering you a clue. You taking it?"

50

GRANT ISLAND, FLORIDA – 6:43 PM
TRIP ODOMETER – 873 MILES

"ONE CLUE?" Ben asked, his eyes burning.

"Take it or leave it," I said, the wind whipping against my body, sand stinging my cheeks.

Ben looked defeated. "What happens after I get this clue of yours?"

"You follow it wherever it leads, which, I might add, is far away from here. Far away from me. And Josh. When you get there, you'll be reunited with your precious cargo."

I left out the part about the Kentucky State Police. That we'd called in a tip, and they would be waiting to bust Ben and Roller when they arrived at the rest stop to dig up the package. That he would also be dealing with the fallout from the pictures, which Josh and I planned to take to the police as soon as we returned to Oak Grove and talked with Penny's family. Add the Free Agents to the mix, and Ben and Roller were facing a pretty major shit storm.

Ben looked out over the ocean, scraping his hands through his hair. His shoulders rippled beneath the thin fabric of his shirt, and I couldn't help but think of all the times I'd run my hands across the ridges of his body. How I thought he was so good when really he was as messed up as you could get.

"This is not how I expected things to end."

"Of course it isn't," I said. "You thought you'd be the one calling the shots."

"Where's the clue?"

I pointed to the lighthouse door, the one with the sign that said Closed for Renovation.

"At the top."

51

THE WITCHES' TOWER – 6:49 AM

"AT THE top?" Ben stared into the dark opening, his eyes resting on the bottom step of the spiral staircase.

I smiled then, leaning forward, my hair sweeping over both of my shoulders, glinting in the lemon-raspberry light of the rising sun. "You're not afraid, are you?"

Roller started forward, his feet tramping the soft grass. "I don't have time for this shit," he said. "Tell me where it is."

Ben's hand shot forward, grabbing Roller by the wrist and jerking him back.

"What the fuck, dude?" Roller asked, yanking his arm from Ben's grasp, the storm in his eyes raging.

Ben shook his head and stepped forward. "I'll get the clue," he said. "I'll finish this."

52

Grant Island, Florida – 6:49 PM
Trip Odometer – 873 Miles

"A very wise decision," I said, my hair whipping free. As free as Josh and I were about to be.

Ben stepped forward, reaching out, placing his hand on my cheek, the rough skin of his thumb rubbing up and down in slow motion. "You'd better not be fucking with me. If this clue of yours is a trick—"

"Nothing tricky. It's just a slip of paper. You'll find it at the top, weighted down by a rock."

"And how far out of the way is this going to take me?"

"Not out of the way at all," I said, tipping my face away from his hand and taking a step back. "I promise."

"I need this to work. I've spent too much time trying to get myself out of this mess."

Ben turned, pressing his shoulder against the door to the lighthouse, pushing his way into the dank-smelling space, toward the spiral staircase that led to the lantern room.

"Oh, yeah. One more thing."

53

The Witches' Tower – 6:53 AM

"What?" Ben asked. His eyes flared as he turned to face me from the tower's doorway.

"You and me? We're through."

Ben's eyes narrowed and his lips parted, but I never got the chance to hear what he wanted to say.

"Cut the crap," Roller said from behind me, his gritty voice like sand in my ears. "Get your ass up there, Baden, and find her stupid little clue."

I turned to face Roller. Smiled. "I've heard so much about you." The staircase began to creak under Ben's weight. "Too bad it all turned out to be true."

"Watch your mouth." Roller took several long strides toward me, one arm outstretched.

I stepped back, twisting sideways, but my heel caught in the grass. I lost my balance and fell to the ground.

Roller stood over me, his head tossed back, laughing.

54

Grant Island, Florida – 6:53 PM
Trip Odometer – 873 miles

Just as Ben disappeared through the doorway, I turned and raced back to the parking lot, the steady rush of the waves warning me, insisting that I move faster.

I heard him before I saw him, the gritty sound of his angry laughter whipping in the wind, lashing at me, trying to keep me away. But I wouldn't go. Couldn't. Not now.

He was facing the ocean, his back to me, feet spread wide.

I looked for Josh, rounded the car and found him lying on that flowing ribbon of white sand, one hand pressed to his mouth, blood pouring from his lip.

"Get up!" Roller shouted.

His foot jerked away from the ground, a spray of sand arcing in the air, his arms spreading like wings as he kicked back and then forward, and the toe of his heavy black boot crashed into the side of Josh's body.

"Your plan just blew up in your face!" Roller yelled. "I want my shit and I want it now. Understand?"

I watched his hand sweep to the waistband of his jeans, curl under the hem of his hooded sweatshirt, and jerk free.

And then something changed.

His hand was weighed down.

Larger.

When I forced myself to focus, the strawberry-orange glow of the setting sun framed his silhouette.

55

The Witches' Tower – 6:59 AM

"You're crazy if you think I'm just going to let you go," Roller said, his hand soaring above me, the raspberry-lemon glow of the rising sun framing his silhouette—sparking off the gun in his hand. "With everything you know, there's no way I'm going to risk you talking to the cops."

I didn't speak. I didn't dare.

I stayed curled up on the grassy blanket beneath me, wondering if Roller could possibly be as crazy as everyone had always said.

"I'll figure out a way to keep you quiet later. First, let's start with the basics. I want my package. And you're going to give it to me. Now!"

I looked at his feet, at the glimmer of dewdrops shining on his heavy black boots. "I told you. I don't have it."

"But you know where it is." Roller crouched to the ground. I focused on the veins bulging from his neck instead of the hurricane in his eyes. "Which means you can take me to it."

"I can't. I only know what the clue says. It was a precaution. In case something went wrong. You can't have the package until we get away."

Roller cocked his head to the side. Bared his crooked teeth.

"We?"

"*I*," I said. "Until *I* get away."

Roller reached out with his free hand and grabbed my arm, yanking me to my feet, pulling me against his body.

I heard it then, the groaning protest of the spiral staircase, just before Ben raced out of the door, hand held high, fluttering a single sheet of paper in the air. "Got it," he said. "It's close to . . . Whoa, dude, what are you doing? I told you, she's off-limits."

Roller pressed the gun to my temple. "We're not alone."

"I'm right here." Josh's voice broke the morning in two, rippling in waves that seemed to come from a million different directions at once. "Come and get me, asshole."

Roller shoved me forward into Ben's chest and spun around just as Josh stepped out of the shadows, one arm raised, his hand outstretched, flashing in the light of the sun.

It didn't make sense, the fire and light, fractured and shattered.

Then my eyes focused, and I saw it.

The shiny smooth surface protruding from the tight clasp of Josh's hand.

The barrel of a gun.

56

Grant Island, Florida – 6:59 pm
Trip Odometer – 873 miles

"Stop!" I yelled, the wind stealing my voice.

I shoved my hand into the pocket of my jacket, my fingers stretching and wrapping, pulling and jerking until they were free.

"Roller!" I yelled, raising my arm, the gun heavier than I expected, its weight threatening to pull me to the ground. "I said *stop*!"

I narrowed my eyes, seeing through the blur of my lashes. And I aimed, ran my thumb down the slick surface of the safety, unlocking the trigger.

He turned then, the wind blowing his hair wild around the frame of his face, his eyes going wide.

"Hadley!" Josh yelled, rising up on his knees, falling forward, grabbing Roller's legs.

Then came the fireworks—the *flash-pop-bang* echoing hard in my ears.

57

The Witches' Tower – 7:01 AM

The cracking sound rocketed through the trees, spiraling around the tower, bursting up to the tie-dyed sky.

I flinched, pressing my hands to my ears, and squeezed my eyes tight, wondering how—why—Josh had a gun.

Everything stopped.

But only for a moment, as the echo of the gunfire tripped up and away.

I heard rustling first, feet in the grass.

And a single, scratchy word. "Fuck!"

Sunlight pierced my eyes as I dared a glance.

Ben was beside me, his back pressed against the tower's curved wall. Roller was running past the BMW, twisting to get one last look over his shoulder.

And Josh, my Josh, lay crumpled at the foot of the sisters, the trunks of their braided bodies pillowing his head.

"Josh!" I yelled, scrambling to him, grabbing his hands, his skin so cold against mine. I pulled him to me, hearing a bubbly wheeze in his throat. Felt something warm spread across my chest and thought it was my heart breaking open.

"You okay?" he asked, his words hot and wet, his eyes shining bright.

"I'm fine," I whispered, gripping him tight. "And you will be, too."

His head fell back onto my leg, and I boosted it up, cradling it in my arm, scooting closer. Shifting sideways, I found Ben still pressed against that glittering stone wall, his face white.

"Call for help!" I shouted.

He parted his lips, his eyes flashing wild. "I don't have my phone," he said. "You do."

"I *don't*!" I shouted, my mind twirling and whirling back and away.

And then it was there, all of it, rushing me, the jagged pieces of a thousand dreams.

The picture of me on Facebook.

The tower, the moon, and the glittering green of Josh's eyes.

The drugs and the girls and Penny with her million goodnights.

The rest seemed mixed up—there was the vibration of tires on pavement, the glow of headlights on an interstate sign, the feel of my fingers digging in dirt, and the salty scent of the ocean.

But none of that mattered at all. Nothing. Nothing but Josh.

I turned, my hands frantically searching, remembering the back pocket of Josh's shorts.

"Hadley," he breathed, his eyes a blazing green fire.

"Don't talk." I reached underneath his body, grabbing his phone and pulling it free. "Just breathe."

Hands shaking, slick with blood, I powered the phone on, pressed the nine and the one and the one. My voice shook and it echoed. It tore through the light.

Josh widened his eyes, raised one hand, his fingers spread wide.

The calming rhythm of the operator's voice called out from the grass. ". . . already en route . . ."

His fingers were ice, roaming my cheek, his palm shivering softly against my skin.

He parted his lips, offering me three words. The faintest whisper.

"A million times . . ."

And then it was raining, my tears on his face.

I wrapped my arms around him so tight I thought he would never slip free.

But still, the light drained from his eyes.

The life soared from his body.

And I folded myself in half, covering him until the sirens came and they pulled me away.

58

Grant Island, Florida – 7:01 PM
Trip Odometer – 873 Miles

A white-hot fire ripped through my chest, a streak of lightning knocking me down.

My face hit a pillow of scratchy sand. My teeth bit into my tongue.

And then he was there, leaning over me, his hands fluttering, his voice shaking.

"Hadley," Josh's eyes blazed green fire. "Hadley?!"

I tried to find words, to force them out, but something heavy pressed on my chest, my throat closed tight, and I was cold. So cold.

Josh looked over his shoulder, the ocean breeze tossing his hair. He shouted something about a phone.

Mine was still in the console of the car.

Or in the ravine.

I wasn't quite sure anymore.

"Jesus Christ!" I heard. Ben—his voice faint as a whisper. "What did you do?"

I wondered if he was talking to me. Or the shadow looming behind Josh.

But nothing seemed to matter. Not as I looked into Josh's eyes.

"Hang on," he said, his voice cracking. "Just hang on, Hadley."

I smiled.

Reached a shaking hand to his face, my fingers grazed the velvety fabric of his skin.

"Goodnight," I choked out.

Josh's voice spiraled through a tunnel of wind that smelled of trees and dirt and tears.

I wanted to tell him. I needed him to know. But I felt dizzy and faded, like the wilting shades of purple and blue that someone had streaked across the sky, the echo of promises whipping away on the waves of the ocean.

59

Seven Months Later

"It's in," Mia said from behind me, the two words nearly masked by a steady hum of tires running along the pavement below us.

I sat shotgun in Brooklyn's parents' minivan, acting as if I hadn't heard. Everyone was waiting for me to respond.

Instead of speaking, I pressed my finger against the switch that opened the window, closing my eyes against the crisp November air. The surge of sound that streamed through the car was deafening, just as I had hoped. My hair whirled around my head, whipping my face. The feeling was familiar, but I couldn't quite place it. I didn't try. I stuck my hand out the window, palm curved, and watched it ride the air.

"The verdict," Mia said, her voice loud but tight. Shaky. "It's in."

"I don't want to hear it," I shouted over my shoulder. "That's why we're here, right? Instead of the courthouse. We all agreed."

"We did," Brooklyn said, her voice coming from behind me. Behind Mia. "You didn't want to be there. So we're here instead, ditching class for a week. Supporting you all the way."

"Just like always," Mia said. "But we never said we were

going to ignore the outcome. I mean, this is huge, Hadley."

"I know." I looked out the window, my eyes gliding over the arched *M* of a fancy-looking McDonald's. "I just don't think I can."

"Well, *I* want to hear it," Tyler said from beside Brooklyn. I looked back, past Mia in her bucket seat, to the third row. "I want us all to hear it. Right now. Together."

"He *should* have a say in this," Sam said from the bucket seat next to Mia. I tipped my head toward her, thinking for the millionth time that she was incredible, that I would never be able to repay her for what she had done.

"I suppose you think you have a say in this, too?" I asked. "After all you did with Ben's computer. You broke the whole thing wide open. Handed the police a virtual road map of that stupid club."

"Piece of cake." Sam shifted in her seat, raising one leg to rest a heavy black boot on her knee. "Tyler's the one who had the biggest impact. The way I hear it, that judge was so mesmerized when Tyler was on the stand, he didn't even blink."

"I was prepared." Tyler gazed out the window, sunlight casting a golden glow on his face. "Ben and the Free Agents targeted Penny because I turned them down. I knew exactly what I needed to say."

"You were the most important part of the prosecution's case," Brooklyn said. "Everyone's saying your testimony was the strongest."

"I just wish Penny were here to see the way it all turned out."

I closed my eyes against the November air, feeling my hand tossing in the waves of wind that rushed past the car as we drove and drove and drove.

"She would be proud of you," Mia said. "And glad you had her back."

"It's over now," I said.

"It's not over." The voice was soft, but strong. Sure. "He deserves to know."

I looked to my left, taking him in, the way his hair fell into his eyes, how tightly his fingers gripped the steering wheel. He reached out, his right arm twisting until his palm faced up, dropping an open hand on my knee. My eyes followed the gentle slope of his wrist, the tight curve of his muscles, and the small circular tattoo centered on his inner biceps.

One single Penny.

Heads.

Up.

I placed my hand in his, lacing our fingers together.

"We all deserve to know. You, because you're one of the—"

"Don't even think of calling me a victim." I spun my silver and turquoise ring around the middle finger of my right hand.

"I would never," Josh said. "We've already established why Tyler and Sam deserve to hear the verdict, but we've forgotten Brooklyn and Mia. They're the ones who stole Ben's phone. They found his pictures. Without that, none of this would have happened."

"You're mixing things up again," I said. "*I* stole his phone. When he locked me in the bathroom at the party. *I* was the one who found the pictures."

"Are you sure?"

I looked at him. I would never be tired of looking at him. "Yes. And at the end of the night, you took the video that they used in court. Just before you were shot. You died out there in the woods, *at the tower*, Josh, and—"

"I still don't understand how I could have been at the tower. Or how I was shot."

"Those parts don't matter anymore. The paramedics brought you back. Now you're healing, and that's the end of that story."

"But the other story," Josh said, "it's still going, Hadley. We should hear what happened today."

"Oh my God, enough," Mia said. "He's *guilty*."

"Mia!" I yelled, reaching between the front seats and smacking her leg. "I said I didn't want to know. I didn't want anything about that trial to ruin today."

"Just because you were scared. You thought he might get off. I've seen it in your face—before the trial, during the trial, and the entire time we were planning this trip. But you don't have to worry anymore. His parents couldn't fix this, not even with the Baden fortune at their fingertips. Ben is guilty. As sin."

"For sure?" I asked.

"Yeah. They haven't scheduled the sentencing hearing, but there's no doubt Ben will be locked up for years. For the drugs and how they were used. For photographing you and the others. A bunch of the other members are going down, too. The fact that their group was posted on the Internet as a game makes the charges even harsher. At the very least, most of the members are looking at sexual battery and being registered sex offenders for the rest of their lives."

"I guess that's good," I said. "Still, it just doesn't feel like enough."

"Don't forget the wrongful death suit my parents filed

against Ben," Tyler said. "There's so much proof that Penny did what she did because of him, starting with the note you found in her room."

I watched Tyler's reflection in the rearview mirror. He was sad, but he was strong. It would take some time for him to adjust, but he would be okay.

"And then there's Roller," Mia said, scrolling down the news feed on her phone. "The article mentions that he was one of the original members of the Free Agents. He's not only going down for the girls he targeted, but there'll also be some level of accountability for all of the others. Obviously, the worst will be the charges he's facing for shooting Josh.

I felt myself breathe—in and out—realizing I hadn't, not really, since the gunshot and the blood and Josh going still in my arms.

Josh rounded a turn in the road, and a bridge rolled out before us like a silver beam of moonlight stretching from one piece of land to the next.

"It's over," I said. "It's really over."

"You're the one who made it happen," Josh said. "It all came down to you. You were brave enough to face it."

"I had no idea how big *it* was. Besides, my decision had more to do with you. And Penny. Everyone had to know the truth. The two of you deserved that much. Not to mention the girls—I had to keep them from hurting more girls."

I looked out the window, over the rail of the bridge, at the open water glinting below, slow waves churning, making me think that everything might have a chance of being washed clean.

"That," Josh said, looking ahead, "is Grant Island."

We were halfway across the causeway when he said it, the words floating through the car and giving everything a slow, dreamlike feel.

"It's the place I've been telling you about," Josh said, glancing over at me. "I swear to God, we were here. That night."

"And I keep telling you, *no*. We stayed in Ohio. We ran from them all night long."

"We ran *here*," Josh insisted.

The tires clipped a chink in the road, and the sound rocketed through the minivan. We had arrived.

"I've seen it," Josh said. "All of it."

"You were dreaming."

"He wasn't dreaming, Hadley," Sam said with a chuckle. "He was knocked out on a morphine drip those first few days in the hospital."

"Look, I know it doesn't make sense, but I swear it's true. We were here. Me and Hadley. That night."

"Right," Brooklyn said. "You stole Ben's car."

"Headed to Cincinnati, where you left me and Brooklyn," Mia added. "As if we'd ever allow that."

"Then spent the entire night driving," Sam said. "All the way to Florida."

"Straight to this island," Brooklyn said.

"Where you set them up," Mia added.

"Just like you did in real life. In *Ohio*," Sam said.

"I know it doesn't make any sense." Josh guided the minivan off the main strip, onto a road that gave me an odd sense of déjà vu. "But I'm telling you. I've been here before. There's a big twisted tree right around this curve. It looks like it's dancing."

We were quiet then, waiting, maybe even hoping, for Josh's sake, that it would be true. But there was no way.

And then, when we rounded the bend, we saw it. Everyone went silent. Thoughts whipped through my mind.

What if?

Could it really be?

Because he was right.

There was a tree—a very twisted tree—with thick branches spiraling outward, like arms spread wide in an invitation to join the dance.

60

Grant Island, Florida

We were standing at the top of the lighthouse, the ocean breeze washing us clean. Josh's hands gripped the railing as he gazed out over the open sea.

I stood there, watching him, the way the wind moved through his hair, the gentle sweep of his lashes as he blinked in the light of the fading sun.

Josh had gone quiet as he parked the minivan in the deserted lot, as he opened the driver's-side door and swung his legs to the pavement. He'd flinched as he slammed the door closed, the still-healing wound from the gunshot smarting as it always did when he moved too quickly. I hadn't wanted him to drive, but he'd insisted. He'd said he had to be the one to take us over the bridge, the one to cross us over to the island.

Josh had stopped to kneel on the pavement, all of us waiting behind him. The muscles of his back had clenched with a memory I wasn't sure I wanted to know. And then he'd stood and taken my hand, crossing from the pavement onto sand that stretched all the way to the water, where rolling, white-capped waves tossed themselves against the beach.

I thought he would lead me there, to the strength and calming rhythm of that ocean. Instead, he took me to the lighthouse and pulled me right through a little door wearing a sign that said Closed for Renovation. Past an abandoned umbrella that was cinched tight, leaning against the brick wall, glowing in the sunlight. We climbed up a set of spiral steps, my hand feeling the tingle of recognition as it slid slowly along the gritty surface of the banister. At the top, we made our way out of the lantern room, to the wraparound platform, and stood against the rickety railing.

The others were in the water, just past a pile of hoodies that had been abandoned on the beach, jeans rolled up to their knees, leaping and splashing, their laughter riding the wind that rippled across the sand.

"You're quiet," I said. "Are you okay?"

Josh cleared his throat. He looked back at me. "I'm remembering."

I shook my head. "There's nothing to remember."

But I didn't quite believe that. Somewhere, on the fringe, just out of reach, I remembered, too.

The salty taste of the air was familiar. So was the jagged-edged rock sitting near the toe of my sandal, and the slip of paper beneath it, flapping in the wind. I bent forward, feeling a hot, searing pain slice through my chest. I ignored it, knowing it wasn't real.

But the rock. And the paper. Those were.

I reached down, the rock's surface scratchy against the tips of my fingers as I rolled it away. With my other hand, I grabbed for the paper. I wanted—needed—to see what it said. But the wind caught it faster than I could, tossing it away. I watched the tattered note take flight, whipping across currents of air until it disappeared.

"It's better, right?" I asked. "This. Here. It's better than your dream?"

Josh reached for my shoulders and turned me toward him.

He smiled, his entire face tinted purple from the glow of the setting sun.

"Yes."

His hands gripped my waist, pulling me close.

And he kissed me.

It was soft and slow, the silky feel of his lips reminding me of moonlight and starlight, the echo of promises, and of fading away.

When he pulled back, he tipped his forehead against mine.

Looked me right in the eyes.

"A million times yes."

Acknowledgments

A Million Times Goodnight was inspired during a girls' night (on the farm) while I was sitting around the most magnificent bonfire of all time, hanging out with a bunch of the finest sister friends a girl could ask for. So much love to my sweet, beautiful, sassy friends, who deserve all the credit for igniting the idea that eventually became this book. (Enough said, right? Because, what happens when you're with the girls *stays* with the girls.)

It's possible that a million people helped me along my journey while writing this book, from the first creative spark by that bonfire to the final version of this final draft, but I don't have enough space to get through that kind of list, so I'll stick to the basics:

A million thank yous to those who read various drafts as I created, tore apart, and recreated this intricate plot—Lori Behm, Janet Irvin, Katrina Kittle, and Sharon Short. But most of all, Melanie Singleton, who I believe read every single draft multiple times.

A million Holy-Crazy-She-Liked-It! leaps for joy in honor of my ever so talented, insightful editor, Alison Weiss, whose guidance brought additional depth and clarity to each draft. Also to Bonnie Cutler, a member of Egmont USA, who supported this title from the very start. And finally, to the entire team of Sky Pony Press, including Julie Matysik, Georgia Morrissey, Sarah Brody, Karla Daly, Denise Roeper, and Joshua Barnaby, I cannot express how much I appreciate the time and support that was offered during each step of this process.

A million and one moments of gratitude to my super-agent, Alyssa Eisner Henkin, who patiently encouraged me through every draft, offered creative suggestions for improvement, and ultimately helped me see the dream of this book through to publication. (We quite possibly logged a million hours on the phone during the process.)

A million thanks to my father, Keith McBride, for many discussions exploring the complexities of time and time travel. Analyzing both reality and fiction with you will always be one of my favorite things in life.

A million hugs to Diana Dermody and Maxine Purnhagen for helping wrangle the kidlings while I wrote, rewrote, and rewrote again. Friday afternoons at Grammy's quite literally saved this book's life. And playtime with Grandma Di is always the best distraction.

A million kisses to my children and husband for all of their patience, understanding, and love as I locked myself behind closed doors and hunkered over the screen of my laptop, typing away. You make leaving the world of my imagination and coming back to reality the most beautiful part of it all.

A million cheers to *all* of my readers. Thank you for believing in me and for helping me believe in myself. Much love.